three

black

swans

OTHER BOOKS BY
CAROLINE B. COONEY

three black swans

CAROLINE B. COONEY

DELACORTE PRESS

Copyright © 2010 by Caroline B. Cooney

All rights reserved. Published in the United States by Delacorte Press,
an imprint of Random House Children's Books,
a division of Random House, Inc., New York.

Delacorte Press is a registered trademark and the colophon is a trademark of
Random House, Inc.

Visit us on the Web! www.randomhouse.com/teens
Educators and librarians, for a variety of teaching tools,
visit us at www.randomhouse.com/teachers

Library of Congress Cataloging-in-Publication Data
Cooney, Caroline B.
Three black swans / Caroline B. Cooney. — 1st ed.
p. cm.
Summary: When sixteen-year-old Missy Vianello decides to try to convince
her classmates that her cousin Claire is really her long-lost identical twin, she
has no idea that the results of her prank will be so life-changing.
ISBN 978-0-385-73867-5 (hardcover trade) — ISBN 978-0-385-90741-5 (glb)
ISBN 978-0-375-89568-5 (e-book) [1. Triplets—Fiction.
2. Sisters—Fiction. 3. Adoption—Fiction.] I. Title.
PZ7.C7834Th 2010
[Fic]—dc22
2009041990

The text of this book is set in 11.5-point A Caslon Regular.

Book design by Marci Senders

Printed in the United States of America

10 9 8 7 6 5 4 3 2 1

First Edition

But the future isn't a hat full of little shredded pieces of the past. It is, instead, a whirlpool of uncertainty populated by what the trader and philosopher Nassim Nicholas Taleb calls "black swans"—events that are hugely important, rare and unpredictable, and explicable only after the fact.

—*The Wall Street Journal*

For Beverly Horowitz, with whom I have worked on thirty books, and whose friendship, conversation and unpredictable ideas are a great joy in my life

CHAPTER

TUESDAY
October

MISSY VIANELLO AND her mother were running errands. Mom was in line at the post office sending a package while Missy walked down the block to the dry cleaner's.

The front door was propped open. Missy entered a large hot space, full of clothing, empty of people. The old-fashioned floor fans rotated slowly on their heavy metal posts. A radio sat on a sorting table. It was small and black with a long cord, and probably as old as her mother. It was tuned to a talk station. A doctor was chatting excitedly about babies.

Missy did not care for talk shows. Politics and angry raised voices did not attract her. Gentler topics—gardens to visit; diseases to worry about—offered nothing to a sixteen-year-old.

On the counter sat a small bell for customers to ring. Like the swirling fans, it was something from a schoolroom in another century. Missy had the odd sensation that she had fallen out of her own time. She tapped the little bell, which made a pleasing musical ding.

Missy was mildly impatient. Usually the couple who ran the shop were so attentive.

The interview on the radio station continued. At first, the doctor's remarks stayed outside Missy, hanging there like the clean clothes dangling from ceiling racks. And then the meaning of his statements penetrated Missy's mind. If there had not been a counter separating customers from the workspace, Missy would have snatched up the radio and pressed it to her ear.

She who had never given a thought to babies, who wasn't interested in babysitting, who hadn't even met any infants lately—she was stunned by what the doctor was saying.

The fact that had kept Missy safe, the fact that had allowed Missy to laugh at her crazy guesses for the last few years—was that fact a lie?

This doctor is an expert, she thought. He knows what he's talking about. Or does he? Can I trust him?

A clerk she did not recognize hurried over, smiling, saying how are you, good to see you, but Missy, transfixed by the talk station, did not answer. The clerk took the small white ticket from Missy's hand and went to find the clothes.

The interview ended. A new voice discussed weather. Missy found herself holding a stack of neatly folded, plastic-wrapped sweaters. She handed over the cash and even managed to say thank you. She left the dry cleaner's. On the sidewalk, she could no longer hear the radio, but the words had come outside with her.

Missy Vianello had not fallen out of her own time.

She had fallen out of her life.

* * *

WEDNESDAY
The following day

MISSY HAD NOT slept well. Every time she lay down, some internal engine propelled her back off the bed. Half the night, she stood in the dark, while the facts of her life sorted themselves like a pack of cards being dealt. In school, though, she was surprisingly alert. The lines from the radio vibrated in her head, and yet she was able to participate in class and do her work. She felt weirdly multiplied by the new information.

By the time it was third period and biology class had begun, Missy's energy was fading. Mrs. Stancil discussed fake science, describing a hoax in which the perpetrators aged bits of human skull and jawbone, buried the bone fragments and then arranged for them to be dug up. They convinced museums and anthropologists that these were the remains of an ancient humanoid. They called the "fossils" Piltdown Man and the world was enthralled by what seemed to be its new ancestor.

Maybe what Missy had heard on the radio was also pretend science. Maybe her new "fact" was as silly as Piltdown Man.

Mrs. Stancil adored classroom discussion. She was delighted when Graham argued with her. "I love archaeology," he said. "I read about it all the time, and that hoax wouldn't work, Mrs. Stancil. You'd test the bones for fluorine, uranium and nitrogen. You'd know immediately how old those bones were."

"Now you would. But this was 1912," explained Mrs. Stancil. "Those testing techniques were unknown."

The class had only six weeks' experience with Mrs. Stancil, but they knew already that she preferred projects that were "outside the box," and quickly tired of projects that were "in the box."

In Missy Vianello's mind, a hoax blossomed. She could see the entire hoax from start to finish. It would be cruel. But it would work. She said softly, "What hoax would you do, Mrs. Stancil, if you could pull one off? A science teacher would be so good at hoaxes. A scientist like you could offer a string of lies, but package them so believably that the public would accept your story as fact."

The kids were on board immediately. "Let's do a class hoax," said Anthony. "We could pretend that a lamb bone from somebody's dinner roast is the shin of a pterodactyl."

"And get very scientific about it," agreed Kelsey. "Buttress our claim with bone details, like porosity, and present the measurements of real pterodactyls, or pretend to, and establish that we have a match."

"I think the hoax should be more trendy," said Carlotta. "How about a fake alternative fuel for cars? We could print pages of chemical testing we haven't done, and convince people we can make fuel from, say, pond scum."

Mrs. Stancil was excited. "People! This is truly outside the box. If we format our project so that our research provides us with a deep understanding of the truth, it will be a fun approach. I like Carlotta's idea. Corn is being used for ethanol, so it's not outrageous that we too could create a vegetable fuel."

"That's not my kind of hoax," said Zach. "I'd rather have a murder victim and convince people it was suicide and get away with murder."

If Missy shouted her own idea out loud, the class would be impressed. But a hoax worked only when nobody suspected. *Nobody*, thought Missy, already feeling guilty; already aware that her hoax might destroy instead of reveal.

"I wouldn't actually have a corpse," explained Zach. "I'd just pretend to. I've seen at least a thousand TV shows with this plot, so I've pre-researched and I'm ready to go."

"Let's do hoaxes in groups," said Emily. "People who like bones can be in the bone group, people who like murder can be in the corpse group and people who like fuel can be in the pond scum group."

In science, what mattered was truth.

But in life? wondered Missy. What mattered most in life?

* * *

EVENING
The same Wednesday

CLAIRE LINNEHAN WAS doing her homework.

Only six weeks into the school year, Claire loved all classes and all study. The textbooks still felt like treasures in which fascinating topics were waiting. Usually this feeling lasted through Thanksgiving. By December, when it got cold and dark early in the day, and she began hoping for snow and ski weekends and wanted to shop for more sweaters, the books felt used up; Claire would have mined the vein of gold that had been so promising and she'd be ready to move on.

Her cell phone rang. The ring tone was her cousin Missy's,

but Claire would have known who was calling anyway. She and Missy could practically read each other's minds. "Hi, Missy." Claire settled in for a long talk. She and her cousin texted on and off all day long, but also had to hear each other's voices at least once every twenty-four hours.

"Hey, Clairedy." Missy had a very chipper voice; very upbeat. People said that Missy and Claire sounded exactly alike, but Claire disagreed. Her own voice was slower and deeper. "Listen," said Missy. "I need an identical twin."

Claire laughed. "Even on the Internet, Missy, there aren't that many identical twins being auctioned off."

"In biology," said Missy, "we've been assigned to pull off a hoax."

"Like filming Bigfoot? Or finding Paleolithic writing on a stone in your backyard?"

"Exactly. Here's what I've decided for my hoax. Out of nowhere, like an asteroid in the night falling through my roof, I will suddenly meet my long-lost, totally unknown identical twin. Everybody will believe my hoax because I will bring my identical twin to school."

Claire was giggling now. She never giggled with anybody but Missy. "When *I* took biology," said Claire, who was a junior while Missy was a sophomore, "we learned *facts*. A hoax assignment is pointless. Guess what, Missy? This morning when Aiden and I happened to enter the building at the same time, he said hi to me. And then he smiled." Arriving at high school at the same moment as Aiden had not been accidental. Missy had been part of the planning. Discussion of boys was a major portion of the cousins' nightly talks.

"Nobody cares about Aiden right now," said Missy. "We care only about my assignment. You have to be my identical twin, Claire."

There was a strong family resemblance between the cousins. When they were little, maybe seven or eight, Missy and Claire used to dress the same, wear their hair the same and loudly pretend to understand each other's thoughts and finish each other's sentences. "We're twins!" they would lie to anybody paying attention. People didn't fall for it, because Claire was taller and heavier, but the girls thought they had a great act. Their parents tired of it and put an end to the fake twin thing. Even now Claire's mother could get bent out of shape if she perceived Claire copying Missy or the other way around.

"There is a strong family resemblance," agreed Claire. "But I'd need plastic surgery to be a perfect match, even if I *wanted* to look exactly like you. I think *you* should have the surgery and look exactly like me instead."

"There isn't time for surgery," said Missy. "The project is due."

A phone call with Missy was relaxing. Claire wouldn't even know she was tense until she heard Missy's voice, felt her body soften. She could get so relaxed that if she was sprawled on the bed, she'd fall asleep, and Missy would yell into the phone, "Hey! Clairedy! Wake up!"

"Identical twins have to be identical," Claire pointed out.

"There's the problem that I am a year ahead of you in school, an A student, in six activities, on two teams, and planning to be a doctor, whereas you—I'm sorry to put this so bluntly— are an average student with no activities except communicating and shopping."

They laughed. In fact the cousins were pretty similar. But with one cousin a sophomore and the other a junior, and living in different states with different curricula and exams— Missy was in Connecticut while Claire was in New York—comparisons were iffy.

"You can dumb down, Claire," said Missy cheerfully. "Here's my plan. I go to school tomorrow sobbing and trembling and tell everybody that my missing identical twin has just shown up."

"Meaning me? Finding me makes you cry?"

"Okay, I'll clap my hands and dance in little circles."

"Better," said Claire. "Now, where will you do this? Biology lab?"

"No, no. Our school—being superior to yours—has an in-house television broadcast. I happen to be friends with the morning announcer. His sister is in my Language Arts class and I was over at their house once. I'll call Rick and regale him with my astonishing news, and arrange for him to interview me."

"They do interviews during your school announcements?"

"They never have before, but they've never had a long-lost identical twin before. I can talk Rick into it. It's quite a story, you know. He'll be all over it. The thing is, Claire, I can't use photographs of my identical twin. Anybody can show up with two photographs of herself and pretend that the picture on the left is her twin. You will be my living, breathing proof that I have an identical twin. You and I are going to have an identical twin debut."

With Missy, either in person or on the phone, Claire felt safer. The sensation was always present, and Claire could never quite get hold of it. Safer from what? But now the safe feeling drained away. "I don't think so, Missy."

Missy was not deflected, which was typical; she was a pit bull. "I saw a TV show once," said Missy, "where they found identical twins who had been separated at birth. The show brought them together for the first time when they were in their thirties. Can you imagine? These two men showed up wearing the same shirt, and here they had the same bowling score, and had gotten married the same month of the same year, and had even married women with the same first name. But they didn't know the other one existed. That's how bonded identical twins are."

Claire could not work up any interest in thirty-year-old men with identical bowling scores. "Missy, get real. I can't show up at your school in the morning. I have school of my own. I live twenty miles away. And I don't drive." Her parents had finally agreed that next spring she could get her driver's license. Sometimes Claire couldn't eat or read from the excitement of picturing herself in her own car, driving to her own destinations, the little plastic ID window in her wallet holding a license and a credit card for gas in the opposite slot.

9

But the thought of driving did not excite her this time. She sat down on her bed and pulled her feet up, as if nightmares under the bed might yank her down by the ankles.

Missy, who usually picked up any mood of her cousin's over the phone, did not notice anything. "Your father can drive you, Claire. Uncle Phil is always obedient to your wishes. School announcements are nice and early. They're over by seven fifty-five so the first class can start at eight, but since your school starts at eight-thirty, you'll almost be back in time. Tell Uncle Phil I need help for one minute on a biology project. Come on, Clairedy. How many people get to be identical twins for a day?"

Becoming an identical twin sounded like quite a step to Claire. Like marriage, only more so.

What was an identical twin, anyway? At conception, it was a single, which then split in two. At birth, the babies had separate bodies and souls, yet they had once shared the exact same body. Or egg; Claire was a little vague. "Do fraternal twins instead," she suggested. "If your hoax is about fraternal twins, you can use anybody. Remember how in your kindergarten there were two sets of fraternal twins and nobody even believed they were related?"

"It wouldn't be fun with just anybody, Clairedy. It'll only be fun with you. And how exciting are fraternal twins, anyhow? People daydream of being identical twins."

"Speak for yourself," said Claire, whose daydreams involved Aiden, a wide assortment of other cute boys, and of course cars. "Anyway, there are flaws in your plan. What about your friends who know me? I'm always at your sleepovers and I've gone to lots of school games with you."

"That was middle school. That was years ago. I haven't given a party in ages. Literally a thousand kids at my high school have never seen or heard of you. And back when they were coming to my parties, you and I didn't look this much alike."

That was true. Missy's low birth weight had resulted in years of illness and slow growth. But by ninth and now tenth grade, the puny cousin had caught up.

"You and I will wear exactly the same stuff for the interview," said Missy. "I'm thinking the pale pink cashmere sweaters we both got for our birthdays. Our hair is the same length now, and we'll wear the same color ponytail holders, and the pink and silver bead earrings we got at the mall a few weeks ago. When I instruct people to see identical twins, they will. That's the essence of a hoax. Obedience to the hoax master."

Claire felt unsettled. Missy seemed too enthusiastic. "Are you sure you understood the assignment, Missy? You're in high school biology, not summer camp."

"I admit I'm not following the guidelines. Mrs. Stancil wants us to be very scientific. Like if you're pretending your lamb bone is actually the shin of a pterodactyl—assuming pterodactyls have shins, which I don't happen to know—you need the right dimensions and bone porosity and all that. We're supposed to do our hoax in groups, but I got assigned to Carlotta's and I don't want to make pretend alternative fuels out of pond scum."

Claire couldn't laugh. The hoax disturbed her. But there was an easy way out. "What do your mom and dad think of your plan?" she asked.

Claire adored her aunt and uncle. They were totally fun people. Former elementary school teachers, they lived in a welter of projects. Even now, when their daughter was sixteen, there was always some family project going on, like making bookmarks or birdhouses or even bricks. A visit to Uncle Matt and Aunt Kitty's was like changing planets. Claire's parents shared stuff like cooking and cleaning—"Let's vacuum!" her mom and dad would say to each other—but Missy's parents would say, "Let's weld our own garden sculpture!"

Missy lowered her voice. "I wasn't going to bring my parents into this."

"When identical twins are first revealed," said Claire, "viewers want to see how thrilled the parents are that their long-lost daughter is found." Claire was confused by her own statement. Under what circumstances could a daughter be lost?

"Why would the parents be thrilled?" countered Missy. "Obviously they didn't want you. If they had wanted you, they would have kept you. And here you are, like a lemon of a car, back from the garage again."

If twins were separated, Claire reasoned, then one of them had been adopted. Claire pictured a teen mother surrendering her babies. Perhaps with so many would-be parents in the world, the social worker had divided these pretend twins in order to satisfy two families instead of just one.

Claire imagined a heavy middle-aged woman, a Department of Social Services name tag pinned lopsidedly to her ill-fitting shirt, holding a blanket-wrapped newborn in each arm, tossing one baby in one direction and the other baby in the opposite direction. "Good luck!" she called, making a quick entry in her handheld computer.

That would be the end of twins. Babies who had been conceived with a life companion—an in-house best friend, as it were—would grow up alone.

Would they feel the loss?

How could they? Those thirty-year-old men Missy had seen on television hadn't known they had an identical sibling. And yet their bodies and lives had gone on behaving like twins, even to the point of bowling scores. Spooky.

Claire's mother and Missy's mom were sisters. The two families were close. Just about every Friday night either Claire stayed at Missy's house or Missy went to Claire's. Claire and her cousin were more intensely connected than most sisters she knew.

It was something she didn't talk about with her other friends. At age six or ten or twelve, it was okay for your cousin to show up now and then for a sleepover. But Claire Linnehan was nearly seventeen. At seventeen you did not look forward with longing to spending your Friday night with your cousin. A seventeen-year-old wanted parties and boys, movies and gangs of friends. Claire had those, but not on Fridays, which were Missy time.

For years, both sets of parents had been trying to dull the ex- cessive friendship between the cousins. You don't need to show up weekly, they would say. How about once a month instead?

Claire could get clammy hands thinking about lasting four weeks without Missy. Maybe their parents were right. Maybe the degree of friendship they shared was a little off. Normal teenage girls did not consider a cousin's visit the most important event of the week. If Claire pretended to an entire high school that she was actually Missy's identical twin, it would be off the charts.

It was also the ultimate don't-we-look-alike? fantasy. Claire was attracted to that. And if Missy and I were identical twins, thought Claire, nobody would say it's weird that we need each other. They would say it's a biological imperative.

"Parents do pose a hoax problem," Missy admitted. "But I don't need to bother with details, Claire. People just have to believe me for a little while. They don't have to believe me forever. Biology is third period, so my hoax only has to last until ten-thirty."

"Short hoaxes are probably the best kind," agreed Claire. It could be fun—just the kind of crazy thing she and her cousin would do. "Okay. Call me back if Rick says yes, and I'll work on Dad for a ride."

* * *

Missy never postponed a task. She was a full-speed person, which was the main reason her parents were not allowing her to drive any time soon. Missy did not slow down for corners.

She called Rick, who was startled to hear from her: he was a standout senior and she was an ordinary sophomore. They were in no classes together. They knew each other because one day she was at his house doing homework with his younger sister Alaina and Rick had gotten Missy a soda out of his refrigerator. That was exaggerating. He had been getting himself a soda, and when Missy said she was thirsty, he silently delivered a can.

"Rick, you won't believe it!" cried Missy now. She ran her sentences together to give him less time to think. "The most amazing thing has happened! Oh, Rick, I'm so excited I'm ricocheting off the walls. I have the best news in the whole wide world and I have to share it with everybody. I think the way I want to announce this is, I want to be on TV with you in the morning."

"I don't have live guests, Missy. Or dead ones. I sit there and read announcements."

"This will boost your ratings."

"My ratings are one hundred percent. I'm on the air in every classroom every day."

Missy lowered her voice. She gasped for breath. "Rick, a girl got in touch with me. She found out that she was adopted. *She's my twin.*" Missy let herself sob. "And what's truly unbelievable, and shocking, and I don't even know how to think about it yet—we are *identical.* When we met—oh, Rick!—it was like seeing *myself* walk toward me. She's me. I'm her."

"You are a separated twin?" said Rick. "I can't even picture that. Missy, you're so beautiful. There are *two* of you? What did your mother and father say? I mean, if your twin is adopted, you must be adopted, too."

Missy was derailed by the news that Rick thought she was beautiful. The hoax did not have its previous appeal. She wanted to discuss Rick's feelings and go to a movie with him, instead of sit in a high school TV studio pretending to be a twin. But it was imperative not to let Rick dwell on details like who was adopted by whom. Missy hurried on. "Rick, she's coming to school with me tomorrow. My twin. She's going to attend class with me so we can start getting to know each other."

"Wow," said Rick. "Are your mother and father okay with this?"

Missy found it annoying that the only person she knew with a broadcast position was giving her a hard time rather than seizing on this incredible scoop. "Rick, here's the truth," she said, preparing her biggest lie. "This is scary. I'm so thrilled I can't sleep, but the thing is"—she whispered, as if her identical twin might overhear—"I'm a tiny bit skeptical. *I* can't compare how we look. *I* can't inspect both of us. But if we're on TV, even for thirty seconds, the viewers will see immediately whether or not we are identical. If we're not—if she's just some girl with the same hair and eyes—the whole school will tell me so. This is my test."

"I think you should go with DNA," said Rick. "And they do specific blood tests for identical twins. They analyze more than a dozen aspects of blood chemistry. We learned that in anatomy and physiology. Identical twins have to be identical right down to—"

Missy burst into tears without even trying. "Rick, please!

She'll be here tomorrow! I want the ice broken. I need you to introduce us at the beginning of the day so I don't have to make explanations every single minute. I need you, Rick. I'm not brave enough to do this alone."

Missy felt brave enough to run the world alone, and often regretted that she was not in that position. But she could not run the high school television studio alone.

"I'd better ask Mrs. Conway first," said Rick dubiously.

Mrs. Conway was one of two assistant principals. She ran a number of student activities and was the sharpest knife in the faculty kitchen. Hoaxes required people to be gullible, or not have time to think clearly, or to be coaxed to think in the wrong direction. Mrs. Conway would not do any of that, since her main occupation was seeing through students' fibs and excuses.

"Rick," said Missy sternly, "you're a senior. You've run the studio for two years. If you can't make this decision, what *do* they allow you to do? It'll just be for one minute. Sixty seconds."

"Tell you what. If you and this girl come into the broadcast room tomorrow morning at seven thirty-five, ten minutes before I begin, and if I can't tell which of you is which, we'll do it."

* * *

Within moments, Claire had second thoughts.

Being best friends with her cousin was one of the nicest parts of Claire's life.

She could not remember refusing her cousin anything. On the other hand, she couldn't remember Missy asking for anything so off the wall.

Claire prided herself on her sharp mind, her easy grip on theories and theorems, her total recall of dates and data. But now thinking did not happen. Low-level anxiety occupied her body.

Missy called back, bursting with the news that Rick was on board. Claire nerved herself. "I'm not going to do it, Missy. I can't lie to Dad and ask him to drive me twenty miles each way during rush hour while I miss some school and he misses work."

Actually, Claire's dad was pretty much her slave and believed that anything Claire did was perfect. Her mother was the digger-out of detail. Mom led Jazzercise classes that met at dawn, midmorning, in the afternoon and in the evening. She kept track of Claire via texting, phone calls and interrogation and wouldn't settle for a meaningless line like "I'm helping Missy with something." But Mom would be at the community center when Claire needed this ride.

Missy was beside herself. "Claire! Rick said yes! It's all set! Find your cashmere birthday sweater."

"Our birthdays are two months apart, Missy. I'm older and I look it. Mrs. Stancil won't buy a fake twin act."

"That's my difficulty, not yours. Tell me the real problem, Claire."

Claire had never been able to say no to Missy. It was as if

Missy had a route into Claire's heart and mind that Claire could not protect. "I hate getting caught doing something wrong."

"It isn't wrong, Clairedy. This is an actual assignment, which I will carry out brilliantly. Nobody will be in trouble, especially not you. Mrs. Stancil and the whole school will believe me. They'll be impressed at how well I pull off my hoax. All you have to do is stand there and be photogenic."

Claire sighed.

Missy correctly read this as surrender. "Be on the curb outside my school by seven-thirty."

"I need an alias. I can't use my real name. Maybe you could call me Wanda or Annabel. That will give me a little distance from this nonsense."

"Wanda or Annabel? Where did you come up with those? I can live with Annabel, I suppose. Do you want a new last name too?"

"Griffin."

Their mothers had been the Griffin sisters, Frannie and Kitty. The sisters were not as close as their daughters. Oh, sure, they talked and gossiped and the four parents went to the movies and football games together and everything. But *needing* to see each other—no.

"Annabel Griffin," said Missy. "The long-lost identical twin. It's perfect."

"And when your buddy Rick, who obviously has the brains of a canned pea," said Claire, "asks how I found you, or where I live, or who adopted whom—do you have answers ready?"

19

"Of course I do. Hoaxes are all about clever answers. My middle name is clever. Remember, we have to fill only a minute, Clairedy. How much can go wrong in sixty seconds?"

* * *

EARLY MORNING
Thursday

CLAIRE'S FATHER PULLED into a visitor slot at Missy's high school. It had not crossed his mind that his sweet little girl would lie to him and so it did not cross his mind to quiz her. "I'll just sit in the truck with my coffee and my paper," he told Claire. "If it's going to take longer than fifteen minutes, phone me. I'll come in, and that will hurry things up. I know how Missy can chatter." Her father fussed with the sip opening on the lid of his take-away coffee cup, which refused to snap into place. He didn't pick up on Claire's anxiety.

She headed toward the front doors, leaving her book bag and purse in the truck. She felt naked without them, as if she had no business being here.

And I don't, she thought.

She had never been in this building. Missy's school system had only tenth through twelfth grades in the high school, and it was only six weeks into Missy's sophomore year. Claire had not yet attended any of her cousin's school games or activities.

The front steps were imposing but shallow. Claire stumbled, which demolished her poise. The years leached away, and she felt like a newcomer on the first day of seventh grade, wearing the wrong clothes.

It was 7:37.

At 7:45 would come the Pledge of Allegiance followed by the announcements, presented by Rick.

Claire paused on the last step.

There was something dreadful about hoaxes: the perpetrator planned to make suckers out of her very own friends.

I can turn around, she thought. Go home. Text Missy so she has time to cancel with Rick.

Claire could not imagine letting Missy down. Furthermore, she could feel Missy's excitement. She and Missy were already breathing in synchrony. She even knew that Missy's panting was from eagerness while she herself was gasping from worry.

I don't *know,* she reminded herself. I just know Missy well enough to guess.

How odd that Missy had even noticed the hoax assignment. Missy did not care for biology. She did not care about Mrs. Stancil. Why was Missy going to such trouble?

The glass-walled foyer faced south and had collected the heat of the sun even at this early hour. Claire was immediately uncomfortable in her pink cashmere sweater. It was too dressy. She had a flicker of surprise that Missy hadn't thought about this, because Missy had excellent fashion sense. Then she thought, Missy wants people to see clothing instead of us. Helps the hoax along.

Claire threaded through strangers, unpleasantly aware of her hot clinging sweater.

"Hey, Missy!" came a shout.

Oh, good. Her cousin had come to get her. Claire looked around.

A total stranger was waving and smiling. "You finish your essay, Missy?" he called.

Missy was not in the foyer. Only Claire was in the foyer.

The boy was laughing now, and two girls standing near him began to laugh too. "Yes, you, Missy," said one of the girls. "Love the sweater. You going somewhere special?" The girl walked up to Claire and hugged her lightly.

Missy and this total stranger were close enough friends for hugs? How could such a friend be so clueless? How could she literally touch Claire and still not know she wasn't Missy? "There is a special event coming up," Claire said nervously.

"We'll want to hear all about it," said the girl. She and the other two students drifted away.

Maybe Mrs. Stancil's hoax assignment was not so stupid after all. People needed to pay attention. Ask questions. Accept nothing without careful examination. This would be a wake-up call.

The foyer had largely emptied. Missy had told Claire to turn right and follow a long straight corridor. Claire obeyed. She turned into a dim corridor and saw a distant pink sweater.

The pink sweater approached.

Claire had the oddest sense of seeing herself in a mirror. Herself was walking toward her. That was her own thick ponytail swinging back and forth, her own earrings bouncing on her own small earlobes. Her own head was tilted slightly to the side. That was her own wave, long fingers not relaxed and curved, but held stiffly, as if lacking a middle joint. Now Claire's smile burst on the other face and Claire's laugh came out of the other mouth.

Claire's eyesight blurred. Her steps grew uneven.

This is a hoax, she told herself. This is pretend. *I* can't be the one who falls for it.

"Could you cheer up a little, Clairedy?" teased Missy. "You're thrilled, remember? There will be witnesses in the studio, so don't goof up. You just have to hang on for a few minutes. I'll do the work."

Missy flung open a door and pulled Claire into the studio. Claire was now facing a wide plain desk on which lay a thin sheaf of papers. Flanking the desk were an American flag and a plastic fig tree. On the wall behind the desk was a blown-up photograph of the high school, with today's date tacked on the blue sky.

Standing at the desk was a short cute chunky boy wearing heavy black-framed glasses. He looked like a 1950s singer inventing rock music. "Wow!" said the boy, his jaw falling open. "Wow," he said again. "Missy," he said to Claire, "this is—I don't know. I mean—I never believed you for a minute. But . . ." He was half laughing, half horrified. "Missy," he whispered, "I actually can't tell which one is you."

Claire felt herself shutting down. The lights in her brain were going off.

"*I'm* Missy," said her cousin. "You're talking to my long-lost identical twin, Claire."

There were gasps from the students behind Claire, who were manning cameras and control panels. "How did you find each other?" demanded one of them. "It's like a miracle," whispered another.

"It *is* a miracle," said Missy, turning slowly to look into Claire's eyes.

For years, Claire had been the tall one. This year she and Missy were the same height, so their eyes were exactly even. Missy's were the same color and shape as her own, deeply set and perfect for eye shadow. Claire was inches from the exact same complexion, pointy chin and full lips. Inches from identical thin eyebrows, such a contrast to the extra-volume black hair.

Nothing is identical, Claire told herself. We share a strong family resemblance. People often comment on it. We are not twins. I am two months older than Missy. Miracles happen, but not the kind where the mother fails to give birth to the second twin for eight weeks. Anyway, my parents are my parents. Missy's parents are her parents. Nobody is adopted.

Missy, when she was nervous, always yanked out her ponytail. At the exact same moment both cousins pulled out their pink hair elastics, shook their heads in the same way to free up their hair and re-ponytailed.

"Isn't it time to do the Pledge of Allegiance, Rick?" asked Missy, yanking out her ponytail a second time, which meant she was really nervous.

Claire locked her fingers to prevent herself from yanking out *her* ponytail a second time. I am not Missy's mirror image, she reminded herself. This is a game. All I have to do is smile. Only Missy has to act.

Rick studied them minutely and then shook himself like a spaniel coming out of water. "After the Pledge, I do my regular stuff, and then I cut to you, Missy. You'll have about a minute. Margaret here will do a countdown, so you stop at the exact right second." Rick checked his lavalier mike, straightened his shirt and sat behind the desk.

There were no adults present. Either Missy had contrived to get rid of supervision, or Rick and his crew were so trusted that advisors didn't feel the need to be here. They might change their minds now. Claire whispered to her cousin, "What happened to Annabel Griffin?"

"I forgot about her." Missy squeezed Claire's hand. It gave Claire the oddest sensation that Missy was the older one. She was guided onto a stool, and a tiny mike was fastened to her sweater. She could not suppress a shudder.

"And roll," called out one of the crew.

Rick smiled at the cameras. "Good morning, friends."

Claire could not smile. She could barely stay attached to the stool. A series of memories passed through her, like the flipping of old snapshots. Mom refusing to let her dress like Missy anymore ("Baby-girl outfits are fine for Missy, but you need something tailored, Claire; something mature."). Mom insisting she could not wear her hair the same as Missy ("That looks sweet on Missy, but you need something more sophisticated.")

or participate in the same activities ("Don't copy Missy. Don't be a sheep in a flock. Strive to be different."). She remembered herself laughing. "Mom, I'm not copying Missy. All girls my age have long hair. I'm just part of the crowd."

"Is that the best thing, dear?" her mom had asked.

"Mom, it's hair. It does not predict my future as a clone of society."

A clone, thought Claire.

Hideous deep panic crawled into her heart.

When Missy began to talk, Claire was startled. Announcements were over already?

"Hi, everybody," said Missy, beaming at the cameras. "I'm Missy Vianello. I'm a sophomore here. And I have the most wonderful, amazing, beautiful thing to share. My identical twin just surfaced. We just found each other! Can you believe it? I have a long-lost identical twin. And this," said Missy, touching Claire's shoulder, "this is my twin, Claire."

A sob formed in her throat. Claire choked it back. She pressed her lips together and then her jaw. It was like squeezing a tube of toothpaste. Tears spurted out the top. "We shouldn't have done this," she said to Missy. Her voice sounded like gravel. "I shouldn't have agreed."

Missy ignored her. "Claire's going to attend school with me today," she said, perky as a cheerleader, "and this seemed like a good way to let everybody know who she is and why she's here."

Claire felt as if her bones had cracked. She tried to find something to hold on to, but for once it couldn't be Missy.

Missy was a stranger. What does she know and didn't tell me? thought Claire. We've always shared everything.

And then she thought, Or have we?

Claire could not control her tears.

Missy was shaken. "I guess this wasn't such a great idea after all. Rick, just cut our segment, okay?"

Rick was pale. "This is live, Missy. We can't cut anything. But we welcome you, Claire, and we're thrilled for you both, and this has definitely introduced you to the entire high school. It's seven-fifty-five, people. Have a nice day."

The passing bell rang immediately. It sounded more like an air-raid siren than the pleasant musical chord at Claire's school. A camera kid handed her a box of cheap tissues. She mopped up her face.

Claire's mother liked to repeat everything three times. "I'm busy, busy, busy," she would say. I'm okay, okay, okay, Claire told herself. I am not Missy's twin. I know all the family stories. My parents tried for years to have a baby, and when I was born at last, I was strong and healthy and Mom was thrilled, thrilled, thrilled. Missy was premature and had to stay in the hospital for weeks and weeks. Uncle Matt and Aunt Kitty hovered over her teensy little crib night after night, full of fear and prayer. We are not twins.

"That was something!" said Rick. "Thanks for letting me be part of it. I'm happy for both of you. I have to run. My first class is all the way on the other side of the school and up two floors."

"Thank you, Rick," cried Missy, cheerful as a Christmas elf.

Claire felt as drained as a tub.

"Nice to have you here, Claire," said one of the camera girls. "Good luck. See you later." And then they were all gone, rushing to their first-period classes.

Claire and Missy stood alone in the well-equipped studio. Missy shut the door. Claire pasted the tissue over her face.

"We'll wait until the hallways are clear," said Missy, "and hope the principal doesn't come racing down for some personal interviewing of her own. I think it went well. What did you think?"

I'm thinking that was not a hoax, thought Claire. But it has to be a hoax. If it's true, both of our parents lied all these years, along with all our relatives. If it's true, even my birthday is a lie. Or Missy's is.

But these days, no one kept adoption a secret. If you adopted a baby, you bragged about it. "I chose you," the parents said to their adopted child. "We chose our baby girl," they proudly told other parents.

Obviously your parents didn't want you. If they had wanted you, they would have kept you. And here you are, like a lemon of a car, back from the garage.

Who didn't want me? thought Claire.

"Somebody's coming," said Missy. "I don't want to talk to any teachers." She turned off the studio lights. In the pitch dark, the girls pressed themselves against the wall.

The door swung open and hid them. If the person pushed hard, Claire's foot or face would be smashed.

Nobody stepped inside. The door closed.

"Probably the principal," murmured Missy. "Or the advisor. It's dark in here, so they think we left. Hope they don't lock us in. That would be crummy."

How casual Missy sounded. Maybe she really felt casual. Maybe it really was a hoax.

Missy opened her cell phone. The girls stood in the dark, watching the tiny cool light of the screen, and its digital clock. Missy's cell displayed a photo of the two of them. It was not recent. Claire was visibly older and taller.

The vicious siren blatted the end of passing period.

"I'll walk you to the front door," said Missy. "Then I have to last through two class periods, and then comes biology, and then I fess up."

How awful if I were adopted, thought Claire. I want to be the daughter of the people I'm the daughter of. I want Missy to be the daughter of Uncle Matt and Aunt Kitty. I want both of us to have the same parents we've always had, forever and ever.

Missy opened the studio door and peeked out.

If we are actually separated twins, thought Claire, Missy and I *do* have the same parents.

We just don't know who they are.

Chapter

EIGHT A.M.
Still Thursday

CLAIRE AND MISSY walked silently to the foyer. Sunlight poured over them and dust motes danced around them. Claire loved the sun. Sometimes she thought of sunshine as her second-best friend, after Missy. Not that Missy felt like a friend right now. But in the soft yellow heat, the doubts Missy had sown disappeared. Claire was able to smile at her cousin. "See you tomorrow night."

Missy did not return the smile. She seemed to be waiting for something. Did she want compliments from Claire? ("Hey, good hoax, Miss.") In an oddly formal voice, Missy said, "Thanks for coming, Claire," and walked away.

Claire hurried to her father's truck. The shallow steps were as hard to go down as they had been to go up. She was surprised to find huge clay pots of gold chrysanthemums lining the brick path. She had been so anxious coming in that she had not seen in color.

The windshield of her father's pickup had collected a layer of leaves. In the cab, her father dozed, head back, mouth open, newspaper draped over the steering wheel. He was perfect, except for getting up to a weight that was dangerous.

This is my father, she told herself. I am not adopted.

Claire opened the passenger door. Hot air from the closed cab enveloped her like a hug. "Hi, Daddy." She yanked out her ponytail and let the thick black hair fall forward to hide any trace of tears.

Her father woke up and rubbed his eyes. "You finish bailing out your cousin?" He yawned, swigged a little coffee and frowned at the cup. It had probably gotten cold. He started the engine and backed out of the parking space.

"I finished," she told him. "Everything's good. Now I'm worried about how late I am. Drive fast, Dad. I don't want to miss my second-period class. It's Latin, and I did the entire translation perfectly and I want to get called on so I get a check-plus for the day." Claire did not usually ramble, nor was Latin a class that usually led her to tell anecdotes, but she babbled on. "We've been doing comparatives, Daddy. Like in the Latin motto for the Olympics? *Citius, altius, fortius.* Faster, higher, stronger."

"I love that you're taking Latin." Her father drove with the one-handed ease of somebody who is behind the wheel all the time. "School was hard for me. I couldn't wait to drop out. For years I was mad at my dad because he forced me to stay in school after I turned sixteen."

Claire's grandfather Linnehan had died last year after a long illness. Her grandmother had stayed in Arizona, where she was content to play endless card games in her retirement center. At most, Claire had seen her grandparents annually. Now she thought, If I'm adopted, Nana isn't Nana.

Her father accelerated onto the turnpike ramp. "Truth is, I barely graduated. It's so great to see my daughter be this terrific student who even enjoys Latin." Merging with I-95 traffic took his attention. He could only partially turn toward Claire and she could only partially see his grin.

No, she thought. It's a partial grin. He's faking as much as I am. He can't know what Missy and I just did. What is he upset about?

She lifted her hair out of the way and studied her father. There were lines in his face she hadn't noticed before. Gray patches in his hair she hadn't seen, and a sag to his shoulders. She had known her father could get heavier. But it had not occurred to her that he could get older.

The drive was difficult. Claire could not allow silence because her father might remember to ask what Missy's project had been about. It was surprisingly hard to engage him in discussion about his construction jobs; it was impossible to keep her mind off Missy's hoax.

The two families lived only twenty miles apart. Or so the parents claimed. Claire happened to know that the shortest route was actually twenty-two and six-tenths miles. In some parts of the country that was nothing. But in the suburbs of New York City it was major. There were few routes, and all had heavy traffic. During commuter time twenty miles could take an hour, a long time to sustain a conversation about Latin.

The questions Rick could have asked if he had done a proper interview—the questions anybody would ask if they considered Missy's presentation for a single minute—sprayed Claire's mind like insecticide, killing normal thought.

If she and Missy were identical twins—which was impossible, since she was older, but just pretend—then probably the biological mother was some poor teenager for whom having a baby had been the end of the world, not the beginning. Maybe she'd entrusted her twins to an adoption agency that by a wild coincidence had divided the twins between two adult sisters—Frannie Linnehan and Kitty Vianello.

What beautiful symmetry, sisters adopting twins.

But it did not add up. Couples who adopted told the whole world. They threw parties and held baby showers. They designed special birth announcements. They celebrated.

If Missy and Claire were twins, the Linnehans and the Vianellos had kept it secret.

What if there had been no teen mother? Both Claire's mother and Missy's mother had had trouble getting pregnant; years had passed without success. What if one of them had never gotten pregnant, while the other had given birth to two babies? What if Claire's very own mother and father had had twins and had given one to the Vianellos, or the other way around?

Claire tried to imagine her mother lying in the hospital bed, saying to the doctor, "Listen. I just want one. Call my sister. See if she'll take the extra kid."

Nobody would do that. And Dad would have been standing

there, wouldn't he? Didn't all fathers attend their child's birth? Dad would have said, "What are you talking about, Frannie? Two beautiful girls? And you want just one? I don't know what kind of postpartum depression that is, but get over it. I'll buy a second crib and we're all set."

It's insane even to think about this, Claire told herself. I am two months older than Missy. We are not twins. There's a strong family resemblance, that's all.

"We're here," said her father, smiling.

She ripped out a sheet of notebook paper and her father wrote her a late excuse. They kissed good-bye and Claire hopped down from the truck. In the office, the administrative aide gave her a late pass. She did not dawdle.

One good thing: Claire had definitely found out that she was susceptible to suggestion. Let somebody say to her, "You're an identical twin," and she was hypnotized and bought into it and became one.

This did not bode well for adult life, when Claire needed to be skeptical and careful because the world was full of bad guys and loser guys and greedy guys. Some lowlife would lean over her, saying, "I'm perfect, and you want to spend your life with me," and Claire would be hypnotized and agree, without even knowing the guy's name.

Claire wanted to share these thoughts with Missy, her response when anything happened in life and plenty of times when nothing did. But she was only steps from her classroom.

She remembered that she had a crush on Aiden, and that Aiden also took Latin. Since she was late, all eyes would turn toward her. Aiden might look interested, and she might text him during class.

She opened the classroom door. Sure enough, Aiden was smiling at her.

In her mind's eye, his clothing fell away.

If Missy and I are identical twins, she thought, we not only had a teen mother, we had a teen father. Some Aiden out there had sex with that girl. They could have been younger than I am now! Fifteen. Or even fourteen. I suppose they could have been thirteen! They smiled at each other across a classroom and one thing led to another and the next thing you know, they're having twins.

In that case, I am nothing but an error. Missy and I were a burden and a mistake. Just a set to be divided.

Claire could not look at Aiden. No matter how much the pretend teenage mother had enjoyed herself with her Aiden, the result wasn't pretty. A pregnancy was not an overnight thing. For nine months that girl had had weight gain and ankle swelling, fatigue and complications. Urine tests and blood tests, ultrasounds and internal exams. No more cool clothing for that girl; she had to shop for ugly, shapeless maternity clothes. But not baby clothes—she wasn't going to need those; she was giving her baby away. Then came the delivery, a postage-stamp word for a very scary event. Two scary events, if she'd had twins. Then this teenage girl had had to look at these two babies she'd created, shrug and go home. To what parents or relative or dorm room had she returned? To what welcome or anger? Then she'd have had to lose weight and try to feel like a kid again. Attend school again, but not as a kid. No matter how young she was, a mother was not a kid.

Claire could not look at Aiden, or at any other boy. She was the first to flee when the bell rang. She took refuge in the nearest girls' room. She wet a handful of paper towels, regretting that the school used rough gray recycled paper instead of nice soft white. She pressed the cold wetness against her feverish eyes.

Lilianne followed her into the bathroom. Claire and Lilianne had been in classes together since nursery school, but Claire did not want her company now.

"Claire?" said Lilianne softly. "Did you just find out?"

Claire stared at Lilianne. The hoax had been at Missy's school, which was in another state! How could Lilianne possibly know about the TV interview?

"My father, too," said Lilianne. "There just isn't any work. They're all just driving around in their trucks, pretending they have jobs, pretending they have income."

* * *

Rick's first-period class was advanced physics. It turned out that the physics teacher was himself a twin, although he was a fraternal twin and his twin was a girl. Mr. Shemtov had done a lot of reading over the years about twins, a fascinating subject, and especially about identical twins, who were even more fascinating. But most of all, he liked to read about identical twins who had been separated at birth.

"To a scientist," Mr. Shemtov told his class, "identical twins separated at birth are the ultimate biological test group. Studying that very small, very exceptional group allows the scientist to address huge questions. For example, what matters most in how a person turns out, genes or environment? Inherited traits or upbringing?"

It turned out that there were enough sets of identical twins separated at birth to use them in genetic, medical, nature/nurture and psychological studies. Rick could not imagine having major medical centers and universities call to ask if you would participate in a study about intelligence or schizophrenia or body fat.

"Rick," said Mr. Shemtov, "we have to interview these two girls. This is a crucial project even though it's a biology topic and this happens to be physics. It's too extraordinary to pass up, and you're first in line."

Missy does like me, thought Rick. And now she owes me. She's excited about this, even though poor Claire fell apart. Missy will cooperate in a research project. In fact, I bet that's why she did it. Not to introduce Claire, but to show off how interesting she is.

Rick was already full of ideas for what direction to take, eager to read other twin interviews. He yearned for the end of class and a few hours on his laptop.

Lucie said in a slow contemplative voice, "You know what, Rick?"

Rick adored Lucie, who never spoke to him except when necessary. "What?"

"There's a moment in your video where the viewer first real-izes that these two girls really and truly are identical twins. I had the sense that it was the first time the two of *them* really knew. It was so emotional when Claire started to sob. Your video is so powerful."

My video, thought Rick.

"Put it on YouTube, Rick," said Lucie. "It'll be the hottest video out there."

* * *

Missy's first class after the interview was gym, which had to be the world's worst scheduling, because she got sweaty and disgusting before the day had even begun. She entered the girls' locker room, wishing she had not chosen the pink cashmere sweater after all, and was assaulted by a chorus of questions and congratulations.

"Missy, where's Claire? I want to meet her!" "Missy, this is so exciting!" "Missy, how did you find each other, anyway?"

Missy peeled off her sweater. The air-conditioning was defective in this locker room. She hid under the wool for a moment, wondering how to answer.

"Missy, did you know already that you were adopted?" "Missy, that was unbelievable. You two were clones." "Exact images of each other, even the way you held your fingers and tossed your hair!"

The phrase "identical twin" was romantic and rare. The word "clone" was disturbing. A clone was an experiment. A test tube occupant. An aberration. Missy had never considered the idea of clones.

"I thought Claire was attending class with you, Missy!" "I can lend her shorts and a T-shirt."

What was Missy supposed to do now? If she said, "Her dad is driving her back to her own high school," everybody would want to know what high school, and what the dad thought, and whether Missy liked the other family. "Claire was a little shaken up," said Missy finally.

"A little! She was practically fainting." "Those tears just poured out!" "You'd have thought she didn't know what you were going to say."

And then standing in front of her was Rick's sister Alaina, weeping.

Was Rick in trouble? Trouble so bad that his sister had burst into tears? How could that have happened so fast? How could it happen at all? If anybody were to get into trouble, wouldn't it be Missy herself? "What's the matter, Alaina?" Missy asked nervously.

"Nothing's the matter. I'm crying for joy. I never saw anything so beautiful or so emotionally intense. Think of the odds against you two finding each other!" said Alaina. "And when poor Claire began to sob—my heart absolutely broke for her. Where is she? I'm dying to meet her. I want to see you two next to each other!"

The gym teacher blew the whistle she wore on a lanyard around her neck and the girls chugged out onto the gym floor. Although Ms. Nelligan taught gym, she was not in good shape.

Her nickname was Nelly Belly. "Where's Claire?" cried Nelly Belly. "You are so athletic, Missy, and I am so interested to see if the two of you share athletic abilities the way you share facial features!"

Even when the class divided to play two sets of half-court basketball, questions showered over Missy. No matter how many she brushed away, more fell.

"What do your parents think?" "Did you already know that you're adopted?" "Do you and Claire know who your real parents are?"

Every morning when Missy left for school, her father would yell down the stairs from his home office, "Knock their socks off, Missy!"

Missy had knocked the socks off every kid in school. A thousand teenagers were barefoot.

* * *

When Claire's father dropped his daughter off at her high school, he had nowhere to go. House building ran in cycles. You had your terrific decade and then you had your lousy decade. You had too much work for anybody to do, and then you had none.

This was a none time.

Phil Linnehan mainly did rough framing on houses for which he was the general contractor. This fall, few new houses were being constructed, and those jobs didn't need him. Usually in the afternoons, he coached. He'd started with T-ball back when Claire was hardly big enough to hoist a plastic bat. But this fall so many fathers and mothers were out of work that a large pool of adults was available for coaching. Phil was not needed.

An ardent Yankees fan, he usually managed several games a year. Nothing compared to Yankee Stadium. This year he could not afford tickets. He was at the place where even in coffee shops, which he hit several times a day, he bought only a cup of coffee—no eggs, no donuts—and left a tip so small it embarrassed him.

He was so proud of Claire. He loved looking at her and thinking about her. He loved watching her read or study, and oddly, he loved watching her send text messages. She adored her cell phone. There was no time when she wasn't texting Missy. He dreaded telling her that he had to change telephone plans and that she would have to drop out of the texting scene. He really dreaded the possibility that he and Frannie could not send their daughter to the college she deserved.

His wife worked harder than anybody he knew. An amazing number of women wanted to get their exercise in before work. Frannie led Jazzercise classes at six a.m. and throughout the day at the Y, the community center and a spa. Frannie still looked great in leotards. She had the cheerleader personality required to keep twenty or thirty women dancing, sliding and weight lifting for an hour.

But Frannie was tired. She and Phil were close to fifty. She couldn't keep this up. What would she do instead? What would either of them do?

Phil sipped cold coffee from the bottom of his paper cup. He wondered vaguely what his niece had needed help with. Missy was not the type to need help. Tiny as she had been at birth, Missy had nevertheless yelled since she could talk, "I'll do it myself."

He considered the coming weekend.

Frannie didn't have Jazzercise Friday evenings because nobody cared about exercise after twelve noon on a Friday. Friday evenings were special. If Claire stayed over at her cousin's, Phil and Frannie would go out for dinner and a movie. They loved movies. They loved popcorn. They loved holding hands.

Phil Linnehan didn't have the money for a movie and popcorn this week.

He hoped it was Missy's turn to come here, and they'd all play board games—fitting them in around the girls' texting, of course—and have fun without money, and he could last another few days without admitting to his family just how deep their troubles were.

* * *

When the passing bell finally rang, Missy sprinted out of the girls' locker room and down the hall. Halfway to her next class, she ran into Jill, who had attended every birthday party Missy had ever had, and certainly knew Claire. Missy expected Jill to stalk up, roll her eyes and scold her. "Oh, please," Jill would say. "That was your cousin. You thought you could fool us by wearing the same sweaters? What a hoax."

Sure enough, Jill raced up to Missy. But she flung her arms around her and whirled her in a wild excited dance. "Missy! I'm so stunned and thrilled and weepy! I mean, I can't believe it. You two are absolutely totally identical. I didn't know identical twins would be *that* identical! I mean, call me stupid, but I thought *I'd* be able to tell which one was you."

Missy gaped at her.

"And here your cousin is also named Claire! I mean, talk about coincidence. But they do say identical twins separated at birth lead very similar lives! Isn't it spooky?"

Missy was speechless.

Wendy—who had also been to many a sleepover at Missy's—Wendy, who had once shared a toothbrush with Claire—walked up and said, "I'm still trembling, Missy. Did you know that I'm adopted, too? If you ever need to talk about it, I'm here for you. It's a wonderful thing, and you're proud, because you sort of own the outlines of your life more than other kids do—since you're a gift and a choice, the way regular kids aren't."

Missy imagined Wendy's parents repeating those lines. It was a little insulting, actually. As if "regular" children weren't also a gift and a choice.

"But still and all," said Wendy, "sometimes you want to cry, because your real mother couldn't keep you."

Missy felt damaged.

"You two are so identical!" kids kept saying. As if there were varieties of identical and some twins were more identical than others.

"Did you ever suspect you had a twin?" they asked.

"Do you have the same hobbies?"

"Did your paths cross before and you didn't even know?"

"Did your parents know that they adopted half of a set?"

* * *

Rick returned to the high school TV studio, copied the relevant sixty seconds of video and uploaded it to YouTube.

He didn't want his video just sitting there, unknown and unviewed. It had to get attention. Rick was a busy guy; colleges liked busy guys and Rick was determined to get into a terrific college. In a few weeks, he would mail his applications. He just had a couple more essays to write and then he was done. His friend list included every acquaintance from every activity, class or sport he'd ever been in. He sent the link to all of these people then, did the same with his e-mail address list.

He imagined his video becoming the most viewed of the week and morphing into a future job in television journalism. He imagined Lucie asking for updates.

"And your explanation for being in a room you don't need to be in when you ought to be in class?" said Mrs. Conway, opening the studio door.

Rick grinned at the vice principal. "YouTube," he said, waving at the computer screen. "The identical-twin reunion."

"No, Rick. Not yet. Not unless it's okay with the parents."

Rick did not know Missy's parents, but the fact was, they

weren't her parents. Some other people were her parents. "I already did," he told the vice principal. "See?" He played the video.

Even Rick was shocked when he watched the video. The girls caught their breath in the same way. Turned aside to hide emotion at the same angle; displayed the exact same curve of cheek. Both had the same habit of yanking out and then re-making their ponytails. At the exact same moment, each girl's eyes filled with tears. Claire's spilled over; Missy's didn't.

Lucie was right. This was wrenching.

Rick exulted. Nobody would see this video and not forward it.

* * *

The high school Missy and Rick attended was a historic building, constructed long before anybody worried about wheelchairs and stairs. Elevators had been added later. Missy never used them. They were slow and Missy did not care for slow.

Now her energy failed her. The biology lab on the third floor seemed as hard to reach as Canada. She felt like a windup doll that might achieve a final gurgle and a last twitch, then fall to the floor.

Her classmate Devlin held the door for her. Boys rarely did that. It was disorienting. "I heard your new twin went on home," said Devlin. "You look as if you should go on home, too. How are your parents doing?" he said, almost tenderly.

Missy had guessed wrong about how this would play out. She had been mesmerized by the identical-twin aspect. Her classmates were mesmerized by the parents. Identical twins were exciting, reunited identical twins were thrilling, but the parent aspect was heartbreaking. Real parents had lost, or not wanted, or could not keep their own two daughters. Adopting parents, who would surely have taken both, had they but known, got one.

"So there are actually six parents," said Devlin. "Your adoptive parents, Claire's adoptive parents, and the real parents."

Devlin had some nerve treating her life as public property. Then Missy remembered that she herself had put it in morning announcements. It *was* public property.

The rest of the class was already seated. Every eye was on her. Mrs. Stancil clapped. "Missy!" she cried. "I am so thrilled for you. What an event! Identical twins are one of the most interesting biological twists in nature."

Normally Missy would have found that a hoot. She would have been texting her cousin: *We're twists, Clairedy.*

Mrs. Stancil stopped talking. Nobody spoke, moved, tapped a pencil or turned a page. They waited for Missy Vianello to talk.

Missy had assured Claire that nothing could go wrong in sixty seconds. She had forgotten that plenty could go wrong after that. She had wanted one consequence, but she was getting a dozen. Her smile wobbled. "That was my hoax. Claire is my cousin. We don't even look that much alike. There's just a strong family resemblance. You were expecting us to look exactly alike because Rick fell for it, and you believed him, and so you believed me."

For a moment the silence continued and the faces were still eager. Then they became furious.

"It was a scam?" said Carlotta, outraged.

"That was incredibly rude of you!" snapped Kelsey.

"I *believed* you, Missy. And all along you were a fake!" said Devlin, as if they had an ongoing relationship and she'd been deceiving him for months.

"I thought you'd be on talk shows and become a celebrity," said Angela resentfully.

"Missy! You giggled at that TV camera and your cousin pretended to sob and all the time it was a joke?" demanded Emily.

It had not occurred to Missy that people who got duped would be angry when they found out. "It wasn't a joke," she protested. "It was our assignment. Remember? The hoax assignment?"

Mrs. Stancil, who always taught standing up, sat heavily on her desk. "Missy, how could you? I'll have to tell the principal."

"You wanted us to do it," protested Missy.

Graham said in a belligerent voice, "Let's run the video again. I believed it this morning, and I believe it now. You two are mirror images of each other, Missy."

Carlotta corrected him. "Not mirror images. That would mean, for example, that if Missy's hair parted on the right, then Claire's would part on the left, and so forth. They are not mirror images. They are clones."

"I am not a clone," said Missy.

"That's what identical twins are," snapped Carlotta.

"Not precisely," said Mrs. Stancil, picking up her cell phone. "Janet?" she said to the principal's secretary. "See if I can have five minutes at the end of the period. Yes, the twin situation is exciting. It is also a hoax. They're just cousins."

"You're in trouble now, Missy," said Kelsey gladly. "The principal will call your parents."

If Missy had had any exuberance left after her moment on live TV, it was over.

What *would* her parents do? What would anybody do if they found out their only child had stood in front of a TV screen and claimed to an audience of one thousand that she had been adopted?

Technically, Missy hadn't claimed that. She had claimed to have found a lost twin. But every kid in high school instantly glommed on to the parent problem. Namely, who *are* the real parents? Not the ones Missy used to claim. And Rick had instantly assessed the other parent problem: Would Missy's adoptive parents be okay with this revelation?

Who could be okay? Kitty and Matt Vianello had built their lives around Missy. No. They wouldn't be okay.

Missy's parents had home offices. They were tied to the house like dogs on leashes. Although their jobs were unrelated, if one of them had to go out, the other would answer both phones. The family had a total of three cell phones, a landline for the house, two business phones and two fax lines. Something was always ringing or humming or buzzing, as if a dozen people lived there instead of three.

It was an ordinary house. Her parents had the big bedroom with its own bath and walk-in closets, and Missy had the medium bedroom. The two tiny bedrooms were offices. All day long, her parents roved through the house, making coffee, working on the same crossword, reading the paper, jotting down lists. Against school rules, they texted Missy on and off all day. You were supposed to read messages at lunch or during passing periods, but Missy read them when they were sent, holding her cell phone under her desk.

At home, there was constant dialogue. The Vianellos were never silent. Missy would walk in the door after school to hear her father yelling downstairs to her mother, "I used up the last of the milk. Put that on the shopping list!"

"I'm not in the kitchen," Mom would shriek. "Add it your-self when you're down there."

"Missy, did you just come in?" her father would holler. "Write milk on the shopping list."

Unlike parents on TV talk shows or in women's magazines, Matt and Kitty Vianello did not hold deep conversations. They held millions of trivial conversations. Nobody discussed truth or beauty. Nobody discussed politics or current events, except to say "Can you believe that?" or perhaps "I can't stand it!" Missy did not use Twitter, but the word was perfect for her family—beautiful birds in a small cage, singing to each other, completely wrapped up in their twittery lives.

Other families discussed things over dinner, but the Vianellos did not even sit down for dinner. They rarely cooked. They were users of delicatessens, caterers, salad bars at supermarkets and a slew of take-out restaurants. Groceries were delivered. They had a dining room, but used the table for packages and piles. Her parents could extend a meal for hours, nibbling at vegetables, picking at cheese, buttering a roll, returning an hour later to reheat an entrée in the microwave. Missy often filled a plate only to forget about it, wander back later and get something out of the freezer instead.

They had a cleaning lady one day a week, which was good, because otherwise they would live in squalor. The cleaning lady scrubbed the bathrooms, mopped, vacuumed and did laundry. She was not patient. She would yell at Missy's parents, "Get out of the way! Pick up your junk! Bring your clothes to the washing machine, I'm not getting them off the floor."

Claire's house was a complete contrast. Uncle Phil and Aunt Frannie were excellent cooks. Dinners included a vegetable, salad and dessert along with the carefully considered main dish. Every dinner was eaten at a table, and the Linnehans had several: kitchen, dining room, sun porch, deck. Nobody watched television as they ate. Nobody interrupted a conversation; everybody waited patiently for one story to end before adding his or her own thoughts. They even chewed slowly. Missy always felt as if she were traveling between planets when she stayed over at Claire's.

And yet their mothers were sisters. It was why Missy and Claire looked so much alike; they had half the same genes.

Or not, thought Missy.

Their dads had nothing in common. Claire's dad was a huge

sports fan and followed beloved teams in several sports. He had all the T-shirts and read all the blogs. Missy's father was largely unaware of sports and when forced into a conversation would say, "What a game!" which saved him from having to know whether they were talking about soccer or baseball. Uncle Phil was always outdoors coaching kids or else framing houses, but Missy's father had no interest in fresh air and owned one tool—a screwdriver that was never the right type or size.

When the two families got together, it was difficult to believe anybody was related to anybody.

Missy did not think they were.

* * *

"Grace," said the principal to Mrs. Stancil behind the closed doors of her office, "you actually gave your students an assignment to create a hoax?"

"The theory was that the kids would do serious research—dinosaur bones in Montana or peat bog burials in Denmark—and with that research, buttress a pretend discovery. I thought it would add a little spice and get everybody excited. We weren't going to fake anything to the public."

"I have already had phone calls from two school board members."

Mrs. Stancil stared. "How could they know?"

"Grace! What century are you in? Rick put it on YouTube. Kids texted their parents! Our student test scores slid this year,

SATs are down and dropout percentages continue to swell. Now one of my teachers has abandoned the biology curriculum for a hoax assignment?"

"Missy didn't do what I asked," protested Mrs. Stancil. "She just pulled off a prank."

"A prank that is your responsibility."

Grace Stancil did not want responsibility. "I'll withdraw the concept, and that will be that."

"Grace, I cannot correct YouTube. The world is going to think that our school reunited lost identical twins. What's more fun than that? What TV talk show wouldn't want two beautiful, tearful girls who just found out they're separated identical twins?" The principal stood up. "The parents have to be informed."

Grace Stancil left the principal's office. She would make Missy call. That would be easier, and blame would lie where it belonged.

Then she thought, Tomorrow is Friday. I can let it go over the weekend. It'll fizzle out.

* * *

Shortly before the end of the school day, Mrs. Conway's voice came over the public address system. "I'm sorry to break in, people. May I have your attention, please. This morning we saw on our in-house television what we thought was an emotional and stirring reunion between identical twins. In fact, Missy Vianello was perpetrating a hoax using her cousin.

Missy regrets having misled us and hopes you had a good laugh. The girls are not identical, they just have a strong family resemblance, and I'm asking students please not to spread rumors about identical twins."

But Mrs. Conway, like Mrs. Stancil, was occupying another century. Rumors were no longer spread by word of mouth. Hours had gone by. Several hundred kids had already forwarded Rick's video to everybody they knew.

CHAPTER

THE SAME THURSDAY
After school

MRS. CONWAY'S OFFICE was large. Missy and Rick were seated at a distance from the vice principal, and from each other.

"Melissa," said Mrs. Conway.

Nobody called her Melissa. She had always been Missy. Her parents often talked about the terrifying days and nights they'd spent in newborn intensive care, hanging over their sick little girl. It was the nurses who had begun to call the tiny baby Missy.

Claire's right, thought Missy dully. Adoptive parents don't visit NICU. I've made this all up. I relied on a stupid talk show, when I didn't even hear the beginning or the ending of it, and it probably had nothing to do with me anyway, and now I have to pay the price.

"Melissa, what were you thinking?" demanded Mrs. Conway.

I was thinking, thought Missy, that Claire would weep from joy when she grasped that we are not cousins after all. Instead, Claire wept from horror. I was thinking that this television moment would corner my mom and dad, and Claire's mom and dad, but most of all, Claire.

What was the point in proving you were identical twins if the other twin didn't want to be one? Missy had known she might hurt somebody with this hoax, but she had not expected to get hurt herself. She had once read a remark made by an identical twin: "If you're an identical twin, you're never alone." Wrong, thought Missy.

"Melissa, I am disappointed in you," said Mrs. Conway. "Why on earth did you perpetrate this hoax?"

"It was not a hoax!" said Rick. "Those two girls are identical. Missy, stop denying it. Just look at this frame, Missy. I've paused it where you and Claire face each other."

Even from Claire, with whom Missy supposedly shared everything, there were secrets. Missy had a hole at the bottom of her heart. The hole was a slit, as if left by a knife blade. Sometimes she could feel it when she breathed—a cold spot in her soul. At the dry cleaner's, Missy had realized that the cold place was not a slot. It was a slice. Something had been cut away, as if her heart were a pie, and a fraction had been served to somebody else.

Claire was that fraction.

Claire was the deep member of the family. Claire read classics and booklist books of her own free will—from the difficult antique phrasing of *Robinson Crusoe* to the horrors of *The Gulag Archipelago* by Solzhenitsyn and *Man's Search for Meaning* by Viktor Frankl.

Missy kept up with *People* magazine.

Claire's books were about finding truth. Missy's were about nontruth, about celebrity and scandal.

And yet it was Missy who was desperate for truth. Now she was humiliated by her fantasy. It was pitiful.

"Missy!" yelled Rick.

Missy had been there. She didn't need to see the video. But she was trapped. She watched Rick's video. Two utterly identical girls looked back at her.

"Melissa," said Mrs. Conway, "the resemblance is certainly there, but what a cruel punch to your own family! And a low trick to play on your school. Furthermore, it's now online. Melissa, do you understand what the Internet *is*?"

"Yes, Mrs. Conway. I realize that Rick's video is irretrievable."

In their home offices, Missy's parents sat at computers all day. It was possible that they had already come upon the video, or that it had been forwarded to them and they were only a click away from viewing it.

If I'm really their daughter, thought Missy, I have to face them with what I've done. But if I'm not their daughter, they have to face me.

In the end, Mrs. Conway did nothing to either student, because there wasn't anything to do. Rick and Missy left the vice principal's office and walked out of the building.

Almost never did seniors take a school bus. Rick was the rare exception. His parents did not spend their money on cars and car insurance. Rick's father had a traveling hobby: he wanted to visit every football and major league baseball stadium in America and every NASCAR track, and also fish in a hundred remote but famous streams. Rick and his father were always flying to some distant venue for some great clash of athletes or else for trout. Rick was an interesting guy.

As for Missy, she was the last bus pickup in the morning and the first drop-off in the afternoon, making her bus ride quick and easy. Yet another reason why her parents were not about to let Missy have her license. Why pay for cars and insurance when you had free transport at the front door?

The buses were long gone. Rick and Missy could hike home or call their parents. Missy was not ready for parents. "I guess I'm walking," she said to Rick.

"I'll walk with you."

Missy set a fast pace.

"You can't outwalk me," said Rick. "You two are identical twins. I'll buy you a Coke if you tell me the real story."

"I have a refrigerator full of Cokes at home," said Missy, although at the moment she could think of no one she'd like to share a Coke with more than Rick.

"I'll give you more airtime."

"Thanks. I had all I needed."

"Missy, you owe me. I want to do a real interview. With you and Claire. How does the weekend look?"

The weekend did not look like the usual sleepover. Why wasn't Claire glad? thought Missy.

At the next intersection Rick had to walk in a different direction. "Think about it, okay, Missy?"

She smiled at him. He was nice. This wasn't his fault.

He smiled back. "Say hi to your sister."

Missy had used the word "twin." She had never used the word "sister." *I have a sister.*

How dare they? she thought. How dare my parents separate us?

* * *

Claire's last class on Thursday was math, which came easily to her, and her best friends and the adorable Aiden were in it.

The hoax had thrown her into a tailspin and now Lilianne had spilled the unemployment news. It had never occurred to Claire that her father had problems. What else had never occurred to her? Certainly not adoption.

Claire walked into math class with her eyes averted so she would not see all these boys who were capable of being fathers and giving their daughters up for adoption. She wrenched her mind off the choreography of sex.

This was the moment Aiden chose to rush over. "Hi, Claire!"

In middle school, Aiden had been a loser. A lot of boys fit into this category in seventh and eighth grade. But by junior year, Aiden was tall, lean and sophisticated.

Claire tried to look like a girl with no concerns, a girl who was fun. Immediately the word "fun" felt like a substitute for the word "sex," which rushed toward the appalling concept of teen fathers who abandoned their daughters.

"Remember Ashley Moore?" said Aiden excitedly. "Remember she used to live next door to me? Remember she moved away?"

Ashley had been both a cheerleader and a member of the dance team, which hardly seemed fair. Claire loved to dance, and of course Jazzercise used dance steps, so Claire had grown up at the feet of a dancing woman. But even with all that exposure, she was not a fine dancer. She and every other girl in school had been envious of Ashley. Had Ashley come back to snag Aiden?

A huge grin spread across Aiden's face. "Ashley sent me the video."

Ashley was sending Aiden videos?

"Ashley says hello. She says congratulations."

Claire was thinking of dance. Of Ashley. And then it came to her. She, Claire Linnehan, who loved Facebook and YouTube and all the other social networking sites, who could hardly wait for the next download, had thought of her sixty seconds at Missy's high school as a contained and finite event. A little box of time now closed. Sealed. Done.

But nothing stays in a drawer in a studio in another state. Nothing filmed is ever over. Of course there was a video. Of course it was online.

Claire yanked her ponytail out. Set her books down on her desk. Repaired the ponytail.

"A girl Ashley roomed with last year in cheerleading camp forwarded it to her," explained Aiden, "because she remembered Ashley used to attend this school."

This school? But the video had been filmed at Missy's school. In another state. Claire said thickly, "I don't think I mentioned my high school."

"No, you didn't. But it's one of the tags the announcer Rick used. It's so exciting about your new sister."

Sister.

Claire felt as if weight were actually falling off her. If she looked down, she would see pounds of flesh lying on the floor, like locks of hair after a cut.

"That TV interview was so tough on you," said Aiden. "I don't blame you for sobbing."

Claire would have said that a tear or two might have leaked out of one eye. She had sobbed?

The math teacher began teaching. Aiden lowered his voice. "I think identical twins are fascinating. I mean, the whole concept. Being exactly, totally the same as another person."

Claire remembered the math. The indisputable eight-week age gap between her and Missy. She clung to the fact of the age difference.

I am not exactly, totally the same as any other person. It is impossible for us to be sisters. Aiden succumbed to the power of suggestion because Missy and I have a strong family resemblance.

The teacher raised his voice. "We will put today's exercises on the board to observe how each problem is solved. Claire, will you begin?"

Begin what? And why? Who cared?

Now that Claire thought about it, who was it that she and Missy were supposed to resemble? Claire didn't look a bit like either of her parents and Missy didn't look a bit like hers. The strong family resemblance was strictly between Claire and Missy.

Claire needed to talk to Missy. Needed it like oxygen.

She stomped on the thought. I do not *need* Missy. She is not oxygen to me. I am complete without her.

But was she? Saturdays, when they parted company for another week, when Missy disappeared from sight, Claire would feel as if one of her limbs had been amputated.

Roberta, who sat behind Claire, leaned forward to tap the first exercise on the homework sheet with her beautiful fingernail. Roberta's nails were black today, and featured tiny silver fir trees. Claire managed to walk to the board and write out her work.

Thinking about identical twins gave her vertigo. If she tipped close enough to the concept, she and Missy might merge. There would not be two of them. There would be one of them.

"Perfect," said the teacher. "Any questions, people?"

Claire made it back to her seat. "How long is the video?" she whispered to Aiden.

"Maybe a minute. When did you find out, Claire? How are your parents handling it?"

My parents are going to see that video! It isn't just me on the receiving end of Missy's hoax. It's Mom and Dad. It's my aunt and uncle. They'll be crushed.

Roberta whispered, "You're going to go bald yanking at your hair like that."

Claire could handle a new identical twin more easily than going bald. She re-ponytailed and locked her fingers together.

Usually she would be texting Missy about now, but she had

turned her phone off, which was like having her mind off or her pulse off.

Tomorrow was Friday. Sleepover night. Missy used to call them Claire-overs. When things in Claire's life went wrong, Missy's presence would remove the sting every Friday night.

Now Missy was the sting.

* * *

Missy stood on the front steps of her house, unwilling to walk in the door.

Melissa, what were you thinking? Mrs. Conway had demanded.

She had been thinking of an afternoon at the mall in August, only a few months ago. Both the Vianellos and the Linnehans had been considering new appliances. Was there anything more boring than reading refrigerator energy-use tags? Missy and Claire had abandoned their parents and sped to a clothing shop too expensive for their parents to consider. For a lovely half hour, the cousins tried stuff on.

The saleswoman could not figure out how one customer changed so fast into so many outfits. Missy was emerging from the dressing room when the clerk spotted Claire poking through the accessories. "Why, you're identical twins! You're adorable," she cried.

Over the last few years, the girls had often been asked if they were twins. They would haul out the "family resemblance" line.

But this was different. This was a woman who did nothing all day but scan bodies.

Claire laughed. "We're just cousins."

The saleswoman snorted. "No way. You are identical."

Claire ignored this. "I absolutely have to have these earrings," she said, handing the clerk a shiny card from which pink and silver bead earrings dangled. The woman was already holding a card with the exact same earrings, which Missy had picked out earlier.

"See?" said the clerk to Missy.

Missy saw.

Claire didn't.

Missy's mother had been horrified when Missy related this anecdote, and had returned to the same old topic of tapering off the cousin activity. "It's not healthy to rely so heavily on a cousin," said Missy's mother. "No more sleepovers."

"Fridays are sacred," protested Missy.

"Sundays are sacred. Fridays are habit. In just a few years, Claire's going to college. And here you are, depending on her like a toddler with a blankie."

That night Missy had researched identical twins.

Surprisingly, experts couldn't always tell by sight whether twins were identical. Fraternal twins could look very much alike, and might be called identical twins until blood tests proved this incorrect. Parents who had identical twins might not see them as being exactly alike; they would magnify the slightest difference between their children. The difference might be attitude or personality or a chipped tooth, but it loomed large for the parents. As for the twins themselves, it was not unusual for identical twins to think they only mildly resembled each other. They would insist they were fraternal twins.

There were ways to determine whether two children were identical: Comparing ponderal indices. Fingerprint ridge counts. Palm print characteristics. DNA profiles. But even in these, fraternal twins could be confusingly close.

The real test was blood. There were as many as eighteen possible blood tests, and their combined result had a .001 percent chance of error.

Missy not only had no way to check these, she had no need. Claire was eight weeks older. Twins had to be born on the same day. Well—maybe one could be born at 11:59 p.m. and the other one at 12:15 a.m. the next calendar day. But no mother gave birth to Baby A and eight weeks later delivered Baby B. Definitively, Missy and Claire were not twins.

Still and all, Missy could not let go of her twin research.

Girls dream of boyfriends and love, college and careers. They do not dream of being identical twins. If Missy had told anybody about her biologically impossible daydream, they'd probably want to deprogram her.

All through August and into September, Missy did not share her research even with Claire. She tried to match what she knew of her parents' lives with what she learned.

Matt and Kitty taught elementary school and had always spent every vacation traveling. They'd been in each of the fifty states, towing a tent-style camper behind them and staying at parks whose slots they reserved a year in advance.

The day came when they wanted kids and nothing happened. Years passed. No baby. Conception was chaotic for identical twins, but failure to conceive was just as chaotic for the sad, desperate parents. During those same years, Aunt Frannie and Uncle Phil had also had trouble getting pregnant.

Years ago Missy had overheard her aunt exchanging pregnancy stories with a friend. The friend was very emotional over the story of sisters who had managed to get pregnant within weeks of each other. "Oh, the power of sister relationships!" cried the friend. "All that hormone communication and empathy!"

Even then, Missy knew that sisterly empathy did not result in a baby. And yet, the friend was correct. After years of dashed hopes and failed attempts, two adult sisters did have babies at almost the same time.

"Almost" was not "exactly." Twins had to be born at exactly the same time.

And then had come a moment in a dry cleaner's and a few lines on a radio. As talk show topics went, it was predictable. Who didn't wonder what it would be like to have or to be an identical twin?

"Sometimes," said the voice on the radio, "parents do not realize that twins are identical because the babies faced environmental differences. The environment is the mother. There are two babies inside her, and sometimes one baby has less room and less nutrition. One is bigger and stronger at birth and therefore looks radically different from its smaller, weaker twin. It does not occur to the mother or the doctor that her twins are identical. Intriguingly, when identical twins are different in size and weight at birth, the little one almost always catches up to the bigger one, and they will end up identical in weight, height and bone structure after all."

When they were toddlers and throughout elementary school, little Missy had worn Claire's hand-me-downs. But in that dress shop at the mall in August, Missy had shared a dressing room with a cousin who fit perfectly into the exact same clothing. Their bone structure, size and weight were identical.

What if I was the smaller, weaker twin? thought Missy. What if I finally caught up to my bigger, stronger twin? Then my birthday is a lie. What if our parents got away with that lie because I was so small? No one could look at the two babies who were Claire and Missy and see any similarity.

But who would lie about their daughter's birthday? And why? Adoption doesn't just happen. There are documents and decrees, social workers and judges. Every piece of paper, every court hearing and every result requires a name and a date of birth, doesn't it?

Or had the Vianello and Linnehan families skipped all that? Had they acquired a set of twins and divided them? How had they gone about this? Legally?

Missy walked into her house. By now, the school would have contacted her parents.

* * *

At 5:45 that Thursday afternoon, Claire's mother came home carrying two pizzas. One was red, with sausage, bacon, onions and garlic. The other was white, with fresh tomatoes, caramelized onions and capers.

Claire loved pizza. She loved watching her parents eat pizza. They were thin-crust people. Her father folded his wedge and ate it from the inside tip to the crust. Her mother cut off the crust, ate the triangle and then nibbled the leftover edge as dessert.

Claire told herself that Missy was a jerk, and there were real things to worry about now, namely her father's joblessness. She did not want to blurt, "So I found out by gossip that you aren't working."

Her dad wasn't doing anything wrong; it was just wrong to have left her out. Maybe it was a form of protection. A "my little girl doesn't need to worry her sweet little head" act.

I'm almost seventeen! she thought. Don't protect me!

Her father folded his pizza, took the first satisfying bite and grinned through the cheese. There was no happiness like hot pizza happiness.

Mom talked. Frannie Linnehan loved her Jazzercise clients, whose lives were her own personal soap opera. She updated Claire and Dad on women they had never met and never would: June had lost another five pounds; Olivia was going to Tuscany; Suzie had taken up bird-watching and spent a lot of money on binoculars but was bored now; Kate's bridesmaid dress was tangerine, which looked awful on her; Emily had gotten her figure back three years after the birth of baby Austin.

"Emily's blog," said Mom, "has photographs of Austin being toilet trained. Icky, icky, icky."

Claire had to laugh.

"And guess what. Emily's expecting again. She's thrilled, thrilled, thrilled, but afraid she'll gain fifty-seven pounds this time too."

On Claire, that would be half again as much flesh. As impossible as turning into identical twins or being adopted. "How much weight did you gain with me, Mom?"

"Let's not think about pounds. Especially not when I am contemplating dessert."

"I can have dessert," said Claire's father. "I worked hard today."

Claire almost said, "No, you didn't."

But she kept silent.

You aren't a family if you aren't sharing problems as well as triumphs.

Maybe we aren't a family.

* * *

Rick's father was furious with him. "You had to know it was a hoax. Identical twins don't drop out of the sky. You saw through Missy. You just did it anyway. Here you have this terrific record of running that studio flawlessly and you do a stupid thing like that."

"Dad, I don't think it was a hoax."

"They wore the same sweater, that's all. They have the same black hair cut the same length."

68

"No, Dad. They are identical."

"They were using you," said his father.

"For sure," said Rick. "I don't know why. And yes, Missy admitted it was a hoax. In fact, she insisted. But it isn't. Just look at the video, okay, Dad?"

In Rick's house, computers were never turned off; they just slept occasionally. Rick played the video for his father.

His father gasped. "Those poor parents," he breathed.

"Which ones?"

"All of them. Missy's. Claire's. The biological ones. Your physics teacher is right, Rick. You've got to follow up."

* * *

At Missy's house, Dad had reached dessert, Mom was still on cheese and crackers, and Missy, having nuked some leftovers and decided against them, was having an ice cream sandwich. Her tongue scooped out the ice cream close to the edges and she was nibbling the chocolate cookie.

Her parents hadn't seen the video. The school hadn't called. This seemed impossible to Missy, whose cell phone rang continuously. There was only one ring tone she wanted to hear: Claire's. Claire didn't call. All afternoon, all evening, Claire didn't call. They weren't going to talk about how they might actually be sisters? Claire wasn't going to ask what had happened when Missy walked into biology? Claire didn't care whether people believed the hoax? Claire wouldn't think to herself, Maybe it *isn't* a hoax?

Missy's father had dropped into his favorite chair and was reading more of his paper. Matt Vianello worked on his *Wall Street Journal* the way some people work on a cup of coffee, sipping and savoring. Missy couldn't imagine why he didn't read it online, since he sat in front of the screen all day, but he liked it on paper.

Missy was supposedly doing her Language Arts homework, which was about similes and metaphors. She had to fill in the blanks. "The first day of school is like a _____" and so on.

"Hey, Miss," said her father. "You still doing similes and metaphors? Here's one. It's poetic."

"Poetic?" asked Missy's mom. "The *Journal*?"

What was the opposite of poetic? Missy imagined saying to her unsuspecting parents, "I want proof. Give me your blood."

" 'The future,' " read her father, " 'isn't a hat full of little shredded pieces of the past.' Instead, this guy says, the future is a whirlpool populated by black swans."

"What a pretty thought," said Mom. "Although I think in our hemisphere there are only white swans. Australia has black swans. I've always wanted to go to Australia. Maybe a train trip through the outback. What was that movie, do you remember that movie? Ever since I saw that movie I've wanted to go to Australia."

" 'Black swans,' " her father explained, paying no attention to his wife's travelogue, " 'are events that are hugely important, rare and unpredictable, and explicable only after the fact.' "

"I wonder what the airfare to Australia is. Wouldn't that be a good vacation? Of course it would be such a long flight. I wish we were rich and could fly first class."

"Great metaphor, huh, Miss?" said her father. "I think, since it's the *Journal,* the black swan refers to the economy."

"Thanks, Dad," Missy was shaking. She went to her room. Shut the door. Called her cousin. "Hi, Claire."

"I hope you're happy," said Claire. "There's a video. Aiden already saw it. He said he understood why I sobbed. Missy, how could you do this to me?"

I did it *for* you, thought Missy. For both of us. "You agreed to it."

"But I didn't understand! And how are our parents going to understand? And what are *we* going to have to understand after *they* understand?"

"Maybe that we really are sisters?"

"Oh, come on, Missy! You set Mrs. Stancil up. You talked her into that hoax assignment. You staged this. You wanted me to face your theory in public. Why didn't you just say to me Wednesday night on the phone that you don't think we're cousins? That you think we're identical twins?"

"Because you wouldn't have taken it seriously, Claire. You always say we don't even look alike. You laughed at the saleswoman at the mall when we bought the same earrings, just like all the other times we've ended up with the same stuff. I even had you wear the earrings today to remind you. It didn't mean a thing to you. We convinced the whole school, Claire. Every single person believed us. Even Jill thought it was amazing that my new twin has the same name as my cousin."

"It is not true," said Claire. "Our mothers are right. You and I are on some crazy mental cliff. You're trying to pull me off the edge with you. We should have stopped this sleepover nonsense back in middle school. We're stopping now, Melissa. I'm not coming over tomorrow night and I don't want you coming here. I will not be your toy twin."

CHAPTER

MIDAFTERNOON
The same Thursday
Long Island, New York

THE WINDOWS OF Genevieve Candler's high school were not designed to open. With the air-conditioning turned off for the season, the soft warm sun had turned the building into a sauna. Sleepy from the heat, Genevieve drifted down the hall toward her final class.

Normally Genevieve was good at school—academics and friendships, sports and cafeteria dynamics came easily to her.

Today—nothing. She could not get her mind off dinner last night.

According to her best friend, Emma, Genevieve had the least involved parents in New York State. Emma's parents were the opposite. They won the award for most involved. They texted Emma, for example, every passing period to ask how the previous class had gone. Emma could hold lucid conversations while thumbing to a parent, B-plus on quiz. Must look up unicameral legislatures.

Genevieve would have been thrilled if her parents even once

a year noticed what was going on in her classes. Or that she had classes, for that matter.

Ned and Allegra Candler were pleasant to their daughter, as if she were a foreign exchange student who would be leaving in a week or two, and for whom a committee was responsible.

And yet Genevieve always hoped.

Last night her father had shown up with a white paper bag from one of the best delis on the Island. He had produced Moroccan spiced lamb, veal Toscana with leeks and mushrooms, grilled salmon pasta salad, coconut chicken with mango salsa, roasted asparagus, Gorgonzola salad with walnuts and bacon, long narrow golden loaves of bread, an assortment of giant crumbly cookies and gelato in three flavors.

Her parents ate out or didn't eat at all, being extremely concerned with staying slim. Genevieve couldn't remember the last time her father had brought actual food into the house.

Even more amazing, her mother had set the table. The Candlers almost never sat down together. What a treat to see her mother dance around, searching for place mats and napkins for the little round table in the breakfast area, a description they used in spite of the fact that none of them ate breakfast. Her mother even fixed a tiny centerpiece, lit a small fat candle and set a pretty yellow bread plate in front of everybody. Then she poured puddles of rosemary olive oil in the center of each plate and cut thick slices from the golden loaves.

Genevieve dipped her bread in oil, reveling in the presence of both mother and father at the same time.

As usual, Ned and Allegra were looking at each other. They

might be distant parents, but they were not distant partners. "What's our schedule for the weekend, Ned?" asked her mother.

Genevieve's father was in charge of giving away the charity dollars from his corporation. It wasn't a highly paid management position, but it was fun. People were always giving him tickets to golf tournaments and basketball play-offs, rock concerts in huge arenas and chamber music groups playing to six people in the library, museum fund-raisers and historical society lectures. He had his choice of New Year's Eve galas and Fourth of July picnics.

Mom had an immense wardrobe and was beautifully dressed for every occasion. She was the perfect guest. She never forgot who was the chairperson or past president or who had created the delightful favors for some party five years ago.

Rarely did Genevieve's parents ask her to join them at these events. She didn't mind missing an awards dinner at the Chamber of Commerce, but it would have been fun to go to the big tennis tournament with the famous players.

From the bread on her dish, Allegra Candler ate literally a crumb. She worked for a cosmetics and fragrance company in New York and looked like a walking advertisement. She was still a size six.

Emma's mother, on the other hand, had left size sixteen behind and was now shopping at stores where they skipped sizes in favor of letters. She basically bought a variety of tents and swathed herself in glorious fabric instead of trying to lose weight.

Genevieve sometimes wondered if the conditions were related: were skinny adults also skinny with love?

Her parents discussed clothing and weather, which of their cars to take and whether they could come home and change between commitments or needed a wardrobe bag. They would be at events Friday night, Saturday night and Sunday afternoon, while Dad also had an important golf game on Saturday morning.

Over the years, Genevieve had had many babysitters, but her primary refuge was her great-grandmother, for whom she was named. Right up until her ninetieth birthday, the elder Genevieve Candler had had her own beach house, her own sports car and her own ideas about things. Then she'd fallen down the stairs, broken some bones that didn't heal and gotten old. A minute later, or so it seemed, GeeGee was in a nursing home.

Before that, Genevieve had spent most weekends at her great-grandmother's. GeeGee was always ready to host a sleepover or take Genevieve and a friend into the city, or to the movies or shopping. But when GeeGee entered the nursing home, Genevieve had to stay home alone when her parents went out. She expected it to be fun, but it wasn't. Nothing on TV was appealing when she sat alone in front of it. It was hard to buckle down and do homework when she was alone, hard not to be bothered by sounds and shadows. In ninth grade, and to a degree in tenth, Genevieve managed to spend weekends with friends. But now, during her junior year, it exhausted her to make arrangements; to beg, to impose, to feel babyish because she wanted company and ashamed when friends exclaimed, "Your parents are gone *again*?"

If Genevieve implied that her parents didn't pay enough attention to her, Ned and Allegra would snap back. Other parents might coddle, smother and spoil their children, who would grow up to be failures as adults, pathetic specimens at work and play. But Ned and Allegra were giving their daughter wings to fly.

Genevieve felt she had been flying since she was six weeks old, when they had turned her over to the nanny. A little time in the nest with Mommy and Daddy would be nice.

At least she still had time with GeeGee.

Even at ninety-three, the older Genevieve Candler had the most beautiful smile in the world. When her great-granddaughter walked into the nursing home, GeeGee would cry, "Hello, sunshine!" "Hello, sweetness and light!" or "Hello, pride and joy!" Then she would have a hundred questions. "Tell me everything, Vivi. How is your crush on William coming? Is Meghan speaking to you again? Did Tess stay captain of the softball team in spite of her grades? What did the history teacher think of your essay? How did you do on the chemistry questions for High School Bowl?"

Genevieve was her great-grandmother's only frequent visitor. GeeGee's three grandchildren—Ned, Alan and Dorothy— used their grandmother as a bank. Aunt Dorothy was always in the middle of a divorce and Uncle Alan was always in the middle of a career collapse. They showed up routinely to mooch off their grandmother for a month or a year. Like Genevieve's father, Alan and Dorothy needed help with vacations and cruises, new cars and boats, mortgages and down payments. The day came when GeeGee said to her middle-aged grandchildren, "There's no more money. I've outlived it. You'll have to pay my bills instead of me paying yours."

Uncle Alan and Aunt Dorothy no longer wasted time visiting, while Genevieve's father became too busy, and Genevieve's mother said nursing homes gave her the willies. They hardly ever asked Genevieve about her visits and did not know that when the water aerobics instructor quit, and nobody else had the interest or qualifications to teach a class, Genevieve took over because GeeGee loved the water. Three afternoons a week, Genevieve coaxed ancient bodies into the pool.

After half an hour in the pool, and maybe a lesson in card games—because GeeGee felt that bridge, canasta and rummy were crucial to the well-balanced life—Genevieve would jog the half mile home.

Last night at dinner, her father had passed the plastic container of grilled salmon pasta salad. He did not ask about Genevieve's day. She thought of mentioning High School Bowl practice. She knew better than to extend an invitation to the next meet. "I'm in the city at that hour," her mother would say. "Vivi, I'm really stretched for time," her father would add.

There was one thing Genevieve did need to bring up. "I was visiting GeeGee the other day. She thinks it's time we scheduled college visits." Actually, GeeGee felt it was long overdue for Ned and Allegra to do hundreds of things.

Her father shook his head. "You're only a junior."

"I know, Dad, but everybody begins planning now. During vacations, we should visit colleges."

Her mother got up from the table and made a big deal of refrigerating the leftovers. If you could call untouched dishes leftovers.

The conversation did not continue. Ned and Allegra Candler gave each other what Genevieve had come to call their Dark Look: a half-hidden exchange of annoyance. Usually she had no idea what triggered the Dark Look, but this time it was probably money. Her parents worked hard (assuming you could call Dad's job work, which most people didn't), but they spent all their income and more. They were the classic overextended couple. They had probably assumed GeeGee would pay for Genevieve's college, but that was not going to happen after all.

Genevieve tried to maneuver her parents in a college direction. "I don't know enough about colleges to think about a particular school. Which ones do you like?"

She was not sure her parents would take out loans to help her. The reason she studied so hard and had joined High School Bowl was to win scholarships. She liked sports, but had no flair and was not good enough to play at the college level. Her scholarships would have to be academic.

"I haven't thought about it," said her father. "I'll buy you some college guidebooks."

"I don't know about using vacations to visit colleges, Vivi," said her mother. "Your father and I are really booked. How about the virtual campus tours every university has online?"

Her parents exchanged a satisfied look, as if the college question was now settled.

Ordinarily, Genevieve tried to placate her parents. Maybe it was the accumulated hours of being home alone. Maybe she was still hungry. But this time Genevieve had had it. "What is there about me?" she demanded. "Why are you just standing here waiting for me to grow up and go away?"

Her mother snapped the lid of a leftover food container. Her father leaned back in his chair.

Genevieve was furious. "You two always seem to have some other kid in mind. You don't even like being around me. What kid would you rather have?"

They exchanged their Dark Look. It was not annoyance. It was a mixture of apprehension and dislike. Maybe even fear.

Fear? thought Genevieve. Of what? Of whom? Of me? "What family secret are you hiding?" she demanded. "Did I commit a murder or something when I was a toddler?"

"Vivi," said her mother, as if identifying her child at last.

"Did I find a gun and shoot somebody during a play date?"

"Vivi!"

"Don't call me baby names. Give me answers. You don't like to be with me. You never have. Tell me why."

Her father rallied. "Vivi, we adore you. You're the center of our lives. It's a bit of a jolt to realize that our baby girl is ready for college. Are you thinking you'd like to stay near home, and attend a nice small school in New York State or New England or Pennsylvania? Or are you feeling daring, and want to try the West Coast or the Deep South?"

Her mother joined in. "Do you picture a campus with forty thousand kids or five hundred? A big city or a country village? Mountains or shore?" Out of her briefcase, Allegra pulled a yellow legal pad and a pencil, which looked archaic. Allegra's life was conducted on her Treo.

Incredibly, the three of them stayed at the little round table far into the evening, while Dad asked questions and Mom began a to-do list.

Now in the stuffy hall at her high school, midafternoon on Thursday, Genevieve thought that the college talk had been camouflage. Wouldn't normal parents react more than that if their daughter suggested she might have murdered a playmate? At least frown? "Oh, stop it. The worst thing you ever did was bite that nasty little Nathan when he bit you." Or maybe normal parents would tease—"No more true crime television for you, young lady."

As for Genevieve's accusation that her parents had wanted some other kid—wouldn't a normal parent deny that? "Of course we don't want some other kid! You're perfect. Except when you're exaggerating."

But Genevieve's parents were not normal. In the outside world, they were normal: at work, at play, at parties. But they were not normal with her.

A boy's voice startled her. "Genny!"

Genevieve shifted the weight of her books to her other arm.

"Genny!" the boy called again.

Genevieve did not think of herself as Gen and certainly not as Genny, so she still did not turn around.

"Vivi," said Cammy, hurrying by. She tapped Genevieve's shoulder. "Jimmy Fleming is running after you." Cammy beamed, happy for her.

Jimmy Fleming was a big deal—a senior widely adored for his amazing abilities in every sphere: from being captain of High School Bowl to captain of varsity baseball, from winning a Westinghouse scholarship to being president of Key Club. He was cute in a lanky, puzzled way. Jimmy Fleming looked like a boy who didn't have the answer, couldn't catch the ball, forgot his homework.

No.

Jimmy was awesomely prepared on every level, in every subject.

The first time Genevieve participated in an actual Bowl meet, she had gotten flustered. She knew perfectly well that Mozart's *Eine Kleine Nachtmusik* was *A Little Night Music;* that the Union Army general who burned Savannah was William Tecumseh Sherman; that Marcus Aurelius was one of the Antonine emperors. But she had failed to think of the answers fast enough. She had not known how many ghosts visited Ebenezer Scrooge, but at least she hadn't forgotten that the world's largest lizard was the Komodo dragon.

For High School Bowl, the boys wore a suit and tie, and the girls wore a white top, a skirt and high heels. High School Bowl was televised. It was a popular local-channel event. Her parents were never home to watch television, so they did not know how poorly Genevieve had done her first time out, but other parents had been comforting. "Next time you'll show them, Vivi. You had stage fright. It won't happen again."

Genevieve assumed that Cammy's delight was misplaced. Jimmy Fleming just needed to tell her something about High School Bowl. Although usually he texted.

She turned to see Jimmy racing in her direction as fast and thoughtlessly as a three-year-old careening across a room, about to misjudge the distance and hit the wall. He was breathless and excited, which was nearly always the case. "When you fall in love," GeeGee liked to say, "pick a boy with bounce."

Genevieve smiled at the bounciest boy she knew.

Jimmy Fleming skidded to a halt. "Genny!" he said in a low, excited voice.

Genevieve always used her entire name, and never used anything else. Nicknames came from people who resisted long names. Why couldn't Jimmy, who knew all trivia in all subjects, remember that? She corrected him softly. "Genevieve."

"Right. Genevieve." He extended a hand as if to touch her, and then seemed to think better of it. He let his hand fall. He chewed his lip, which she had never seen him do, even when his next answer would win or lose the meet. "Genevieve, remember last year when High School Bowl made the finals? Remember how we had tournaments with the winners from other New York State counties? Remember we played the Westchester County champion?"

They had had a bus, like a sports team, and a cheering section full of friends and parents—not her parents, but enough for the team to feel supported. "I didn't play," she reminded him. "I was new. I sat there."

"That's true, but you sat next to a guy named Ray Feingold."

Ray Feingold had made her laugh so hard she had had to fight for control throughout the meet. Ray Feingold had even more bounce than Jimmy. Ray had gotten in touch with Jimmy Fleming about her? That was so romantic! Genevieve beamed at Jimmy Fleming.

* * *

Jimmy had been eager to chase Genevieve down. He'd looked up her schedule, tracked her probable route and snagged her in the hall with seconds to spare. He stared at her black halo of hair because he could not meet her shining eyes. She had misunderstood why a boy far away in another county was thinking of her.

I don't want to be the messenger, thought Jimmy. People shoot the messenger.

The bell rang the end of passing period.

Jimmy was a fan of almost everything in life. He liked all sports and all academics. He liked all activities and all pursuits. He liked all girls. But there were standouts, and Genevieve Candler was one. Jimmy never saw Genevieve smile without having to smile back. It was a gift, getting others to smile.

Jimmy had been told that not only did this girl visit her ancient great-grandmother in a nearby nursing home most days, but that three afternoons each week, she led water aerobics for ninety-year-olds. What could ninety-year-old people even do? Could they do it more than ten minutes? Could they do it without drowning? What would people that old look like in bathing suits?

Each time Genevieve showed up for Bowl practice, Jimmy thought of the long list of activities on his college applications. Not one equaled Genevieve's stint in a nursing home. It was beyond beyond.

Genevieve was laughing. "About Ray," she reminded him.

Jimmy could think of no way out. He swallowed. "Something went down this morning at a high school in Connecticut. Not Ray's high school, he's in New York State. See, the Connecticut school televises morning announcements. A friend of Ray's goes there, and forwarded him this weird video from this morning. Well, not to Ray in particular, but to everybody he knew."

"Weird" was not the word for the video. "Dramatic and emotional" defined the video.

The weird part was standing in front of Jimmy.

* * *

What could a Connecticut high school video have to do with her? Genevieve had been born in Connecticut, which was annoying, because she could not claim to be a New York native. But her parents had moved to Long Island when she was little, to be near GeeGee. She couldn't remember the last time she'd been in Connecticut. Why would you go there? But she didn't care about some video. "And Ray?" she asked excitedly.

"Ray asked me to tell you about the video."

Genevieve tried to hide a rush of disappointment.

Jimmy flapped his arms, as if starting the chicken dance. "You know what? Let's forget it. Pretend I didn't chase you down, okay?" He backed off, waving good-bye although he was only a few feet away.

"Have you seen this video, Jimmy?"

"Um. Yeah. But it can wait."

Genevieve had never participated in the videos kids sometimes made where they were naked or acting crazy, so this could not be a film that had come back to haunt her. She could not imagine what the content might be. She took out her Smartphone, which was new and had dozens of applications she had not even tried.

"That screen is too small," said Jimmy.

"That's okay. What's the link?"

"There isn't time," said Jimmy. "You have physics."

Jimmy Fleming knew her class schedule? Genevieve found this surprising and delightful. "I can be late. I'll claim High School Bowl had a meeting."

Jimmy was visibly trying to think of more excuses.

She was intrigued. "If it's important enough for Ray to locate me and important enough for you to panic, let's go to the library and you can show me on a nice big computer." Genevieve tap-danced toward the library. Dancing, she had the poise to take Jimmy's hand and haul him along.

"I don't know if it's anything to celebrate, Gen."

"Genevieve," she reminded him. "If you come into the library with me, Mr. Varick will let us sit together at a computer. You're Scholar Number One, you know. Librarians always submit to the will of Scholar Number One."

At the library, Genevieve stopped tap-dancing, because the library was carpeted and because Mr. Varick was a man without humor. They had no library passes, but Jimmy Fleming saluted the librarian and said, "High School Bowl. Fact-check."

Mr. Varick merely nodded.

The large room was almost empty. In a few minutes, the classes signed up for this period would dribble in, but for now Genevieve Candler and Jimmy Fleming were alone among the ranks of computers. Jimmy sat down at one, typed in his student code, logged on to the Internet and went to YouTube.

He looked up at Genevieve, his expression a match for her parents' faces last night. Apprehension. Maybe something worse.

Abruptly Genevieve was afraid. Her parents had failed to deny it when she'd accused herself of crimes. *Were* there crimes? *Had* she done something hideous? Had a video of her crime surfaced?

Jimmy brought up a video. He did not touch the Start arrow. He stood. He gestured for Genevieve to sit down.

Genevieve no longer wanted to know why her parents had exchanged their Dark Look. She wanted out of here. She wanted to be running into the nursing home, where the aides would already have GeeGee and the others heading for the warm shallow pool. Where would pull off her clothes—on water aerobics days, she wore her two-piece suit as underwear—while half a dozen ancient people looked longingly at her body. They too had once been lithe and supple. She would slip into the water and coax them in after her.

She actually heard Jimmy swallow. She stared at the black rectangle where the video would appear. She clicked the Start arrow. The video began.

A boy sat at a table. A blown-up photo on the wall behind him showed the front entry to his school. An American flag and a plastic tree flanked the table. The boy was cute and friendly-looking, with chunky glasses and a shirt that had been ironed. He was setting down a sheaf of paper. "That completes our morning announcements. And now we have a special event. I want to introduce Missy Vianello."

The camera shifted. It focused on a girl.

The girl was Genevieve.

She was looking at herself. In Connecticut.

Herself smiled and then giggled.

Genevieve's giggle.

Herself said, "Hi, everybody. I'm Missy Vianello. I'm a sophomore here. And I have the most wonderful, amazing, beautiful thing to share."

The voice was Genevieve's voice.

The gesturing hand was Genevieve's hand. Genevieve had the same tendency not to relax the middle joint of her fingers. She watched her own stiff fingers toss a ponytail over her shoulder. Her ponytail. Not sleek and shiny, which was desirable, but fat and fuzzy. The Genevieve on the screen yanked the elastic off. A black cloud of puffy hair surrounded the pale triangular face.

Genevieve's hair.

Genevieve's face.

Herself in another school in a different state talked on. "My identical twin just surfaced. We just found each other! Can you believe it? I have a long-lost identical twin."

The camera now displayed two girls.

Genevieve was both of them. They were both her.

Genevieve felt like a Dalí painting. Her eyes popped out the sides of her head, while a clock lived in her throat. An insect crawled through her brain and a pie slice was missing from her neck.

"And this," said the Missy one, touching the other girl's shoulder, "this is my twin, Claire."

But they were neither Missy nor Claire. They were Genevieve.

The Genevieves stared at each other and the Claire one began to cry.

What was going on? Who were these girls? Were they her?

Was she actually in Connecticut with them?

Was she one of them?

The Claire one said, "We shouldn't have done this. I shouldn't have agreed."

The Missy one turned back toward the TV camera. "Claire's going to attend school with me today," she said, "and this seemed like a good way to let everybody know who she is and why she's here."

Sobbing, the Claire one removed her mike and stepped out of view.

Herself said to the announcer, "I guess this wasn't such a great idea after all. Rick, just cut our segment, okay?"

The camera returned to the boy at the desk. He was still cute, but now he was pale, his speech slower. "This is live, Missy. We can't cut anything. But we welcome you, Claire, and we're thrilled for you both, and this has definitely introduced you to the entire high school. It's seven-fifty-five, people. Have a nice day."

The video stopped. Genevieve stared at the silent screen. After a while she played the video again.

When her Missy self appeared, Genevieve paused the video. She could not pick up the pieces of her brain to make anything fit. She played the rest of it. Her Claire self appeared.

In the video, her two selves beamed or wept.

Who were these girls?

Who was she?

* * *

The third time Genevieve played the video, she managed to have a thought: If three girls look exactly alike, perhaps they are triplets.

How could Genevieve Candler be one of triplets? Only by adoption.

Had she, Genevieve Candler, been adopted?

Impossible. Ned and Allegra Candler didn't even like children. They wouldn't adopt one.

And yet, Genevieve remembered something now. Only a few months ago, in August, Uncle Alan had made one of his rare visits to the nursing home. When he found his niece leading a water aerobics class, he said, "You're pretty young to be so conniving."

"GeeGee loves the water," Genevieve had said, wondering if she had the wrong definition of "conniving." "They aren't allowed to go in unless there's somebody here. So I'm here."

Uncle Alan snorted. "Your parents taught you well. You'll be number one in that will. Ned and Allegra only had a baby to please Grandmother, anyway. That's why you were named Genevieve. To get closer to the cash. And there's still cash, believe me. The old bag didn't run out. She just doesn't want to share it."

How dare he refer to her wonderful great-grandmother as "the old bag." How could GeeGee—who was good, funny, nice, cheerful, generous—have a grandchild like Uncle Alan, anyway? Genevieve couldn't stand thinking about ugly people and their ugly thoughts, especially when they were related to her. When Uncle Alan left, she managed to forget about it. After all, nobody had a baby just to get an inheritance.

Or did they? Could Ned and Allegra be just as ugly as Uncle Alan?

Had there been a set of triplets available for adoption? Had Genevieve's parents adopted a girl child in order to name her after the older Genevieve? Had they expected GeeGee to die sensibly at eighty or ninety, leaving baby Vivi her money, which they would then control and spend? And then GeeGee had had the nerve to live long enough to use up the money?

Maybe that's the Dark Look. Uncle Alan was right. I failed to achieve my real purpose. And now I'm going to cost even more. I expect to go to college.

I can't be adopted. I'm GeeGee's great-granddaughter. Her sunshine. Her pride and joy. Her sweetness and light. Or a player in a sixteen-year deception.

She examined the other two Genevieves again.

What a feeble word "triplet" was. Like insignificant music. Or a small fall.

I must be adopted, she thought. There's no other way I can have identical—

This time the word "triplet" did not come to mind; it was too infrequently used. It was alien. The real word was "sisters."

A beautiful, shocking word, one that had never had a use in Genevieve's life.

Those two girls could be my sisters? I could have had company all these years when I was home alone? I could have laughed and shared and argued and shopped with *sisters*?

Genevieve's body had dried out. She could not wet her lips or swallow. She could not blink or speak.

The school day would be over soon. Her great-grandmother would be waiting for her. Nobody could enter the pool unless a certified swim instructor, familiar with life-saving techniques, was present. GeeGee and her aide would sit patiently, awaiting

Genevieve's arrival. Patience was a required skill in a nursing home.

When she was a girl, GeeGee used to swim in Long Island Sound for miles, from one sandy beach to the next. Now she used a plastic water-wheelchair to get down the ramp into the pool, and wore a flotation device that the aide strapped around her middle. The water at its deepest was three and a half feet. Using a pink foam noodle to support her arms, GeeGee would dog-paddle a few strokes.

In normal water aerobics, the water splashed and roiled as people kicked and jumped. In GeeGee's class, the surface of the pool remained flat, because Genevieve's group mainly rested on their foam noodles, watching her exercise but not really exercising themselves. They loved to hear about her classes and friends and activities, and were befuddled by references to Facebook or texting.

Genevieve did not have parents to emulate; she just had parents. Instead, she strove to be like her great-grandmother. It was GeeGee whose life, voice, heart and zest Genevieve admired. She was proud of being Little Genevieve.

What if I'm not? What if I'm somebody else?

Jimmy Fleming said, "You okay, Gen?"

CHAPTER

STILL THURSDAY AFTERNOON

GENEVIEVE COULD NOT recall her last class. Had she attended it? Had she spoken to Jimmy again? Or just staggered out of the building? She stared at her great-grandmother's nursing home. A high wide portico allowed ambulances to drive right up to the entrance, safe from rain and snow. What would it feel like to live in a building where you planned to die? What would it feel like to the older Genevieve Candler when the younger one said, "Guess what? I'm not yours after all."

Genevieve glanced at her watch. Minutes and hours were meaningless now. The time that mattered was sixteen years not shared. Sixteen years when she could have had sisters.

A quick sharp wind showered her with tiny yellow leaves from a thin graceful tree. She caught one in her hand.

Even if I'm adopted, GeeGee will still love me. It'll be a different love, but it'll be just as deep. Adoption won't cancel how much we love each other. Or will it?

Genevieve did not want to be here. She wanted to park herself in front of that video and watch it over and over until she had her other selves in her bones.

On weekdays, her mother did not get home before seven.

94

She could not remember her father's schedule. But both parents were easy to avoid. Genevieve had the upstairs of their little house, a narrow, low-ceilinged set of tiny rooms and closets, which her parents grandly referred to as "Vivi's suite" and which Emma called "the starving poet's attic." They never bothered her up there.

It had become popular to send e-mail questions among her friends. Not dull questions like "What is your favorite color?" but disturbing questions like "What do your parents do that you wish they wouldn't?" Genevieve never replied, although she did read other people's responses. "I wish my mom wouldn't run around the house in her underwear," wrote one girl (quite an image if you knew the mother). "My parents are just right," wrote another girl—sweet and perhaps true, but perhaps a way to stay in the game while avoiding the question. A few weeks ago the question had been: "On a scale of one to ten, how glad are you to have the parents you have?"

Genevieve had slammed her mind shut and deleted the e-mail.

Now the question rushed up like an icon bouncing at the bottom of the desktop, filling the screen of her mind, shouting, *You don't have to worry about the parents you have! Because you don't have them! You are adopted!*

A dreadful thing happened in Genevieve's heart. She rejoiced.

That's the secret, she realized. Ned and Allegra adopted a child by mistake. They aren't the parent type.

She forgave Ned and Allegra a thousand affronts and lapses.

They were not her parents! Whoever the parents were, she shared them with the Claire girl and the Missy girl.

Her restless legs had walked her indoors. The woman at the desk cried, "Gen! How lovely you look today! They're all waiting! You're a speck late."

Genevieve resented being told that she was late. I'm a volunteer, she wanted to say sharply. I'm here because I'm a good person. If it takes me a few more minutes today than it did last time, I am not late. I am on time whenever I get here, thank you. Out loud she said, "Hi, how are you?"

The receptionist pushed the guest log toward her.

I'm a guest, marveled Genevieve. Even in my own family, I'm a guest. Because I'm not theirs.

She floated down the nursing home's long halls, buoyed by the strange and terrifying thought that she was not descended from Ned and Allegra. She arrived at the pool room. When she opened the door, the distinctive scent of chlorine and the hot dampness of evaporating water would envelop her. Genevieve would play ballet with her class. "It's *Swan Lake!*" she would cry. "Arms sweep up! Arms curve down." For a moment, all motion would be graceful. "It's *Coppelia!* We're mechanical dolls! Tiptoe forward! Tiptoe back!"

When she was a girl, GeeGee had loved ballet. She had attended ballet classes in the city for decades and had taken her great-granddaughter to many a performance.

And if I'm not her great-granddaughter? thought Genevieve.

GeeGee might take the news in stride. Age gave perspective. But if you have staked your all on one child and that child isn't yours after all, and the parents of that child have been lying for years . . .

How had Ned and Allegra gotten away with it? If Allegra had not been pregnant but suddenly had a baby, everybody from her employer to her grandmother-in-law would have known it wasn't hers.

Genevieve walked into the pool room.

The smile that told Genevieve she was the most welcome person on earth transformed GeeGee's wrinkled face.

I'm going to sob, thought Genevieve. Just like Claire sobbed.

Am I just like Claire? Exactly, precisely, identically like Claire?

She kissed her great-grandmother and stepped out of her jeans.

Her ancient "swimmers" invariably felt the pool water ought to be warmer, so Genevieve pleased them by jumping into the pool and shrieking, "Aaaaaah!" as if she too were shocked by the cold, although actually the water was annoyingly warm. Genevieve projected her voice to fill the cavernous room and to overcome the deafness suffered by her entire group. "Let's all jog in place for a minute! Remember to breathe!"

The seniors laughed, since taking one's last breath was a big worry in this crowd.

"If you hold your breath because it makes exercise seem easier," Genevieve said for the umpteenth time, "your blood pressure will rise."

Everybody had a noodle, a long plump foam ribbon to help with balance. The noodles were green and yellow and pink and blue. "Rainbow!" called Genevieve, and up went the noodles to form brightly colored arcs in the air. The class stretched left and then they stretched right.

A few summers ago, with both her parents out of town on business trips, Genevieve had amused herself by going through every drawer of the desk and three bureaus in her parents' bedroom. Doesn't every kid do the same? Genevieve had not expected to find treasure or secrets; she just wanted to know what was there.

Jewelry. A stash of cash. Old programs and ticket stubs. Lists. Old passports. Birth certificates, including her own. She couldn't remember it now, so it must have listed Ned and Allegra Candler as her parents, and Genevieve as their baby, or she would have noticed.

I'm not adopted after all, she realized. These parents who are so unparental are my parents. Whoever Missy and Claire are, I'm not related to them. I don't have sisters.

She leaped into action so she wouldn't weep. "Cross-country!" she shouted. "Pretend you're on skis! Lunge forward! Let's try to do twenty! Let's do a countdown! Nineteen! Eighteen! Seventeen! Lucille, you can't drop out yet!"

Lucille yelled, "I'm ninety! I can drop out whenever I want!"

"Not in my class!" yelled Genevieve. "I'm the commander here! Keep up the pace!"

They were all laughing.

I only saw Claire crying, thought Genevieve. I only saw Missy excited. I want to see their smiles. I want to hear them laugh.

Her body exploded. She churned the water, making waves

and whirlpools. I want to see them. I want to be in the same room with Missy and Claire.

Once I see them, I'll know.

Do I have sisters?

Am I adopted?

I'll know.

* * *

Genevieve's walk home was peaceful and familiar. A pleasantly shaded sidewalk led through the village, past boutiques and real estate offices, the post office and a coffee shop. Beyond them were the tracks of the Long Island Railroad. She turned south, walked two long blocks, swung left at a little park and followed this street home.

When she had been young enough to need after-school sitters, Genevieve had not come home to an empty house. Now each time she unlocked the door and reset the alarm, she felt a pang. She acclimated herself to the emptiness and then walked silently into the back half of the house, where there was light. Genevieve loved sunlight. In school, she always wanted a desk by the window. She was vague about her future and could not visualize her life beyond the first week of college, but she knew she wanted sunlight. Texas, maybe. Southern California. Spain.

The Candlers lived in a town of spacious homes, many of them true mansions, and all with generous yards, but their own house was small and cramped, with a living room/kitchen taking up the entire back half, a master bedroom and bath the front left quarter and the garage the front right quarter.

In the large living room/kitchen, the Candlers lived like pioneers in a one-room log cabin, except that their one room had every conceivable electronic delight. If her parents were home and awake, they were here. In this room was life: magazines and mail, microwave and gas fireplace, books and television, movies and radio, sound system and computer. The appliances hummed, waiting for human attention.

Me too, thought Genevieve.

Their backyard was so small it didn't even have a tree, but their neighbors' big yards were filled with massive maples. With no fences, it felt and looked as if the Candlers had a big yard too. The setting sun gleamed through half-bare branches.

She had turned her cell phone off when she arrived at the pool, because when her phone rang, she absolutely could not stand letting it ring. If she vaulted out of the pool to snatch it up, GeeGee was disapproving.

Now she powered it on, watching a photograph appear on the little screen: an above-the-shoulders picture of herself, GeeGee and her parents at their anniversary party last year. Her parents had a good marriage. Maybe a great one. They loved each other's company. Of all the events to which her father received tickets, dances were their favorites. Often the dance floor would clear while people stepped back to admire Ned and Allegra. Her mother loved to talk about these wonderful nights, when she and her handsome husband were the envy of every couple.

On Genevieve's cell phone were messages from both parents.

Her mother's voice was deep, as if she were a heavy smoker, when in fact Mom had literally never touched a cigarette. "I'm afraid of them," she had told Genevieve once. "It looks like such fun waving them around and watching the smoke waft. If I so much as hold an unlit cigarette between my fingers, I'll be hooked and spend my life rushing outdoors in all weather to suck on one."

Genevieve's eyes filled with tears. Yes, she wished her parents were different. Yes, she wished they had more time for her. But she loved them. If only they loved her back.

"Vivi," said her mother's voice, "it's about four. I have a staff meeting I can't skip. I won't be home until nine. Ten if I miss my train. There's plenty to eat in the fridge. I can't take a call during the meeting, but text so I know you got home all right. Love you."

Then Dad's voice, higher than Mom's. He was a tenor, and used to sing in a concert choir but missed too many rehearsals what with all his engagements, and had to drop out. "Vivi. Building committee is tonight. I'll be home maybe ten o'clock. I'm not far, fifteen minutes if you need me. See you."

They do love me, she told herself. They do worry. They just trust me to lead my life while they lead theirs. I've never said to them, "I hate all this independence. Come home. Do nothing for a change. Sit around. Keep me company."

If her parents ever sat around, Genevieve would know they were fatally ill, severely depressed or too penniless to fill the gas tank.

Usually she sent both of them the same text, letting them know that she'd had a good day and was now home studying. I could forward the video instead, she thought. Even on the smallest screen, those girls are me.

It was tempting. Allegra would see the video during her important meeting. Ned would get his during his not particularly important meeting. Would it slap them in the face? Would they crumble? Or did they know already that there were two more of her in the world?

I'm probably overreacting, she thought. It was probably an ordinary mild resemblance.

But both Ray Feingold and Jimmy Fleming had seen Genevieve Candler when they saw Missy and Claire.

The sun went down. The living space was shadowy and silent. Without music or TV, she was alone in the world of her house.

What if she was *not* alone? What if she had Missy and Claire?

They don't know that I've found them, she thought. They don't know I exist. They think they're twins.

Genevieve never did her homework in her bedroom. It was isolated up there. She worked at the kitchen counter, books spread over the expanse of glittering granite, and she ate dinner in nibbles, a little of this, a bite of that, all evening long. Now she prepared her tools: pencils, Post-its, fork and spoon.

Where the kitchen counter turned a corner, a built-in desk held the family computer. Genevieve circled the kitchen island where her books were strewn, sat down at the little desk and brought up the video. Claire's last name had not been given, but Genevieve tried various spellings of Vianello on MySpace and Facebook. And there she was: Missy Vianello, her page closed except to friends.

Genevieve researched. She herself had been born in Connecticut, and the high school where Missy had introduced her twin was also in Connecticut. Genevieve located the Connecticut statute dealing with the birth certificates of adopted children. It was difficult to work through the legal prose. It looked as if a newborn's birth certificate gave the biological parents' names, but once a court decreed the adoption, a new birth certificate was issued. This one had the adoptive parents' names. So the adoptive parents had a legal birth certificate for their baby, but not precisely a true one.

Was that the kind of birth certificate she had found in her parents' room?

It did not look as if any birth certificate would have a line at the bottom saying, "Multiple birth—check for siblings."

Because no matter how many multiples are born, she thought, the babies are separate people. They get their own identities. If I were adopted, though, there would be a court decree. I didn't find that. On the other hand, to keep the adoption secret, you would not store proof in a drawer where the child would find it.

Genevieve imagined her real mother as a young girl in high school, terrified, her future at risk. She imagined the girl sobbing as the social worker whisked away her babies.

I could be older than my real mother was when I was born! That real mother could have been fourteen. What fourteen-year-old could do a good job with one baby, let alone three?

Genevieve found herself weeping for her fourteen-year-old mother. She imagined the mother of this teenager—Genevieve's biological grandmother—saying, "I might help you with one baby, but three? Give them up."

Genevieve didn't like the grandmother.

Maybe the biological mother was much older, in the middle of a spectacular career, already had two teenagers and could not disrupt her life for another kid, let alone three.

Genevieve didn't like them, either. They ought to have celebrated! Rearranged the house! Rejoiced in three new babies!

What about the father? Was he just a kid himself? Or a stranger passing in the night, and the mother hadn't even told him? Maybe she didn't even know who he was so she *could* tell him.

Maybe they were both druggies out on the street and Social Services collected the babies from some slummy room as the parents sat around in a stupor.

Maybe the real mother was married but out of work, and her husband was a paraplegic and they'd lost their house in a fire and had no insurance on their car, which had broken down anyway, and they were using old bureau drawers for cribs, and it seemed kinder and better to let rich people be the parents.

I'm inventing birth mothers like a movie director trying to

find a good scene, she thought. And in Connecticut, Claire and Missy must be lying awake playing the same game.

No—wait—they already had the answers! How had they found each other? What did they know?

She watched the video again.

In the maddening way of television, half the sixty seconds were spent on the announcer. This made Genevieve crazy in nature shows, when the camera cut away from the grizzly bear or the lioness to show the expert. She always wanted to telephone and say sternly, "Nobody cares about you. Get out of the picture."

But she did sort of care about Rick, with his unfortunate glasses and his cute face. He had brought Missy and Claire to her. If only he had given her more time with them.

Enough of this, she decided. I'm wasting time. She texted Jimmy. I have to reach Ray Feingold.

In a minute, Jimmy texted back with Ray's cell number.

Genevieve psyched herself up. Was anybody else in the entire United States asking how to get in touch with possible triplet sisters?

Halfway through dialing Ray's number, she stopped. Once she reached those girls, the truth—whatever it was—was going to exist in this room. It would exist in her life. In her conversations. In her future. Between her and her parents. Between her and GeeGee.

I should sleep on it, she thought, knowing she wasn't going to sleep tonight at all. She was going to be watching herself times two on video.

Mom and Dad will be home before long, she reminded herself. I could be sitting here. I could point to the screen. "Got sixty seconds?" I could say.

But Ned and Allegra's reaction was beside the point. The two people who mattered now were Missy and Claire. Genevieve wanted to touch them and hear their voices and meet their eyes. The parents who had lied could be dealt with later. She completed her call to Ray Feingold. "This is Genevieve Candler," she said, trying to keep emotion out of her voice.

"Hey, it's me, Ray. You saw that video, Genevieve?" His voice was loud with excitement.

"I've been studying it for hours. Ray, I don't have the answer. I don't know what I'm seeing. I just know that I have to call those two girls up. I have to talk to them."

"I agree," said Ray. "I knew you'd be in touch. My friend at Missy's high school gave me Missy's cell number but he didn't have the other girl's. Ready to write it down?"

"I'm ready," she said, although the hand holding the pencil was trembling. At least she didn't have to choose which sister to call first. How could she possibly decide that one mattered more than the other? But what would she say to Missy? A person claiming to be an identical triplet was obviously a lunatic. Missy would hang up on her.

"I did get Claire's last name, though," said Ray. "Linnehan." He spelled it for her. "They're both on Facebook," he added.

"Thanks, Ray."

"I hope thanks are in order," he said seriously. "I'll be thinking of you."

* * *

CONNECTICUT
Friday morning
Before dawn

CLAIRE LINNEHAN HAD had bad dreams. She woke up so wired that taking a shower seemed dangerous: she'd electrocute herself in the water.

Claire weighed herself down with a heavy terry bathrobe.

She remembered buying that robe. She and Missy had both spotted it across the lingerie department and had both lunged for the pale lemon yellow robe. Claire had pretended she really wanted the light blue.

I knew back then, she thought. Normal cousins don't share an understanding that even includes cut, color and texture.

Claire hung the bathrobe back up. She closed the closet door on it.

In the kitchen, shivering in her thin pajamas, she breathed in the comforting scent of brewed coffee. Her mother had left for the early Jazzercise class she taught. The last inch of strong black coffee was still hot in Mom's favorite mug. Claire poured herself pink grapefruit juice. With her bare toe she knocked the pantry door open to gaze upon the cereal selection, and without thinking, she did what she always did first thing every morning. She phoned Missy.

"Now I know you hate me," said Missy groggily. "It isn't even six yet."

Claire hadn't looked at the clock. It was way early. "Sorry. Well, I do hate you, but only sort of."

"Oh, good. Sort-of hatred is the best kind."

They giggled.

Claire was not a giggly girl. In school, she often didn't get the jokes other girls laughed at. But with her cousin, everything was funny.

"And?" asked Missy.

"I was taking the twin thing seriously. I was up all night wondering which of us has a mother who didn't want the extra one." Claire rinsed out her juice glass. She opened the dishwasher and sighed. The dishes sparkled. Claire despised putting dishes away. She set the used glass on the counter and began emptying the dishwasher with one hand while she held her cell with the other. "I know it's a hoax, Missy, but I also know it's not a hoax."

For a long time they were silent.

"You're waiting for something," said Claire.

"I'm waiting for you to tell me you're glad."

Claire could not fathom that. How could either of them be glad that they were adopted?

"It's Friday," said Missy finally. "We need a plan for the weekend. When do we play the video for our parents?"

Claire wasn't ready for the show, the showdown or the explanation. "The video isn't the only thing going on. Guess what else?" Claire told Missy what Lilianne had said about her father having no work.

"That's so scary. Poor Uncle Phil. And just when Aunt Frannie wants to give up the Jazzercise franchise."

"What? What makes you think that? Mom hasn't said anything to me."

"You're kidding. She and my mom talk about it all the time. Your mom is exhausted. She's fifty, you know. That's old old old for leading exercise classes, especially as many as she has."

"Missy, how come you didn't tell me?"

"I thought you knew."

One parent without work. One yearning to quit work. What's the matter with us? thought Claire. Why don't we know anything about each other?

Claire dragged the kitchen footstool under a high cabinet that hung alone on a far wall like a mistake. There was no counter under it. No companion cabinets nestled up to it. Its lower shelf was messy with appliance manuals, receipts and out-of-town phone books. The middle shelf held cookbooks her mother liked owning but never used. On the top shelf was a large plastic container full of important documents. Claire took it down, popped the lid and began leafing through the papers. A paid-off car loan. The title to that car. Her father's expired passport. His new one. A power of attorney for an elderly relative in Florida.

Missy rambled on about running errands and picking up dry cleaning and talk radio. Claire interrupted. "I'm looking at my birth certificate. It's normal. It names Philip and Frances Linnehan as my father and mother. The birth date is my birth date. So we know one thing, Missy. I am who I am. Go find your birth certificate. Birth certificates are absolute proof."

"I hunted for mine," said Missy, "and I didn't find it. Just listen to me, Claire. Here's what I heard on the radio. It was a geneticist who specializes in studying twins reared apart. That's what they call them: twins reared apart. It sounds like horses on their back legs, but it means growing up without each other. Separate houses. Separate lives. Are you listening, Claire?"

Claire pressed her birth certificate against her cheek. I was not reared apart, she told herself.

"This doctor had an explanation for why twins might not seem identical at birth but over the years might become identical in size and weight and shape. When the mother is having multiples, the babies don't necessarily have equal space or nutrition in the womb. One might be born smaller and less strong. One might have more space, right from the beginning."

Claire was horrified. Before babies were even born, one would squish out the other? Grab more of the swimming pool, as it were? Really, nature was hideous.

"That would explain why I was so much littler than you, Claire. You used more space, and I had less."

I was the twin who shoved? thought Claire.

"Remember, I was in Newborn Intensive Care for a long time," Missy was saying. "Mom and Dad christened me when I was still in the hospital. Maybe they dated my birth from the day they brought me home, and that's why I have a birthday eight weeks later than you do. Not because I was born eight weeks later. Because they faked the eight weeks later."

"That's crazy. No matter how long you spent in NICU, your parents would still use your real birth date. Even if *they* didn't, the hospital would. Parents don't fill out the birth certificate.

Document people fill it out. Besides, why keep a baby's real birthday a secret? There is no reason to fake a birthday."

"Unless it's a deep dark secret that girls who are supposed to be cousins are actually twins."

"Our parents aren't the deep dark type, Missy." Claire put her birth certificate back in the plastic box, snapped the lid, slid the container back on the top shelf and closed the cabinet door. She put away the stool, sat at the kitchen computer and Googled "adoption law."

Missy said, "I agree. If you and I are adopted twins, and each adult sister got one of us, our parents would have let us in on it. So maybe even they didn't know."

In the fascinating way of online searches, the results Claire brought up were a mishmash. She could not resist a story in which some woman had babies she then sold. Claire read the story out loud to Missy.

"I don't mind if Mom and Dad paid to get me," said Missy. "I'm worth it."

"Ugh. Who wants to be the child of some creepy creature who offers twins to the highest bidder?"

"Another thing, Clairedy," said Missy. "Every time you and I do something alike, or want the same thing, or buy the same thing, or we're good at the same thing, both your mother and my mother pretend it doesn't mean anything and then—always—they separate us."

Claire was jolted by the sound of running water. She had forgotten how early it was; her father was still home. "Dad's taking a shower," she said to Missy. "Text me later."

She tiptoed to her room, shut her door and climbed back into bed. She did not want to talk to Dad. She wanted him to leave for work, pretend or real.

The online story seemed almost possible. Her parents could have bought her, like an anniversary present. "Here's a little thing I thought you might like, honey."

Stop it, Claire told herself. Adoptions are expensive. Besides, I'm not adopted. I'm the one with the birth certificate.

She had a ghastly thought. If her own mother really was her own mother, and yet she and Missy were twins, then *her* mother was actually *Missy's* mother too, having handed her leftover baby to her sister. Want the runt of the litter? she imagined her mom asking Aunt Kitty.

* * *

THE SAME FRIDAY MORNING
Long Island

LAST NIGHT HAD been a roller coaster for Genevieve. Her heart would race up the incline, staring at the sun and a future with sisters. The same heart would plunge down, nothing but cold wind, brutal metal and ghastly truth around its soft tissue.

She snapped awake like a baseball bat breaking on an invisible fault line.

The house was empty, of course. Allegra had to catch such an early train that Genevieve almost never saw her Monday through Friday mornings. Dad didn't need to be in the office early, but he usually drove away the minute he was dressed to meet his coffee shop buddies. He'd yell up the stairs to be sure she was awake, tell her to have a good day and then slam the door behind him.

She must have slept through that.

There was no dormer in the long narrow poet's attic. There was one window to the east, over her bed, and one to the west, in her bathroom. Genevieve paced back and forth, staring out into the dark predawn, tasting the names Missy and Claire. She had never known anybody with those names. She didn't know anybody except her great-grandmother with the name Genevieve, either.

Today she would call Missy. If she was really rattled, she'd write out the dialogue and read from a script.

Who were we in the hospital? she wondered. Babies A, B and C? We knew each other once. In the womb. When I meet Missy and Claire for the first time, it will actually be a reunion.

Genevieve slipped her arms into a filmy ivory-white robe that swished around her ankles and hid her boring pajamas. Feeling glamorous, she opened the attic door and descended the stairs regally. The stairs were straight and narrow. No large furniture could be brought up unless it was dismantled.

Incredibly, both of her parents were sitting at the breakfast table.

"Vivi, my word," said her mother. "Do you usually dress up like a nineteen thirties movie star for breakfast?"

Her mother was having cornflakes and her father was eating Special K. She would have said neither of them ever touched the cereal in this house.

"You look gorgeous, Vivi," said her father. "And so mature. Twenty-five or something. I'm weak thinking about the passage of years."

Genevieve looked at the kitchen clock. It was an hour and a half earlier than she usually got up. She'd been so grateful to escape bad dreams that she hadn't even looked at the time.

"If she looks twenty-five," said Allegra Candler to her husband, "how old does that make me?"

The kitchen computer was on. They had been checking their e-mail. But they did not act like parents who had just seen a video of their daughter's clones.

"Twenty-nine," said Ned, blowing a kiss over the dry cereal.

Genevieve slid carefully into a chair. Two meals in a row they were all at the same table? It was a record. She said lightly, "Were you talking about college visits?"

"Are you already packed?" teased her father.

Her mother poured her a glass of orange juice. This was amazing. Allegra was not the attentive kind of mother, who measured a daughter's vitamin C intake. She was the casual kind, who figured that if Genevieve had not grasped the principles of good diet by now—oh, well. "Thanks, Mom."

Her mother really did look twenty-nine. Well, from a distance.

Genevieve suddenly saw her mother as brave. Allegra's career had never taken off. She had expected to be a star, but she was only a cog in a machine. She's not going into the city every day for herself, thought Genevieve. It's to provide a house and clothes and a cell phone and college for me.

Her father tapped his newspaper. He loved the *Wall Street Journal*. "I was just reading aloud to your mother. This paragraph caught my imagination. Listen. 'The future isn't a hat full of little shredded pieces of the past. It is, instead, a whirlpool of uncertainty populated by what the trader and philosopher Nassim Nicholas Taleb calls black swans—events that are hugely important, rare and unpredictable, and explicable only after the fact.'"

"At this morning's conference," said her mother, "I might suggest a fragrance line called Black Swan."

"Black Swan sounds more like eye shadow," said her father.

They hugged her good-bye, which was such a treat on a weekday that Genevieve did not want to let go.

When both cars had left, she called Connecticut information. A recording gave her the number for the high school whose name had appeared on the blown-up photograph on the wall behind Rick. She accepted the option to have it automatically dialed. The phone in Connecticut rang.

A melodious recorded voice gave facts about the high school and extensions to dial. Genevieve kept count on her fingers. She didn't need athletic schedules, the attendance clerk or driving directions to the school. She chose option six.

"Good morning, principal's office," said a voice.

Genevieve figured that after such an exciting identical twin reunion, the school might have a press release. It might tell her enough about Claire to locate her too. She did not want to call Missy without calling Claire. Triplets should reunite at the same time, not one at a time. "I'm from the *New York Post*,"

Genevieve lied. "We'd like to interview the newly discovered identical twins."

The secretary laughed. "You and everybody else. Please don't follow up. It was a hoax. The girls are cousins. They have a strong family resemblance. There are no identical twins. It was their idea of a joke."

* * *

Genevieve stood in the kitchen while the cereal softened in the milk and the orange juice grew warm.

There were no twins.

Nobody was identical.

Nobody was adopted.

Nobody was a long-lost anybody.

Sobs wracked her body.

She could not climb the stairs. She kept tripping on the long sweeping robe. She slid out of it and carried the puddled satin to her room, and couldn't make it stick to its special velvet hanger.

A hoax.

She dressed slowly in the dullest clothing she had and then pulled a large plain gray sweatshirt over it all. She needed room in there for a pounding heart and shivering skin.

She ran a brush through her hair, shook her head, caught the hair in her fist, put it in a black elastic and was dissatisfied. She tugged her hair out and repeated the process until it was right. Not too tight, not too loose.

CHAPTER

FRIDAY
Genevieve Candler's high school

THE LOSS OF her sisters was physically painful. Her first class hurt. Conversation hurt. Chairs hurt. The clothing on her body hurt. She had difficulty responding to greetings. "Headache," Genevieve kept saying. "Migraine." She had never had a migraine, but girls who used that excuse were always pitied.

After an assembly, Jimmy Fleming detached himself from a group of friends and trotted over. "What did they say when you called them?"

"I called Missy's high school first. It was a hoax, Jimmy. Those two girls are cousins with a strong family resemblance. There are no twins. There are no triplets. The fact that I look a bit like them is accidental."

"Get out!" said Jimmy. "They're you, Gen. You're them."

She tried to be lighthearted. "It was fun, though. Being an identical triplet for a day."

"No." Jimmy was firm. "I've been studying that video. We were not hallucinating, Gen."

"It's a hoax," she repeated.

Jimmy Fleming shook his head. "More likely, the hoax is a hoax."

This sentence had no meaning. Genevieve was relieved when Jimmy walked on. Her friends clustered around, assuming that Jimmy was interested in her. "Jimmy Fleming?" they said excitedly. "He's awesome!"

He wasn't interested in Genevieve. He was interested in her circumstances. She shrugged. "He was asking about a research project we're doing."

Ellen frowned. "For what class?" Since Ellen was in all Genevieve's classes, she knew that Jimmy Fleming was in none.

"High School Bowl."

"Oh, that."

The Bowl team rarely had a student audience. People who were interested joined.

I can fake conversations in school, thought Genevieve, but GeeGee will see through me. I don't ever want her to know that I rejoiced at the thought of being adopted.

She phoned her great-grandmother. "I can't stop by today after all, GeeGee. I've got so much to do. I'm sorry."

"I'll miss you, darling, but how lovely that you have lots to do. That's what it is to be young. Now enjoy every minute, and since this is Friday, and I don't always see you over the weekend, save up your stories and I'll see you next week."

"I'll be over Saturday or Sunday."

"Nonsense. I'm fine. You're a teenager, not a nurse's aide."

In her next class, Genevieve was tempted to watch the video

on her cell. But what if a classmate or teacher asked what she was looking at? She played it in her head.

If it had been a joke or a hoax, then Claire had been acting. But in her mind's eye, Genevieve saw no acting. Claire had been in a state of shock. When those tears spurted out, Claire hardly knew she was weeping; she seemed almost afraid. It was almost Allegra's Dark Look. What was there to be afraid of?

And then Genevieve knew: Claire was afraid that Missy was telling the truth. The video captured the split second in which Claire Linnehan realized that she really was an identical twin. Whatever the school administration might think, what Claire learned was that she and Missy were not cousins after all.

Jimmy's right, thought Genevieve. It's the hoax that's a hoax. We're all three adopted.

Ray had given her the solution last night; she just hadn't been paying attention. Facebook was the answer. She would friend Missy and Claire, and Facebook would simultaneously deliver the message to each girl. When they went to her page, they would stare at her picture the way she had stared at theirs. They would draw their own conclusions and take their own actions.

Or not.

Claiming a migraine again, Genevieve went to the girls' room. From her Smartphone, she added Missy as a friend. A tiny space opened on the screen. It asked, "Do you want to add a personal message?"

She had to do this right. It was a matter of life and death.

No, a matter of life and birth.

Genevieve composed her message. Facebook informed her that Missy and Claire were now pending friends.

Wrong, thought Genevieve, giddy with joy and fear. They are pending sisters.

* * *

FRIDAY
Missy Vianello's high school

MISSY WAS YELLED at by people who had not wanted that cute little identical twin reunion to be a hoax and yelled at by people who insisted that she and Claire were identical twins and that there was no hoax.

Jill and Hannah showed up with photographs of old birthday parties at Missy's house. They handed around pictures of big tall Cousin Claire having cake alongside shrimpy little Missy. Missy imagined Jill and Hannah sitting down grimly with their mothers' old-fashioned albums, flipping through every page, determined to unearth proof. "You shouldn't play con games on your friends, Missy!" snapped Jill.

"I'm sorry," said Missy.

The kids who didn't yell teased her instead. "Is this Missy standing before me, or her evil twin Claire?"

In math, the teacher worked with a group having difficulties with a particular equation. Missy was not having difficulties. Her group was supposed to finish an advanced worksheet. Missy finished quickly and opened her phone. She had an e-mail from Facebook. A Genevieve Candler had added her as a friend. Missy had never met a person named Genevieve.

"Melissa!" said her math teacher. "Put your phone away or give it to me."

Missy jammed the phone into her pants pocket. "Sorry," she said.

An hour and a half passed before she could check her phone again, and by then she had eleven texts and two voice messages waiting, all more tempting than an e-mail.

* * *

FRIDAY MORNING
Claire Linnehan's high school

WHENEVER A TWIN MOMENT had arisen in the past, Claire found it easy to dismiss. It was fun, cute and meaningless. Aside from the fact that she did not have the same parents as her cousin, she was eight weeks older.

Now Claire swam in a vision of herself, too little to be born but big enough to elbow Missy out of the good space. She saw herself kicking away, getting limber and strong, while Missy was literally curled in fetal position, unable to exercise. She saw herself popping out first, getting a nice lungful of oxygen and opening her eyes to enjoy the world, while Missy emerged blue, with little folded-up lungs that barely inflated.

For Claire, the shock of school on Friday was that nobody knew she'd had a shock. School was ordinary, friends were ordinary, classes were ordinary.

So is my life, she told herself. Even if I am adopted, that's still ordinary. No matter who my biological mother is, Mom is still my mother.

Usually the texture of a Friday was woven into the weekend. Friday classes seemed shorter, and the kids louder and less careful. On an ordinary Friday, Claire daydreamed of being with her cousin, the way a dieter might daydream of an ice cream sundae. She could feel the essential loneliness of the week ending, her heart opening up, ready to share . . . my soul, thought Claire. Do we share souls?

It was a terrifying thought. But identical twins definitely shared more than blood types, fingerprints and hair.

At lunch, Claire and her friends hurried to the cafeteria line, filled trays and dropped into chairs, acting as exhausted as marathon runners. Everybody whipped out cell phones at the same time, synchronized as dancers, and they were all talking, eating and laughing while they sent texts. The five girls with whom she sat had been close friends for years. Micayla, Carter, Steffie, Baillie and Elizabeth were all flutists in marching band, as was Claire. They all took advanced art. Baillie and Claire were in Math Club while the other three girls had attended tennis camp with Claire. She cherished their friendships. But they were incidental compared to Missy. Sometimes the depth of her friendship with Missy frightened Claire as much as it frightened her mother.

Now she thought, Missy has never been my friend. She has never been my cousin. She has always been my identical twin and my heart always knew and I always turned my back on it. On her.

Claire ran her eyes over the list of waiting text messages. The usual set from Missy, which she knew she must answer but couldn't. The usual from various friends, including every girl sitting right at this table. She checked e-mail. Just one. A friend request from Facebook.

Claire loved her friend list and was always willing to expand it. But right now she just wanted to go home. She wanted to talk to her parents about construction jobs that weren't there and Jazzercise classes that were too hard. She wanted to be part of her parents' decisions and their worries. She did not want, now or ever, to be part of a deception begun at birth. Maybe before birth.

Her need for Missy battled with her fury at Missy.

After lunch came math. The teacher was demanding and there was rarely a moment to flake off. Perfect for today's shuddery mood.

Claire always chose a desk close to the window. She loved light and sun. Today she didn't even notice the sun. The unread messages from Missy preyed on her mind.

The math teacher began going up and down the aisles making sure everybody had written out the entire problem and its solution, not just the answer. Claire's row was checked first, giving her a few minutes of freedom. She and everybody else on the window side opened their cell phones.

Claire's pulse was racing. She felt as if her legs would begin to race too. Her body would take off, a human jet driven by Missy's awful stunt. To put her mind on other things, she opened the Facebook e-mail asking her to confirm Genevieve as a friend. Then she read the message sent by the unknown Genevieve Candler.

We have to talk. Here's my cell number. It's a matter of life and birth.

Didn't you usually say "a matter of life and death"? Who would refer to a matter of life and birth? And who would write such a peculiar thing anyway?

A scream rose in Claire's throat. She shut her phone fast and hard. She shoved her chair backward. It screeched against the floor. The teacher turned around. "Claire," she said reprovingly.

"Spiders?" asked one of the boys.

"Claire, are you all right?" asked Steffie.

Genevieve Candler must be referring to the video. If Aiden had seen it, a million people had seen it. Only one would think that a video featuring long-lost identical twins was a matter of life and birth: the birth mother.

What awful words. A female who was the mother only in the moment of giving birth, like a reptile or a fish.

I don't want a birth mother! I want *my* mother! If there is a birth mother, I don't want to meet her, not even online. I don't want an introduction, let alone a relationship. I hate her already. I hate Missy. I'm never doing a sleepover again.

"I'm fine, thanks, Steffie," said Claire.

"You look as if you saw a ghost."

Could that be what identical twins were? Ghosts of each other?

* * *

FRIDAY
The Vianello house

MISSY'S MOTHER HATED to be asked what she did for a living. Even her husband and daughter hardly knew what she did. The shortest explanation put people in a coma.

Kitty Vianello had to break up her workday with little excursions, or she too would have been comatose. She would abandon her office to dart downstairs and check snail mail, boil potatoes for salad, do a load of laundry, fill the bird feeder or knit one row. She would coach herself out loud. "Come on, you can do it! You can work another half hour!"

Her job was to read vast amounts of material from regulatory committees in Congress and summarize it for an online newsletter: fifty pages of changes in OSHA regulations, and Kitty condensed it into two.

Before Missy was born, Kitty had taught fifth grade. Elementary schoolkids were delightful. In her memory, all her students had been brilliant and cooperative, all other teachers fun and interesting and all parents eager to help. But newborn Missy had been fragile, often sick and more than once back in the hospital, and Kitty had wanted to be with her baby girl twenty-four hours a day. She left teaching and went home to live with fear. She was afraid of every illness Missy suffered. There had been more than one night when she and Matt and Missy really had stood at death's door.

When Missy became a toddler, demanding to do things by herself, marching around the house like a tiny soldier, assaulting the rules that kept her down, Kitty found herself with a different fear. Missy was perfect. If the birth mother knew, she would come to the door, and Kitty and Matt would have to give Missy back.

Matt was equally afraid. He wouldn't even confide in a lawyer.

When Kitty tried to talk it over with her sister, Frannie was annoyed. "There was no crime."

"We don't *think* there was a crime." Kitty hated to repeat the rats-chewing-on-her-gut fear that Missy had been stolen.

"You're irrational," her sister would snap. "Missy had hospital staff twenty-four/seven for weeks. They never saw anything wrong. And you and I had the same obstetrician. It's a mess, but it isn't a crime."

Easy for her sister to say. Her adoption was legal.

On the same Friday morning that Genevieve Candler trembled, Claire Linnehan braced herself, and Missy Vianello repeated the word "hoax" over and over, Kitty Vianello raced down the stairs once more, hoping the exercise would keep her body as trim as her writing. But every excursion ended in front of the refrigerator. Stuck to the front of the refrigerator with magnets Missy had made in first grade were the latest photographs of the cousins.

The photographs were terrifying.

Kitty leaned against the cool door of the fridge, her mind on a shopping bag with a ribbon still curly after all these years, sitting on a shelf in a rarely used closet in the dining room, hiding the terrifying evidence from a long-ago purchase in a scrapbook store. Kitty had been seduced by the beautiful paper, and had decided to make a scrapbook of the life of her daughter. She and Matt had taken thousands of pictures of Missy. Kitty remembered or didn't remember to pick them up once they were developed. The pictures lay around the house in their store envelopes, finding their way to a kitchen drawer needed for spatulas and slotted spoons. Missy was nine then, dangerously distant from babyhood, and Kitty was starting to forget when and where all those photographs had been taken.

Many photographs were from the Friday-night sleepovers. Tiny Missy and tall Claire played together with an intensity that made the adults laugh. Missy bore a comical resemblance to her cousin and imitated Claire in everything.

One Saturday morning, when Phil and Frannie came to get Claire, they stayed for lunch. The men played pool in the basement family room, while Kitty and Frannie took over the dining room. With Frannie as her cheerleader, Kitty felt that today was the day. By dinner, she would have a scrapbook. They sent the girls outside and faced a table strewn with years of photographs. Step one was to get them in chronological order.

An eerie problem surfaced.

Frannie and Kitty couldn't always tell which photographs were of Missy and which were of Claire. At first it was funny. Missy was a lot smaller, and therefore wore Claire's hand-me-downs. It was not surprising that there were pictures of Claire at age five in a beautiful blue Sunday dress, and Missy a year or two later in the same blue dress.

What was surprising was that their very own mothers could not tell which girl was which.

"This must be Missy because it's our sofa," Kitty would say. "It could be Claire visiting," Frannie would point out.

The photographs they could not label because they did not know whether the child was Missy or Claire became a stack.

It stopped being funny.

In life, the two mothers saw completely different children. Claire was not a bit like Missy. Claire was sober; Missy was bubbly. Missy smiled a lot and widely; Claire smiled less, and rather carefully. Claire had a large vocabulary and used it; Missy was apt to skip speech in favor of dance or tantrums. Missy was fearless, and threw herself off things and on things and into things. Claire waited.

But in photographs, no difference was visible.

The little girls in these pictures were not similar. They were identical. One of them just had a smaller footprint.

Kitty whispered the terrifying thought. "Did we adopt twins, Frannie?"

"Impossible!" Frannie's arms were folded across her chest as if to protect herself from the mere thought. "Our Claire is older than your Missy."

"We don't know that, Frannie. We only know what Dr. Russo said. And he contradicted himself."

"They're not twins!"

Downstairs their husbands were laughing. On the front porch their daughters were giggling.

After a while, Kitty packed the photographs in shoeboxes. Frannie slid the scrapbook materials back into the handsome paper shopping bag and retied the curly bow. There was a useless closet in the dining room. They put the paper bag on the top shelf and closed the door. But they could not close off their guesses.

Every now and then the four parents talked about it. They could go for months or even years without a discussion, and then the topic would blow up on the horizon like a storm, a hurricane requiring them to nail plywood over the windows.

Claire's mother would say, "The girls come together like magnets. Is that proof they're twins?"

Missy's father would be irritated. "It's because we bring them together every week. They're used to each other. They're not twins."

Claire's parents would say, "Experts want adoptive parents to tell the truth right from the beginning."

Missy's parents would erupt. "We don't know the truth! And you're not in our situation! You're legal! Anyway, all four of us made the same promise. We promised never to tell."

"It was a stupid promise," Frannie would say. "We have to tell eventually. Especially you guys. It's unbelievable that you've gotten away without proper papers for so long. What happens when you run up against a school official who won't buy into your lies and postponements?"

The lies and postponements had been amazingly easy.

Way back when it was time for Missy to attend kindergarten, her parents had enrolled her with a promise to bring in identification. They were lucky. The woman in charge of such things was not competent, and forgot. Every now and then at parent conferences a teacher would say, "We don't seem to have all of Missy's paperwork," and Matt would say, "I'll get on it," and incredibly that would suffice. The school ran from kindergarten through fifth grade, giving them six years of grace. There was a sticky moment when the school demanded a social security number prior to Missy's shift to middle school. Matt replied sharply that this demand was totally unwarranted and he did not intend to hand out such an important number for no reason. The school pressed. Matt demanded to know why they were making an already tough transition from sweet elementary school to the rigors of middle school even more painful for a sensitive child. The Vianellos had their rights, he explained, and privacy was crucial to them. If the school kept up with its invasive nonsense, they would take Missy out and homeschool her.

This was no empty threat. Matt and Kitty were former teachers. They could homeschool Missy if they had to. But Missy—all friendship all the time—would have been crushed by the isolation.

Schools hate homeschooling, so this was an effective tactic. Whenever a clerk phoned or e-mailed to ask again for the missing data, Matt would threaten to file an official complaint. Did the office want to be investigated for incompetence? The poor clerks were dealing with a thousand students. They didn't have the time or energy to fight about one nice little girl saddled with combative parents.

And in middle school, Missy had had her own worries. Was she popular? Was she smart enough? Good enough? Pretty enough?

The answer was no. Missy was gawky in middle school. In body, speech and style, she did nothing but stumble. Then suddenly, in ninth grade, Missy became an independent young woman, at ease with herself, good at anything she felt like being good at. By sophomore year, she was elegant and accomplished.

Where had the years gone? her mother wondered now. It was already time to discuss college.

Maddeningly, Missy wanted to attend whatever college Claire chose, and therefore saw no reason to discuss anything. She explained that after Claire was accepted, Missy would know where *she* was going, too. "You cannot base your college choice on what is right for Claire!" Kitty yelled at her daughter.

"Of course I can," said Missy, not being rude, just stating a fact.

This Friday, Kitty Vianello was eager for the weekend. She straightened up, eager for a nice snack, too. Then she saw that on the fridge door, along with reminders of dentist appointments, the endlessly updated grocery list, the photographs and the phone numbers, was the strange little paragraph her husband had torn out about black swans.

The black swan that could bring doom into her life beat its wings in Kitty Vianello's heart.

Her sister felt that if the birth mothers had wanted Missy or Claire, they would have come by now. But Kitty knew that the ways of the heart were mysterious. Years might pass, but sorrow and regret could swell instead of vanishing. If the birth mother contacted Missy now, Missy was too old to be taken away. But Missy might choose to leave the parents who had lied to her all these years.

* * *

Missy had been texting Claire on and off all day. Claire hadn't answered. Missy kept remembering her cousin's closing statement last night: "I won't be your toy twin."

She did not listen as the history teacher read aloud from an ancillary text. She felt as restless as bubbles in soda, little pieces of her surfacing and breaking through.

The person she cared about most on this earth had been the victim of her hoax. The two people she cared about maybe as much—maybe more; how did you quantify love for your own parents?—sat at their computers, not dreaming that Missy had toyed with their lives. Missy had not had the simple decency just to ask them for the truth. She had seen an opportunity and seized it with no more thought than a toddler seizing a cookie.

The largest thing in life—Who am I? Who are we? Who are you?—and Missy had made it a game.

There was no escape. The video blocked every exit.

And yet at the same time, Missy thought the video was perfect. Her parents, Claire's parents and Claire herself also had no exit. They were locked in that video, and somebody had the answers and would have to tell.

Missy checked her phone again, but Claire still had not

replied, by text, voice or e-mail, which she checked last because it was the least likely. She opened the Facebook e-mail.

"We need to confirm that you know Genevieve in order for you to be friends on Facebook. Genevieve says, `We have to talk. Here's my cell number. It's a matter of life and death.`"

How peculiar. Not at all what a person wrote when she wanted to friend somebody. Missy read it again. Wait. It didn't say "life and death." It said "life and birth."

This is about my birth. Somebody who knows my history saw the video! I bet Genevieve Candler is the doctor who delivered us. Or the nurse. Maybe the aide. I know, I know! It's the social worker who split us up!

Wait.

It couldn't be the doctor who had delivered the twins. It couldn't be a nurse, an aide or a social worker. Even if they could separate in memory a particular set of newborns, they would never remember the names of those babies sixteen years later. And if Missy and Claire were adopted, they hadn't had the names Vianello or Linnehan at birth anyway. A person who had been in that delivery room and then sixteen years later saw a weepy reunion between two cute girls would not connect the video to the birth of one scrawny and one healthy twin.

Except for one person. One person in that delivery room might make such a connection.

The mother.

The real actual biological mother.

Missy was stricken. She had daydreamed about being identical twins as if the idea were a party favor, sparkly and silly and sweet. This message was more like a fire eating a house, suffocating a family.

Missy's family.

Claire's.

The birth mother wanted to be her friend.

Missy's phone sat in her lap like a hand grenade. If she touched it, their lives would explode.

* * *

Aiden said eagerly, "What did you find out, Claire? Have all the parents met each other now? Do you know who you really are?"

Thirty-six hours ago I knew, thought Claire. Now I know nothing.

Claire thought about church. She loved church and yet it bored her. The music predated her grandparents, never mind her parents. She generally read the pew Bible to keep herself going for the whole hour. God and Jesus were always telling people to do things "in my name."

Names mattered. You had to know your name. Of course, all parents have to choose a name because no baby arrives with a tag, like a collectible doll. But if a baby is adopted, its name is more made-up than other kids' names.

How are Missy and I going to get out of this? thought Claire.

What happens when our parents see that video? What names will they give us then? The names of our real parents?

I don't want real parents! I want my parents. I want Missy to be a nasty mean interfering manipulating *cousin.*

In front of Aiden, she hid behind Missy's story. "It was a hoax. I should have told you yesterday, Aiden. Missy had an assignment. I think we got carried away."

"A classroom assignment?" said Aiden in disbelief. "To do a hoax?"

Claire nodded. Her neck was stiff. She was paralyzed from anxiety. "The hoax was supposed to involve science. I guess the science in our hoax is the psychology of fooling people."

Aiden's face fell. "You're not her identical twin?"

"No. We're cousins. There's a strong family resemblance."

Aiden lost interest and walked away. Claire could not figure out how to call him back. She had the oddest sensation that she could not call herself back either. The girl named Claire Linnehan was gone. In her place was a child of unknown origin, waiting to be identified.

* * *

FRIDAY
Three p.m.

WHEN SCHOOL ENDED, Missy had to take evasive action to get away from Rick; Mr. Shemtov, the excited fraternal-twin physics teacher; and Mrs. Conway, who was even more irked today, having fielded questions from national media.

Missy didn't go near the buses. She didn't go near the student parking lot. She slid through the cafeteria and exited onto the loading dock. She passed trucks, a little tractor and some dollies to emerge on the maintenance road, and sneaked off the school grounds.

I expected it to be like confetti, she thought. A parade. Welcome home, identical twins! But I opened the gate and now Genevieve Candler wants to come in.

This time when Missy phoned, Claire answered. "Yes?"

"Are you coming over tonight?"

"Melissa, I told you. I'm ending that. It's twisted us. We're entertaining sick thoughts. Have a nice weekend."

"Wait! Did a Genevieve Candler want to friend you? Did you read the message?"

"Yes, I read the message. No, I'm not going to be the woman's friend. Who can she be, Missy, except the birth mother? I don't want one. What are you trying to do—destroy our lives?" Claire hung up.

I wanted to be twins, thought Missy. Instead, I've lost my best friend.

Missy was home. She unlocked the front door. From the top of the stairs, her father shouted, "Miss?"

Missy usually liked her nickname. She was the only Missy in the entire school system. Her mother always called out "Mih-see" on two different pitches, but her father often shortened it to "Miss," as if she were a saleswoman and he was trying to get her attention: "Oh, miss, can you tell me the price of this jacket?"

"Miss" was what you called a stranger.

Am I a stranger in this family?

Her parents clattered down the stairs from their offices, happy for an excuse to take a break.

"Uncle Phil called," said her mother. "He wants to know which direction you girls are going tonight."

Uncle Phil was the biggest man Missy knew. He could still pick Missy up as if she were a toddler and toss her in the air. Missy had always wanted to be a cheerleader who got thrown into the air and caught by adorable boys in front of great crowds in the gym, but she had never made the squad. Sometimes when her uncle tossed her into the air, her skull would barely miss the ceiling and Mom would yell, "You give my daughter a concussion and you're history!" and Uncle Phil would yell back, "I am history. I'm legend. I am lore."

He'll still be my legend and lore, Missy told herself. Even if we're not related.

She was shocked by this thought. If she wasn't related to her parents, she wasn't related to anybody else, either. Not Uncle Phil and not Aunt Frannie. Not her aunts and uncles on her father's side, not her cousins in Ohio. Not her grandparents in Florida and not her grandparents in Ohio.

"Am I driving you to Claire's?" asked her father. "Kitty, did we get the oil changed in the car?"

"I don't know, but do you want some decaf, Matt?"

"I'm having a Coke. Miss, you want a Coke?"

"Missy," said her mother, "you didn't happen to see my yellow purse, did you? The one I bought on sale that time and it's too small but I love the color?"

"How about a brownie?" said her father. "Your mother and I had a domestic attack. We used a mix and even remembered to set the timer."

"First we had to find the timer," said her mother.

Missy set her book bag down and headed into the kitchen for a brownie. "No sleepover tonight," she called back.

"You're kidding, right?"

"You've been begging us to spread our wings and find other weekend activities," said Missy. "Ta-da! It begins tonight."

Her father followed her into the kitchen and had another brownie. "What's Claire doing instead?"

"I didn't ask," said Missy.

"I don't believe that," said her mother. "You always know every single thing Claire does every single second. You send a hundred texts a day."

"We're going cold turkey. Sort of like cigarette addiction. We're going to de-cousin for a weekend and see how we do. If we go into spasms of agony from withdrawal, there's always Saturday."

Her father was laughing. "Miss, I'm tickled pink. What shall we do as a family, then, just the three of us on a Friday night?"

The correct answer was watch a video, but Missy didn't suggest it. She had dragged Claire into Rick's studio to expose the secret. Now she wanted the secret back.

CHAPTER

FRIDAY EVENING
The Linnehan house

CLAIRE DID NOT turn on the lights in her bedroom. She stood in front of her full-length mirror staring at her shadowy reflection.

Claire could imagine Missy in Mrs. Stancil's class deciding to use the hoax idea. What Claire could not see was the benefit. Wouldn't it have been better to wait for the weekend when the two families were together?

But parents who kept secrets all these years might not yield. Missy's dad might roll his eyes. "Come on, Missy," he might say. Claire's own father might say "Huh?" while he helped himself to more food. Her mother might say, "Missy, don't be annoying. There are enough annoying people in my exercise classes. I don't need it from you." Missy's own mother would not have been listening. "Do you like this salad dressing? I don't usually use lemon juice, I usually use vinegar, but I was out of vinegar and I saw this once on TV and I thought, it'll be mild, but maybe people will like it."

And what would she, Claire, the identical twin in question, have said when Missy presented her theory?

It wasn't our parents Missy needed to convince, she thought. It was me.

Okay, Missy. You did it. I'm convinced.

Claire reached for her cell phone.

Missy answered instantly. "Thank God you phoned! I missed you so much. Don't call me Melissa again. I don't even know who she is."

"I don't know who she is either, Missy. Okay, two things. First, I lied. I knew the instant I left your high school foyer and turned right and looked down that long dim hallway and saw that pale pink blur. I knew who you were. I knew who I was. I just couldn't admit it. I can be a twin instead of a cousin, I guess, but I can't be adopted. Not yet. Maybe tomorrow."

They didn't giggle. But there was a softness in the silence.

"And the other thing?" asked Missy.

"The Genevieve person. I've decided that it's some Internet junkie trying to invade our lives. But it's making me nervous. Let's look at her page together. We'll have a good laugh and go to sleep friends." Claire knew Missy wanted to go to sleep identical twins. But Missy let it go. "Let's get our laptops," she said. "I feel the need for a large screen."

Claire put on her bed light. She got her laptop and arranged herself comfortably in bed. She plumped the pillows. Balanced the laptop on her knees. Tilted the lamp so it didn't glare on the screen.

"Ready?" said Missy.

"Ready," said Claire.

But of course she was not ready.

Who could be ready for this?

Genevieve Candler's Facebook page featured album after album of little square pictures to click and enlarge.

There was Missy standing on white-painted steps leading to a red front door. Claire had never even seen white-painted steps. How did you keep them white?

There was Missy admiring a Christmas tree decorated with mauve and violet silk flowers. Their families celebrated Christmas in green and red. Where were these places? Who had Missy visited? Had this Genevieve person been stalking Missy, secretly taking pictures the way somebody took pictures of every house and road in the nation for Google Maps?

Claire had never met anybody named Genevieve. Did this girl pronounce it French: *Zhan-vee-ev?* Or American: *Jenna-veev?*

She clicked photograph after photograph. Who were those people gathered around Missy, their smiles proud and happy? And where were they? There was no wallpaper in Missy's house, let alone with striped pink roses. Missy had never sat in a golf cart, waving a club at the photographer. Missy had never celebrated a High School Bowl victory.

The cell phone fell out of Claire Linnehan's fingers, making a tiny thud on the thick carpet of her room.

These were not pictures of Missy. These were not pictures of Claire, either.

No, no, no, no, no, no, no, I don't want this.

She shifted her laptop to the blanket. Without taking her eyes from the screen, Claire reached down with one hand and felt around on the floor for her phone. If she slid off the bed, she would be in water over her head. She would drown. Claire hauled herself back to safety. She put the cell close to her mouth but could not summon speech.

Missy was whispering into the phone. "Clairedy."

"I'm here," she whispered back.

"There are three of us. We're all three identical."

Claire was not going there. "It's some video trick. Three people cannot be identical. She downloaded our pictures from the video. From our own Facebook pages. She manipulated them with some program."

"Check out her earlobes. You and I each have one pierced earring hole. She's got three. She isn't us."

Claire gagged.

"Do you think somebody cloned us?" asked Missy. "Do you think we're a set? Did we come in a box? Or a tube?"

"Clone" was a hideous word. It sounded like sheep and laboratories and things forbidden by law. *I* can't be a clone, thought Claire.

"So now we know," said Missy. "You and I are not cousins. We're not identical twins, either. We are identical triplets."

Had Claire ever used the word "triplet"? Did you ever need that word? If three people played instruments, they were a trio. If three people went somewhere, they were a threesome. If something happened three times in a row in a sport, you might have a three-peat.

Only musical notation had triplets: three notes forced into

the space of the usual two. It was a good definition. Genevieve Candler was forcing herself into the space of the usual two.

No, said Claire to herself. I won't have it. She's not getting into my life.

Missy's voice ballooned with excitement. "Clairedy, there are three of us! We have another sister. We're a three-per. We're triplets!"

If Missy was right, this girl Genevieve had been alive for the exact same number of years, months and days as Claire. She had been brushing the same hair, putting polish on the same fingernails, choosing a bathing suit for the same body.

Claire Linnehan was exactly the same as this stranger on the screen.

Not that separated triplets were precisely strangers.

I knew her once, thought Claire. I touched her once.

"Whoever we are," cried Missy—and Claire knew that Missy was dancing, because that was what Missy did when she was excited; she leaped and spun—"whoever we are, we have the same parents!" Missy sounded thrilled, as if she did not realize this meant that the parents they'd lived with all their lives were fakes.

Claire knew adopted kids. Their parents loved to talk about how they had lined up and begged and pleaded and gotten interviewed and waited for years, all for the privilege of having this particular child. But if Claire was one of three identical babies, she was not a particular child. She was a group. You might as well say you wanted the orange on the left instead of the orange in the middle. Who could tell? Who even cared?

143

How simple and pleasant her earlier guesses seemed. As adopted identical twins, they would just reset the same group of six: Claire and her wonderful parents plus Missy and her wonderful parents. Oh, sure, they would have to sort things out and admit stuff and wonder about biological whatevers, but they would still be who they'd always been.

Wrong.

There was a third person.

In Language Arts, you learned about "person." There was first person, as in the sentence "I am loved." There was second person, as in the sentence "You are loved." First person and second person were always standing right there. You were them or you could see them.

But third person was somebody else, as in "She is a stranger."

There was now a third person. And a third family.

"Let's call her up!" said Missy. "She gave us her cell number! Let's call right now! She practically says it's a matter of life and death! I can't wait to hear her voice!"

Claire would have screamed, but she did not want to wake her parents. "Are you nuts, Missy?"

Her father would call this a can of worms. It was one of his favorite phrases, used to describe everything from failed economies to political scandals.

In fact, Claire's family ate very little out of cans. They certainly didn't buy cans of worms. When were worms canned? Perhaps you saved your empty baked bean can and used it for the worms you caught for your fishing trip. Claire pictured the worms as fat and gelatinous and wriggling. Piled on each other, suffocating each other, each little squirmy head trying to get free. She pictured the can falling over and the worms slithering out.

"Genevieve will be awake, I know she will," said Missy confidently, as if she and Genevieve had known each other for years.

And maybe we have, thought Claire. Maybe she will be just like us. Like those thirty-year-old guys with the same bowling scores.

The can of worms emptied in Claire's hair, crawled into her brain and down into her heart. "I will not get in touch with her. I do not want to know her. I want her to go away."

"She won't go away. She must have as many questions as we do. She's awake, Claire. She's staring at her cell phone, wanting it to ring, just the way I was staring at my cell phone, wanting you to call and forgive me. The three of us are doing the exact same thing at the exact same time because we *are* the exact same. She's our sister, Clairedy."

"I'm not ready to be your sister, never mind hers."

"But aren't you excited, Clairedy? Aren't you dying to meet her?"

"No. It could still be some elaborate hoax. Or confusion. Or coincidence."

"Then we have to see her in person. The moment we see her, we'll know if she's our twin. I mean, triplet. And if she is, we'll run toward each other and merge."

As if Claire wanted to "merge" with anybody. As if it could be a good thing for these sickeningly similar creatures to meet.

145

Not to mention that three families would be shredded now. Why stop at three? Maybe there were four or five. If you were going to clone or multiply, why not really go for it? Maybe every few years, another Claire would pop up.

* * *

Already the name Genevieve seemed soft and familiar, like Missy's favorite old velvet pillow on the downstairs sofa. Lying on her stomach on the bed, she Googled every clue from the pictures. "Genevieve isn't that far away in miles," she told Claire. "I just found her high school Web site, which I got off her High School Bowl pin in that photograph. The White Pages show two Candlers in that town, and now I'm doing Street Map, and I'm guessing our Candlers do not live in a nursing home, so ours is the one on Bayberry. Okay, I'm bringing up a map. Our house is one mile from the beach here in Connecticut and where we live, it's maybe thirteen or fourteen miles to cross Long Island Sound, and now I've found her street, and she's four or five miles inland. So technically speaking, although not by road of course—by road it's a couple of hours—we're about twenty miles away from Genevieve."

She and Claire were also about twenty miles apart.

Missy considered geography. The metropolitan area around New York City was complex, and water, either Long Island Sound or the Hudson River, divided everything. There were three states involved: New York, New Jersey and Connecticut.

Some of New York State abutted New York City, like Westchester County, where Claire lived. Long Island, where Genevieve lived, began with Brooklyn and then stuck out into the Atlantic Ocean to the east, parallel to Connecticut's shore. Commuters into New York City went by car, train or bus. Trains entered one of two stations. Westchester and Connecticut riders ended up at Grand Central Terminal, New Jersey and Long Island riders at Penn Station. Buses had more freedom, and cars just needed to decide which bridge or tunnel to use.

"It's Friday night," said Missy. "You and I never plan anything for Saturday morning except each other, Clairedy. Let's call Genevieve and arrange to meet under the clock in Grand Central tomorrow."

"No! We have to wait and think this through."

Missy began singing football cheers under her breath. "*Motivate your feet, get the rhythm, get the beat!* Clairedy, I have to see her. I have to breathe her air. I have to touch her. *One— let's scream! Two—let's shout! Three—come on, let's shake it out!*"

Claire did not take up the cheer. "If you and I are twins, we get an equal vote. I vote no. That means it's a tie."

"But we're not twins, Clairedy. I was wrong. I always knew there was a hole in my heart and this is it. It's Genevieve! She used to be here. My heart knew. You and she and I are triplets. So you get one third of the vote, and we already know Genevieve's vote, because she got in touch with us first. So it's two against one, you're outnumbered."

"I won't be part of it. Don't you ruin my life!"

Missy tried to be patient. "It won't ruin anybody. It'll be an addition. We'll have another sister."

"I don't want any sisters. Not even you. You make a great cousin. I don't want a twin. Even when I admit it, I don't want it to be true. Missy, slow down. I just found out that my mother is too tired to keep working and my father doesn't *have* work and they aren't my parents anyway, I'm adopted, and my cousin is actually my twin—and now you want me to stalk some stranger?"

"What is your problem?" demanded Missy. "I did want answers from our parents. But now that I know about Genevieve, I don't care about explanations and documents. I want to be with her. Clairedy, the moment I am with Genevieve Candler, I will know who we are."

"Don't call me Clairedy. Don't call me Claire, either. It's some made-up name stuck on me by parents who aren't my parents. I probably don't even have a name. Listen, Missy. Today has been one ice bath after another. Don't call this girl! If you do, don't tell me. If you meet each other, don't include me. I'm not part of it!"

* * *

FRIDAY NIGHT

IN SPITE OF the fact that she had been lobbying for this for years, Claire's mother was unsettled that the girls were not getting together. Claire was studying? Claire never studied on a

Friday night. Fridays were reserved for Missy. The girls' need to talk and share surpassed anything Frannie had seen in years of watching women gather to talk and share. Sometimes the girls literally talked the whole night. Other times they baked cookies or played board games or rented movies. They could talk through an entire movie. Her husband couldn't stand it. He had to leave the room.

Frannie knocked on her daughter's bedroom door.

"I'm busy," said Claire.

Frannie did not interpret this as "Don't come in." She opened the door and said, "Want to have a midnight snack with Dad and me?"

Claire did not glance up from her computer. "It's nowhere near midnight. Anyway, I have too much to do."

Frannie sat on the bed. "Clairedy, did something happen between you and Missy?"

Claire looked at her mother as if smelling roadkill. "I have a project I cannot postpone."

"What's the project?"

"I'm still choosing a topic."

"Which class?"

Claire looked her mother up and down as if she were an insect to be stomped on.

It's here, thought Frannie. The awful adolescent dislike of parents everybody talks about. I've lost my sweet baby.

Claire heaved an irritated sigh. "Language Arts," she said finally.

Frannie almost apologized for being interested in her daughter's life. She found her husband. They went to a movie without Claire. When they got home, Claire was still in front of her computer, still grumpy.

"It's late, honey," said Frannie.

"It's Friday," said her daughter, in the voice of one dealing with stupid people. "It doesn't matter how late I stay up."

Frannie bent to kiss her daughter good night. Claire did not return the kiss.

* * *

STILL FRIDAY NIGHT

TRAIN SCHEDULES WERE posted online. Missy found a 9:03 local from Stamford that got into the city at 10:09 a.m. She would need a ride to the train station and a good excuse. She had minimal interest in culture, but she looked up current exhibits at the Metropolitan Museum of Art. One was Byzantine art. What was that? And who cared?

She checked her cash situation. She was in good shape. Tomorrow morning, she would say that somebody had canceled on the art class field trip, making room for somebody else, and Missy was taking advantage of cultural opportunities, and Byzantine art would be broadening. Her parents would be happy that Missy was having a non-Claire event and might end up with a new best friend who was not a cousin.

And this might come true.

Missy Vianello called the cell phone number Genevieve Candler had put in her Facebook message.

The possible sister was up and waiting. "This is Genevieve."

Claire's voice, thought Missy. For a moment, she wanted to hang up. For a moment, she wanted Claire far more than she wanted this stranger. Then she said, "This is Missy."

"Missy! Thank you for calling! I've been sitting up in bed willing you to call. Did you compare pictures? Did you see?"

"I compared. I saw. You're me. I'm you." I know by phone, thought Missy. I don't have to touch her or see her.

Missy wept. Am I crying for a lost sister or a found one?

"I've watched the video of you and Claire about a hundred times," said Genevieve.

"Us too. Claire is opposed."

"She wants her own gene pool?" asked Genevieve.

I'm a born giggler, thought Missy. Is Genevieve?

Born. How *had* they all been born? And to whom? "Claire doesn't want to be part of this," Missy said, and her heart wrenched and a different kind of hole opened up. "She thinks it's creepy."

"It is creepy," said Genevieve in Claire's voice, "but I keep telling myself it isn't *too* creepy."

"How did you find the video?" Missy asked.

Genevieve told her about Jimmy Fleming and Ray Feingold. "Jimmy guessed that the hoax was a hoax."

"He's right. Genevieve, I have to meet you. Now, not some other time. I checked train schedules. What are you doing tomorrow? Can you cancel it? Do your parents let you go into New York by yourself? Can you fib about a class trip if you're not allowed to go alone? Do you have the money? I'll take the train from Stamford that gets in about ten-fifteen. We'll meet under the clock on the upper level at Grand Central." She could hear Genevieve crying. "Don't cry," Missy begged, even though she herself had been crying through the entire conversation.

"I'm crying from joy. I never thought I'd have a sister, let alone one who can't wait to meet me. But what about Claire? I can't not meet Claire. Should I call her? Will she talk to me?"

"I think she'd flip out. She's angry. She says I had no right to drag her into my hoax. She wants the same parents and the same life."

"She gets to keep the same parents and the same life. I won't be in the way. I'll just be an add-on, like an ell off the same kitchen."

"Identical triplets are a little more intense. I'll call her again in the morning and give her a second chance."

"No, call her now," said Genevieve.

It was the first thing that actually surprised Missy: Genevieve expected to be in charge. Because she's the oldest? I wonder if we'll ever know which of us is the oldest. Or is it because her personality is stronger? Claire will be happy to hear that our personalities aren't cloned. She will not be happy to hear that Genevieve is a little bossy.

On the other hand, Genevieve was right. Including Claire could not wait until the morning. "Okay, I'll call her now," said

Missy. "The excuse I'm giving my parents is a school trip to the Metropolitan Museum to see Byzantine art."

"My parents are fine with anything. Long Island trains go to Penn Station, though. I'll take a taxi over to Grand Central and meet you at ten-fifteen under the clock."

Missy started to say "How will I recognize you?" when she remembered that she would be looking for herself.

* * *

FRIDAY NIGHT
Late

MATT VIANELLO HAD known that he would love being a dad, but he had not known how much he would love it. In the lottery of life, he was always so grateful that he had been given Missy.

Scrawny and sickly, Missy had paid a high price for her low birth weight. Colds became pneumonia. Coughs became bronchitis. Fevers were life-threatening. And there had been that bout of meningitis, when he and Kitty had sat at the hospital holding hands, wondering if their little girl would live until dawn. For years, their lives were punctured by illness—days and nights spent rocking, walking, cuddling, soothing, medicating and above all, worrying.

They wanted to homeschool Missy rather than expose her to classroom germs. But Missy insisted on being exactly like her big cousin Claire, and so their fragile child went to kindergarten after all. Missy had known what she was doing, which was always the case. She loved school from the first day and she loved it now. She danced through dozens of activities, spending the minimum amount of time on each, so she never became good at anything, but she sure enjoyed herself.

She was a year older than most of her classmates because Matt and Kitty had kept her home an extra year to stabilize her. Missy hadn't pressed her father as hard as he had expected about getting her driver's license. His line that Missy's full-speed personality was a driving risk had been accepted. But one day he would need paperwork.

Now, Matt Vianello could not fall asleep. His wife and sister-in-law had been trying to end the girls' Friday-night sleepovers for years. Now that it was happening, he felt dread.

All week his daughter had seemed to study him as if he were an arithmetic problem and she was coming up short. There was no affection in her gaze. He had the sensation that he and his wife had fulfilled their purpose and soon Missy would walk away and never look back.

You were supposed to bring up your kid with wings to fly. But flying meant departure. He could not imagine how empty life would be when Missy departed.

A sudden peal of laughter from Missy's room cut through the dark of the house. At this hour, she could only be on the phone with Claire.

Matt Vianello sighed with relief.

He fell asleep.

* * *

FRIDAY
Even later

CLAIRE LINNEHAN SAT as stiffly on her bed as if it were a park bench.

It's two against one, you're outnumbered. How could Missy say that?

It was already coming true. Claire was not part of the first meeting. She'd have to meet Genevieve sometime, because Missy was correct—there was no escape. But Missy and Genevieve would become a pair ahead of her. They'd be sisters while Claire sat alone in a room lit by a glowing computer, as if her only friends were electronic.

She returned to an Internet source she had bookmarked earlier, a site about the biology of multiple births. She had bookmarked the page on twins, but now she scrolled to the page about triplets.

Triplets could be three separate eggs in the mother, in which case they were fraternal triplets. Plain old brothers and sisters who happened to be born at the same time. Missy, Claire and Genevieve were visibly not fraternal triplets.

Triplets could be two eggs, one of which split once, so that those two were identical twins, while the second egg didn't split, making the third baby a fraternal twin. Claire hoped this was not her own situation. How ghastly if even among triplets one could be an outsider.

Or triplets could come from a single egg, which split once, and then one of the splits split again. These were identical triplets.

Claire imagined Missy and Genevieve smiling as they talked.

Each smile would tip outward in the same way, and each girl would very slightly bite her lower lip, so quickly only a mother would see. Their moms would scowl. "Don't bite your lip, honey," they would say.

And Genevieve's mother? Did she have the same complaint because she had the same daughter?

Who was Genevieve's mother?

Who was Claire's?

Claire's parents were sleeping. They were separated from Claire only by closets. They still occupied a world without identical twins and triplets. They knew nothing.

Or did they know everything?

She thought, Missy will invite Genevieve for a sleepover. There won't ever be a Claire-over again.

Her cell phone rang. It was Missy. Claire snatched it up.

"I called her!" said Missy. "Clairedy, it's incredible. I really liked her. Although I think she could be a little bossy. Now listen. We're going in to the city tomorrow morning just like I planned. She's taking the LIRR into Penn Station and we'll take Metro-North into Grand Central. We'll meet under the clock at ten-fifteen. We're pretending to go to the Metropolitan Museum to see Byzantine art."

"What do you mean, 'we'?" said Claire sullenly.

"Clairedy, come on. I'll get the train in Stamford and you catch the same train in New Rochelle. I'll be in the front car, waiting for you."

"How can you be so calm? Our lives were carved up and served separately at birth! You should stay home vomiting."

"Claire, she's our sister, not our death sentence. If we don't meet, how will we know for sure?"

"It sounds as if you've settled that without me."

"She wants to call you, Claire. Would that be all right?"

"Missy. This is not a cute little excursion into a cute little past with a cute little triplet. This is the end of our families. We have to stay home tomorrow and sit with our parents while they see the video."

"I don't care about them right now," said Missy. "I need Genevieve."

CHAPTER

SATURDAY MORNING
Long Island

NED CANDLER'S GOLF game had been canceled. He stared out the kitchen window at the pouring rain. Ned didn't like being home. He liked leaving home. He liked parties and movies, action and games, dinners out and dances. He told himself to make a list: Chores I Have Put Off Long Enough. There wasn't a chore out there Ned felt like doing.

The coffeepot stopped sputtering. Ned poured himself a cup, added sweetener and milk, stirred and sipped. No matter how much money you spent on your coffee maker, it didn't compete. Coffee from chains, diners and restaurants was always better.

Now what? The Candlers had Saturday newspaper delivery, but he wasn't in the mood to trot down the driveway in this pouring rain. He turned on the kitchen computer and checked the news. Many things in the world were going wrong. He felt unable to read the details. He had problems of his own.

He and Allegra fell into a maligned category: people who live beyond their means. They lived in a town they couldn't afford, drove cars whose payments they could barely make and wore fine clothing they had to charge. Now he couldn't even ask his wealthy grandmother for help. She wasn't wealthy anymore.

But the big worry was Vivi, who had become an academic star, something she certainly had not inherited from her parents. Vivi would want to go to a top college, which would cost top dollar. Ned didn't have medium dollars. He didn't have *dollars*. He had debts.

He checked his e-mail. He always had a huge number of messages waiting. Corporate Giving was a strange little department. It didn't "lead" anywhere. It just sat on the edges of the real activity. When they were young, he and Allegra had been sure their jobs would "lead" somewhere. They expected to be movers and shakers. Instead, Allegra was just another drone, working hard to achieve little, while Ned had the same responsibilities he'd started with twenty years ago. He loved what he did and was proud of it; he truly helped people. It would never pay more, but he couldn't stand the idea of changing jobs. He and Allegra had a social calendar to die for. Keeping up with the invitations was not cheap. He couldn't afford to take Vivi to look at colleges, never mind pay for her to attend one.

He hardly knew Vivi anymore. Back when she was little, just another skinny dark-haired child, the whole thing seemed like wallpaper. The decision he and Allegra had made was background. Elevator music. The older Vivi got, the less that seemed to be true. When Ned looked at her now, the decision would rise up and look right back at him. He would feel a low-level panic, knowing what people would think. He would look at his beautiful wife, for whom he would do anything. He and Allegra almost never talked about it. They didn't need to. They could tell when the other was panicking.

Allegra's panic was deeper. She was the mother. She would be judged more harshly.

Ned Candler did not believe that conspiracies could last. There was no such thing as a permanent secret. One day their own secret would be exposed.

Since he couldn't drink coffee without reading a paper, he scanned a half-read *Wall Street Journal*. The paper was folded open to a strange and beautiful phrase he had circled with the thick blue tip of his favorite fountain pen. He knew what his Grandmother Candler would say about that: "You could have bought a single plastic ballpoint pen, but no, you have to have a dozen fountain pens, each of which costs a fortune."

He couldn't concentrate.

The black swans in his life kept swimming into view.

* * *

SATURDAY MORNING
Connecticut

MISSY SKITTERED INTO the kitchen. She felt as if her fingers and eyes and hair were separating from her body, about to float around the room and attach themselves elsewhere. She wanted to be with Genevieve Candler so much it was like starving to death.

"Hi, sweetheart," said her father. "You're up early."

I'll get him to drive me to the station now, thought Missy. I can't wait here. I'm about to meet the long-lost identical twin I faked. I can't look at Mom and Dad or even talk to them. And if I'm going to coax Claire into coming, I sure can't have my parents listening in. "Morning, Dad."

"We're working on vacation plans," said her father.

"I was thinking of Savannah," said her mother. "Isn't 'Savannah' a pretty word? There was a girl named Savannah in your first grade, Missy. Whatever happened to Savannah?"

"But is there a lot to do in Savannah?" asked her father.

Missy could not take more twitter. "There's a trip into New York today. People are going to the Metropolitan Museum to look at Byzantine art. One kid canceled and I get to go. All you have to do is drive me to the train station."

"Oh, Missy, that will be such fun!" cried her mother. "Or will it? Isn't Byzantine art mostly sad thin saints? I always want a saint who's happy. But I think they often die difficult deaths, and naturally they're a little depressed."

Oh, my God, I love my parents, thought Missy. They're nuts, but they're mine. I have to get out of here now, before I'm crippled by loving them.

"You'll need money," said her father. "Train, subway pass, museum fee, lunch." He peeled off tens and gave them to her.

If she told Dad she didn't need money, it would draw attention to the expedition. She took the cash. "Thanks."

"Keep your cell phone on," said her mother.

"And stay with the group," said her father.

"Who's the teacher?" her mother wanted to know.

"I'll stay with the group," she promised, avoiding teacher identification. She hated lying. Of course, they had lied every single time they claimed to be her parents.

They'll still be my parents, won't they? Our family won't dissolve, will it?

Not surprisingly, her mother had difficulty locating her purse. Her parents discussed possible purse locations, a routine conversation that normally made Missy crazy, but this morning she wanted to weep.

Half of her yearned to spill everything. Half of her was desperate for Claire to come too. Half of her was sickened by the physiology of this. Was she really identical to two other people, from her freckles to her toenails? It was unnatural. Half of Missy didn't want a molecule of her life changed, and the other half had already planned how to change every bit.

That was too many halves for one body. She was exploding from the pressure of her halves.

And she had to admit the possibility that there were no identical triplets, that Genevieve and Missy were drama queens with big hair.

At last, Missy's mother located her purse. Yes, the wallet was in it. Yes, her driver's license was there too. She even had the car keys! What a good day this was shaping up to be.

Kitty Vianello was a poor driver. She tapped the accelerator instead of leaving her foot on it, so the car lurched. She slowed down too early for curves and remembered to look one way but not the other. Missy was grateful for the invention of airbags.

Stamford station was elevated, spreading high across the tracks, with escalators going up and down to the New York–bound or Boston-bound trains. Groups would gather on the upper level. Missy's mother would not realize that no other classmates were here. Yet her mother seemed vaguely aware that the situation was odd. Missy distracted her. "Does Aunt Frannie still want to quit Jazzercise?"

"You can only do something for so long," said Kitty Vianello, "and then it feels like a rat trap. Plus, when you're hitting fifty, you're stir-crazy. Your aunt Frannie needs a change. We all need a change."

You're about to get one, thought Missy.

* * *

Frannie Linnehan was yelling at the top of her lungs. She had good lungs, from shouting over loud music all week long. "I can't do this anymore!" she informed her household. "I can't get up at dawn one more time! I can't be a cheerleader for one more hour! I'm giving up today!" She slammed the skillet around. "Philip! Do you want eggs?"

"You can't quit," said her husband. "We need the money. I'll cook the eggs. You get ready."

Frannie was grateful. Cracking eggs this morning struck her as dangerous. She might hurl them across the room just for the joy of the splat. Phil was right. They needed the money. She knew that Phil had little work. She knew how discouraged he was. She knew how he worried about their brilliant

163

daughter, and the college Claire deserved, and the cost of such a college.

They had saved and saved, but after all that saving, they had only enough money for one year at an ordinary school. Claire deserved four years at a great school.

Frannie paused outside her daughter's closed bedroom door. She knocked lightly. Claire was probably still asleep. Frannie would tiptoe in, reassure herself that all was well—

"What do you want?" snapped Claire.

"I'm leaving," said Frannie through the door.

"And?" said Claire.

Not once, not ever, had Frannie Linnehan heard that tone of voice from Claire. "And I want to hug good-bye, honey."

"I'll be up in a minute," snapped Claire.

"You don't have to get up, honey, I'll come in and—"

"I *said* I'll be *up* in a *minute*."

Frannie retreated.

In the kitchen her husband was beaming. "Tommy called," said Phil excitedly. "He has work for me! Tommy's going to need me for the rest of the month."

Claire stomped into the kitchen.

"Eggs?" said her father.

Eggs made her think of human eggs. Of clones. Twins. Triplets.

Claire adored two television shows in which the families had many children: one family where they had them one at a time, and just never stopped, and were now up to sixteen or eighteen kids—more kids than were in some of Claire's classes—and another family that had a series of litters—two here, six there. Who could live through a pregnancy of six babies all at once? How did the *babies* live through it? It must have been tight in there.

If Missy's theory was correct, then Claire had elbowed Missy around, breathed her oxygen and taken her nourishment, so that Missy emerged a pitiful miniature who took years to catch up. But if babies had personalities in the womb, wouldn't Missy have been doing the elbowing? Wouldn't Claire have been the little shriveled one? And who was this Genevieve? Another big shoving kid or another squashed little one?

"I'm not in an egg mood," she said to her father.

"What's going on?" demanded her father. "You lost your rhythm or something?"

I've lost my twin.

I've lost my triplet.

I've lost my mind.

You two are liars. You're not even related to me.

My triplet is stalking me.

My cousin-twin and the triplet are becoming best friends while I sit here watching fried eggs get cold.

Claire would test whether a high-pitched scream really could break a window. That was probably true for old-fashioned, single-pane windows, not the energy-efficient layered windows in this house. She could probably scream all day and the windows would just stare reflectively back. "Nothing's wrong."

"You're not acting normal," said her father.

And separating triplets is normal? Taking one third of a

triplet set is normal? Never telling your daughter she's adopted is normal?

Claire pretended to study cereal boxes on the shelf. Mostly she was just turning her back on her father. Who wasn't a father.

She chose the dullest cereal: shredded wheat. A cereal that truly had nothing going for it. Not even looks. She opened the little interior pack with the three cereal slabs and crushed one into a bowl. *That* was what it had going for it. You got to crush something.

"Dad's working today, Clairedy," said her mother. "Do you want to do something special when I get home? Maybe drive up to Clinton and Westbrook to the discount malls and buy clothes?"

"No."

"We could call Missy and see if she can come too."

"No. I'm doing a project with Wanda and Annabel."

Frannie had never heard of Wanda or Annabel. For years she had pushed Claire to develop other friendships and spend less time with Missy. But was it wise after all? What was wise, in their situation?

What *was* their situation? The dark fear that could still envelop Frannie after all these years invaded the room. Now, she thought. I should tell Claire the truth now.

But now was impossible, just as it had been impossible a thousand other times. Phil was grabbing his Carhartt jacket and his keys. Claire was pouring juice.

Frannie wrapped her toast around the egg and bacon to make a sandwich and rushed to the car to eat as she drove.

* * *

Allegra Candler liked to sleep in on Saturday mornings, but the pounding rain woke her. I'll fall asleep again, she told herself, snuggling back down.

But sleep did not return. She felt as drowned by her problems as the backyard was by rain. Back when she was young and it didn't matter whether she wore it, she had loved makeup. Now she had to wear it. She had to color her hair. She had to search carefully for fashions that did not date her. She had to deny herself all desirable food. She was surrounded by young women who were beautiful, thin and ambitious. They expected to overtake Allegra easily. She expected it, too.

On the train every day, going into and out of the city, she was forced to listen to dozens of cell phone conversations. There were three topics: work and gossip, which she could filter out, and parents checking on their children, which she could not. "Hi, Jacob. Did you get your homework done?" "How was your piano lesson, Max?" "Go ahead and defrost the burgers, Emily." "I don't *think* so, Devon. In a million years, you're not getting permission."

Allegra rarely checked on Genevieve, who seemed to lead a life that did not require parents, just a house. Vivi had been a grown-up from the start, a sturdy, reliable child who needed little attention. And this was a good thing, because the mother with the twelve-hour day and the father with the evening and weekend commitments had little to spare.

Small children were cute and sweet and they loved Mommy

and Daddy and were busy learning to ride a bike or else read. They all looked alike to Allegra. On the rare occasions when she showed up for a school activity, she couldn't tell the other children apart. Mostly she was grateful that she didn't have a fat one.

The teenagers looked alike too. The girls had long hair, usually flat and shiny and caught up in a ponytail. They dressed alike, they talked alike. Vivi was exceptional. Even her hair had personality—thick, wafting black hair that took up space and could not be tamed like the hair of other girls. Her decisions were astonishing. By the time Vivi was a junior, she had chosen an academic sport as well as athletic sports and had even taken over the nursing home water aerobics class.

Who *was* this girl?

And sometimes, Allegra would think . . . Who were the others?

The decision, which Allegra hardly thought of when Genevieve was small, and which she could tuck away for months or even years, now smacked her in the face every day. When Allegra checked the back of her mind, where the decision lay, she saw how immense it was. A river she could not recross.

Yet the decision had been easy to make. Allegra could no longer imagine how this could have been the case. Surely she and Ned had wept and clung to each other and made lists of pros and cons?

No. They had just done it. And since they had never told anybody to start with, nobody had asked.

The rain pounded relentlessly, as if it planned on coming in the house.

Allegra considered various robes. Her favorites were satin and lace, but the day was damp and chilly. She settled on a chrysanthemum-print fleece. She didn't usually care for fleece, which quickly looked ratty, but the robe was cozy. She fixed her hair, put on some makeup—because she never appeared anywhere without makeup, even her own kitchen—and slid her toes into small woolly slippers.

Their little house had two bedrooms: she and Ned were downstairs in a charming space without enough closets while Vivi was upstairs under the eaves, a funny little suite with low ceilings and small slanted closets. Allegra rarely went up there. Vivi did her own cleaning, changed her own bed and carried her own laundry down to the cellar, where the washer and dryer were hooked up.

At this hour on a Saturday, Vivi would be asleep upstairs.

Allegra Candler smelled coffee. She smiled happily. Ned's golf game would be canceled. Maybe they could go shopping. She loved shopping. Vivi would be busy; she was always busy. It was one of her most attractive features.

* * *

Kitty Vianello managed to find the correct one-way entrance to Stamford station. She was proud. She glanced at her daughter.

Gripping the handles of her purse so hard her knuckles were

white, Missy was staring at the station as if expecting a rock star to get off a train. Her eyes burned feverishly. Her teeth were actually chattering. When Missy leaned over to kiss her mother good-bye, the lips that touched Kitty's cheek were cold.

"Sweetheart, are you feeling all right? You're not coming down with something, are you?"

"I'm fine, Mom." Missy vaulted out of the car. "See you later." She slammed the door, ran across the sidewalk, hauled open the glass door and darted up the stairs to the station.

Somebody was honking. Cars were piling up behind her. Kitty drove away.

I should be proud, she thought. I brought up a daughter who can sashay into the city without a backward glance.

But Missy had been glad to get away from her mother.

Kitty felt herself being drawn into the unfinished scrapbook. The shoeboxes of photographs that still sat on the high closet shelf. The truth.

A past she could not change and a future she could not predict.

* * *

It's Saturday morning! thought Genevieve, coming up off the bed as if catapulted. And I have sisters!

She hugged herself and darted to her sleeping computer. She brought up the precious video and watched it twice.

What to wear?

She stared in the mirror at a body exactly like the bodies

occupied by two other girls. Those identical bodies had slept last night, would shower this morning, put on clothing and swallow juice. She would believe this if she saw herself across the room at Grand Central.

I'll call Claire now, she thought. We need to be all three of us, not two minus one. But Missy told me not to call.

Genevieve had forgotten to ask anything important. Do you know who our parents really are? Did you know you were adopted? Do you like Chinese food? Do you hate sandals where the strap divides your toes?

She and Missy had simply talked, as if they had known each other all along. As if they were sisters.

Genevieve had to wrap herself in a towel for a while, and dry her thoughts out as well as her hair. She was too wired to face her parents. Even the least involved mother and father in New York State might notice her excitement. But Saturday mornings, from early spring to late fall, her father had breakfast with golf buddies. As for Allegra, Saturday mornings were a precious chance to loll around, and she rarely rose before eleven.

Genevieve did not need permission to go into the city. Her parents expected her to make her own decisions. Still and all, they liked to know where she was. She decided to leave a note on the kitchen counter. Later she would text, to be sure they had read the note.

What to write? It must be impossible to check, and yet reasonable, so they wouldn't worry. Not that Ned and Allegra were worriers. "We trust Vivi completely," her parents liked to say, and other parents were cowed, because they didn't trust their kids an inch. But trust was not involved. Her parents simply didn't think about Genevieve that much.

Which would she rather have—two new sisters or parents who cared?

It isn't a choice, she reminded herself. My sisters exist. I have them whether we meet or not. As for my parents—they are who they are. And they're not actually mine.

I'm adopted.

The shiver of rejoicing was followed by a shudder of shame. It would be her lifelong secret—that when she realized Ned and Allegra were not her father and mother, her heart had leaped with joy. She would not even tell Missy or Claire, assuming the girls became close. It was a black mark next to her soul.

She brushed her hair, thinking of the identical hair of Missy and Claire. Her analysis didn't feel right. Why would Ned and Allegra, whose interest in parenting was low, have bothered to keep adoption a secret? In fact, why would they have adopted?

Ned and Allegra were not attracted to children. They didn't volunteer in school, help with a club or assist a coach. They barely knew the names and faces of Genevieve's classmates, whereas her friends' parents tracked Genevieve along with their own kids.

Genevieve could not picture Ned and Allegra at the moment of her adoption, clasping their new baby to their hearts, crying, "At last! We have our own child!"

Had adoption been trendy that year? Were all their friends having babies? Was Genevieve just a way to keep up?

Genevieve watched the video again. She had forgotten to ask Missy why the girls had even done that interview. What had they known, or guessed, to make them throw their situation into the air like that?

She found an umbrella. She could walk to the train station as easily as she walked to GeeGee's nursing home or high school. She planned to go early. She would wait inside the station, out of the rain.

How would she and Missy greet one another? Would they scream? Weep? Laugh? Would they know each other, bone to bone, soul to soul, the way identical twins supposedly did?

What would they do about Claire?

* * *

Claire Linnehan stood alone in the kitchen. What was she going to do all day? Why did it have to be raining? How was Claire going to survive college if she couldn't even get through a weekend without Missy?

If she's my cousin, and I need her like a blood transfusion, it's warped. But if she's my identical twin, and I need her, all of a sudden it's normal.

I will not go on a crying jag, she told herself. I will get busy and do interesting things.

Compared to a long-lost identical triplet, not much was interesting.

Her cell rang. It was Missy's ring. Grief choked her: fear over who she was or wasn't; pain over what Missy had done, or was doing now.

Claire let Missy's call go to voice mail.

* * *

Ned Candler looked up from his newspaper.

His daughter walked into the kitchen, looking beautiful in long pressed pants, a long gauzy shirt and a long wafting jacket with a tiny trendy vest over it. "You look terrific, Vivi. What's up?"

She seemed rattled by the sight of him. "You don't have a golf game?"

He pointed out the window at the rain.

"Oh," she said. "Well. Um."

He had to smile. Vivi was still just a kid.

"A bunch of us are going into the city," she told him. "Metropolitan Museum. Some kids have an art assignment. The rest of us are tagging along."

Ned couldn't stand museums. He was bored before he paid the entry fee. Five minutes of walking through those halls and his legs were tired. They should have golf carts in museums. You'd purr past the dull parts. Which would be most of it.

"Can you drive me to the station, Dad? Since it's raining?"

"Sure." Ned went to the computer and scrolled through his e-mails, deleting some, reading a few, postponing most. There was a message from Boyd in Connecticut. Boyd had been best man at his and Allegra's wedding twenty-five years ago. Could Ned and Allegra really have been married for twenty-five years? Had he missed their anniversary? No, because he'd be dead.

He counted. They'd been married in December. A white velvet, green holly, red berry wedding—the most beautiful he'd ever been in or been to. He still remembered it with pleasure. He still had the most beautiful bride. Good thing he'd thought of that, because their twenty-fifth *was* coming up. We have to do something special, he thought.

Of course, "special" meant expensive.

Vivi said, "Dad? I have to go."

He clicked on Boyd's e-mail. The message was brief. DID YOU SEE THIS YET??????!!!! There was a link. Boyd was always sending something, as if Ned cared about dancing parrots or abandoned towns in the Northern Plains trying to coax people to live there, or some weirdo who had spent his life reinventing algebra. Ned had long since ceased to open the attachments. He wrote back, Wow!

* * *

Allegra Candler entered the living room/kitchen. Her husband was at the computer. She waltzed over and kissed his bald spot. It was so cute. Every year he was cuter. Whereas she, every year, had to wear more makeup and now had to have her hair colored because of the appalling gray that had begun to appear years too early. She was sure Ned had no idea she colored her hair.

Over his shoulder, she scanned the list of e-mails. "Boyd wrote?" she cried. She adored Boyd, even though Boyd was on his third wife, which cramped their friendship, since wife number one had been Allegra's college roommate.

"Oh, you know Boyd," said her husband. "Always forwarding something nobody cares about."

Allegra turned toward the coffee and there stood Vivi. "Darling, I love the outfit. It doesn't look like your average Saturday morning. Where are you headed?"

"A bunch of us are going into the city."

If Allegra never went into New York City again, it would be fine.

"Metropolitan Museum," her husband added.

Allegra worked in the heart of Manhattan, but never did anything except shop. She was just barely acquainted with the names of museums, never mind the contents. "Do you have enough money, Vivi?" she asked. "Do you have an umbrella?"

Genevieve waved a small collapsible black umbrella.

"Have a good time." Allegra took Ned's place at the computer. Before checking her own e-mail, which was bound to have something depressing from work, she clicked Boyd's message. Boyd could always dig up something fun.

Allegra followed the link.

CHAPTER

LONG ISLAND
Still Saturday morning

As ALWAYS, HER parents' thoughts were elsewhere. Ned was staring at the rain, Allegra at her e-mail. If my parents are sorry they adopted me, thought Genevieve, I have no hope. I will never be closer to them and they will never be closer to me.

For a moment it was hard to stand up straight.

Her father's cell phone rang. He began talking in the loud voice he used only on the cell, as if his model were deficient at carrying sound. "I know!" Ned shouted. "The rain! I don't know what I'm going to do all day long! Okay, that would be great! But first I have to drive my daughter to the train station."

A few hours from now, she thought, all three adoptions will be exposed. Three sets of parents will have to admit the truth, if they haven't already. The evidence is visible. There will be scrutiny from every relative, neighbor and stranger. Maybe even from the media.

What if her parents had even *less* use for Genevieve once the truth came out?

She was zipping a granola bar into her handbag when her mother made a strange sound. Genevieve turned to see Allegra scrambling away from the computer, almost tipping the chair over. Her face was distorted, her cheek twitching. "No!" said her mother thickly, batting at the computer screen as if mice were popping out of it.

"What's wrong?" demanded Ned. "Gotta go," he said into his phone.

"Nothing's wrong!" shouted Allegra, closing the screen. She whirled to face her husband and daughter. She looked like a shoplifter caught by store security. "Vivi, when are you leaving? Ned, get her to the station." Allegra swept them toward the door. "Have a good time, Vivi."

"You're really in a tizzy, Legs," teased her husband. "Midlevel managers are not allowed to have a tizzy. What did Boyd send, anyway?"

It must have been Missy's video, thought Genevieve. That's Boyd's role in life—finding crazy stuff, sending it on. My mother just saw two girls who look exactly like me. She just heard Missy claim that she and Claire are identical twins. Mom thinks I don't know. She's trying to hide the video from me. She's trying to protect me.

How sweet is that?

Genevieve checked her watch. She had a few minutes to spare. "I've seen the video, Mom," she said gently. "I saw it two days ago. Don't worry. I'm okay with it."

Allegra gasped, then crumpled. "Oh, Vivi," sobbed her mother. "I'm sorry. I'm so sorry."

Sorry about what? Adoption was not the end of the world. It was just a different way to set up a world.

Ned frowned. He walked back to the computer, bent over it and clicked, standing until he had brought up Boyd's attachment.

Allegra found a tissue. From the careful way she blotted her eyes, her main concern was her mascara. This was good. Her mother was returning to normal. Appearances first.

I love her, thought Genevieve, slightly surprised. I love them both, just the way they are.

Something hard in Genevieve vanished.

* * *

Missy's train pulled out. The train originated in Stamford, and though it had many stops to make before it reached New York, already the car was half full. Missy tried to save a seat for Claire, but a man talking loudly into his cell phone sat down, flapping his newspaper against her.

Scenery changed swiftly from corporate landscape to golf course, wonderfully green from the rain. At the Old Greenwich station, a swarm of riders got on, with the eager, pleased expressions of people going into the city for fun. The wheels of the train clacked like a song in a picture book. The train stopped in Riverside. Cos Cob. Greenwich. Port Chester. The next stop was the likeliest for Claire.

Get on, get on! Missy prayed.

She had only a partial view of the platform. Was Claire there?

I need you, Clairedy. You need me. You have to come. You can't sit home and watch television.

179

The train departed. Missy sat tall, making herself visible. She looked up and down the aisle for the black-haired, black-eyed cousin who was her identical twin.

Triplet, she corrected herself.

But Claire did not appear.

* * *

Ned sat down so hard on the wooden chair that Genevieve expected its legs to snap. "I didn't know," he whispered. "*I didn't know*. Who could have known? They're identical. Look at them." He played the video again, pausing it exactly where Genevieve had: identical black-haired, black-eyed girls staring at each other, one with joy and one in shock.

"People will know." Allegra's voice broke.

This was Allegra's big worry? Who cared if people knew?

For once think of me first! thought Genevieve. I'm your daughter! Well, no. Actually, I'm not.

She looked at her watch again. She was not going to make the train. Her heart seized up. I can take the next one, she told herself, trembling. Nothing is ruined. I'll text Missy. She'll be okay waiting at Grand Central.

On Saturdays, trains ran hourly. Genevieve would give her parents a few minutes and then walk to the station, no matter how hard it was raining. She was not telling them why she was going into the city. Her sisters were none of their business.

"The moment I saw the video, Mom, I realized that I'm a

triplet separated at birth and separately adopted. Don't be upset. I'd rather be your daughter by blood, but adoption doesn't change who we are. You're still my parents." Genevieve felt as if she were quoting a book on how to be well-adjusted. In fact, in her opinion, adoption changed one hundred percent of who they were.

In particular, it changed who her great-grandmother was.

Genevieve's hope in life was to be as fine a woman as her great-grandmother. The list of GeeGee's virtues was long. Genevieve liked to think that she had inherited some of her great-grandmother's traits, even the same jaw and the same hands.

No.

"Adoption!" cried Allegra, as if this were a new and thrilling word. "Yes!" she said firmly to her husband. "Genevieve is adopted."

"Adopted," repeated her father, sounding confused.

For this she had missed her train? Genevieve was beside herself. Only Ned and Allegra could construct a life built on a lie, and then allow the lie to become so real they forgot about it. A moment ago she had loved them again. Now she despised them again. "You adopted me because GeeGee wanted the next generation of Candlers. You wanted to cozy up to her. Uncle Alan said that was the only reason you had a kid. He was right, wasn't he? You don't even like children! You adopted me to inherit GeeGee's money."

"No," said her father. "You're mistaken, Vivi."

"I'm not mistaken! It's all about money with you two! Uncle Alan told me this summer that I'm just as conniving as you are."

"You've never connived in your life," said Ned. "You are a good person. I'm not sure where you got it from. Your mother and I have not set fine examples."

Genevieve didn't want excuses. She didn't want denials. She didn't even want details. She wanted to meet Missy. "Take me to the station, Dad. Now. Please. We can talk later. You guys work out your story, make sure your versions match and let me know what lies you've picked when I get home tonight. I have to catch the train."

Her father had the nerve to look angry. "Nothing in the city matters right now, Vivi. Let's sit down. There's a lot to cover."

"No, Ned," said Allegra.

Genevieve flourished her umbrella. "I have to go into the city."

"It's more important to see some silly art exhibit than talk with your mother and father about your birth?" snapped Ned.

"If the circumstances of my birth mattered, you would have discussed them long ago. I have an appointment. I'm keeping it." Her father spent his life going to appointments and rarely, if ever, put Genevieve ahead of them. Genevieve opened her cell phone to text Missy.

"What are you doing?" demanded her father. "What is the matter with girls your age? Why do you have to text every single minute to every single person? Put that thing down!"

"People are expecting me. I don't want them to worry. You've had sixteen years to mention this. It can wait another thirty seconds." Genevieve texted: Parent trouble. Taking later train. Will send arrival time ASAP.

Just communicating with Missy lifted Genevieve's heart. It was only an hour. She could last one more hour.

* * *

I'm an idiot, thought Claire. Certifiable. They put people like me in institutions.

Missy and Genevieve will attach to each other, the way a few days ago Missy and I were attached. The rest of my life will consist of two sisters courteously accommodating a third.

Claire dressed faster than she ever had in her life, called the taxi from her cell phone, yanked on pants and fastened buttons at lightning speed. She was lucky. There was a free taxi and it was on the way. This was not always the case; her town had few taxis. She opened her stash of cash from birthday and Christmas presents, poured it into her purse and dashed out the front door, irritated by the time it took to lock up.

She stood on the curb, ready to wave the minute she spotted the taxi, so the driver would see which house. She was not wearing her usual bright colors. In New York, the color of choice was black. Claire and Missy didn't even own black, which did not favor them. Claire had chosen a pair of expensive tailored khaki pants, a white long-sleeved shirt and a pale beige jacket. Clothing covered all but her fingertips. She turned the shirt collar up and left her hair down, so even her throat and ears were invisible.

I'm the color of a sand dune, she thought. I should change. Put on orange or pink or lemon or turquoise or all at once.

But it was too late. The taxi appeared. Claire flung herself into the backseat. "Railroad station, please. I'm afraid I'm going to miss my train."

"You taking the nine-twenty-three?"

"Yes."

"Your only hope is that it's running late. That happens pretty often, though, so cross your fingers."

Claire crossed her fingers. Missy is going to meet Genevieve so they can merge, she thought. I'm going so I can hang on to Missy.

She let a call from her mother go to voice mail. Claire knew exactly what it was about. The Saturday morning Jazzercise classes included Aiden's mother. Aiden would have shared the video with his parents because that was how kids lived: sharing videos. Mom had been ambushed.

Good! thought Claire, astonished at the breadth and depth of her anger. You let *me* be ambushed! You didn't care if *I* was out here without the truth!

The taxi was almost at the station. Claire could see the train, but it was hopeless. Even if they had had a green light, there were three cars between them and the intersection. They watched the train pull out. "I have to get to Grand Central." Her voice was trembling. "Can you drive me all the way into Manhattan?"

"I don't usually drive into the city. Is this a matter of life and death?" He was smiling a little.

"Almost."

"We can race the train," said the taxi driver, "and try to beat it to the next station. Odds are against us. But we'll be able to see how we're doing because the railroad parallels the thruway. Want to try?"

"Yes. I have the money. Go for it."

The cabdriver cut through traffic, leaning on his horn, taking risks and reaching the on-ramp of the turnpike.

It was like a movie. They caught up to the train, and began to pass it. It was going around fifty, while the taxi was doing seventy. Missy was only a few hundred yards to the right of Claire. Claire almost waved. "We're going to make it!" she shouted.

"Probably not. We have to take the exit and go through some traffic and that will eat up our gains. We could drive one more station. It'll cost more, but we get back the minute that the train is stopped here, and the minute it takes for the train to pick up speed again. Fasten your seat belt, okay?"

Now that she considered the possibility of dying in a crash, Claire was more cheerful about being a triplet. She fastened her seat belt, straightened her shirt and jacket and wondered what her cousin and Genevieve had chosen to wear.

More than once she and Missy had found themselves wearing the exact same clothing, when they had not consulted each other. When they were shopping, their hands frequently landed on the same shelf, choosing the same color of the same style. Would Genevieve, who had not grown up with them, dress like them anyway?

* * *

Frannie Linnehan was in cheerleader mode. She encouraged, danced, demonstrated, joked and guided. She sang along with the music, helped the newcomers and complimented the experienced.

When class was over and Frannie was putting away extra weights and mats, Liddy Scott came up. Liddy's son Aiden was in Claire's grade. The mothers often discussed teachers and curricula, happily listing their education peeves. Liddy said, "I can't believe you're here, Frannie!"

At work, it was necessary to be upbeat. So Frannie beamed. "Of course I'm here. I love this stuff."

"I figured you were up all night talking about the video and you'd be too tired for a class. Jack and I were trying to decide, if we were in your shoes, would we want the media involved or not? But it's out there now. You probably won't have a choice. I absolutely never knew, Frannie. I've been in Jazzercise for six years and you never said a word."

Frannie had acquired the skill of making little noises to encourage the customer. "Uh-huh," said Frannie, barely listening.

"Claire told Aiden it was a hoax, but Aiden says it's not."

Frannie was blank.

Liddy Scott said slowly, "You haven't seen it, have you?"

Frannie focused. "Seen . . . ?"

Liddy handed her cell phone over. Annoyed, Frannie watched the tiny screen.

A boy sitting beneath an immense photograph of her niece's high school in Connecticut was making an announcement.

He introduced Missy, who was excessively perky, which meant she was up to something.

The camera shifted. Now *Claire* was there. How could Claire be at Missy's school? Frannie vaguely recalled Phil agreeing to drive so Claire could help Missy on some project.

The girls were wearing the matching sweaters they'd gotten for their birthdays last year. Their earrings also matched, of course. Frannie was sick and tired of all the matching.

Missy twinkled at the camera. "I have the most wonderful, amazing, beautiful thing to share. My identical twin just surfaced. We just found each other! Can you believe it? I have a long-lost identical twin."

In the video, Missy touched Claire's shoulder. The girls faced each other. Even to Frannie, the identical profiles were a shock.

"And this," said Missy, "this is my twin, Claire."

Claire's mother stared at the tiny screen as if she could climb in. Oh, Missy, she thought. Nothing good can come of this. Why didn't you ask us first?

But that was unfair. Whatever happened now—and something would happen—it was not Missy's fault. Four parents had let the girls down.

On the video, Claire sobbed. "We shouldn't have done this. I shouldn't have agreed."

Frannie had to get home. Gather Claire in her arms. Apologize. Tell the truth. Not that Frannie knew the truth. "Liddy, I have a second class this morning. Would you lead it for me? You know all the moves. I've got to get to Claire."

Liddy nodded, and Frannie was out the door and in the car.

187

For years, she and Phil had tried and hoped and prayed for a baby. She had never gotten pregnant. For years Frannie reported in to Dr. Russo, who would suggest another avenue. No avenue, no matter how expensive, exhausting or upsetting, had given the Linnehans a child.

And then one day Dr. Russo telephoned. "We've never talked about adoption, Frannie, but a baby will be born to one of my patients in a few months. The mother wants a private adoption. You won't meet her and she won't meet you. You'd have to agree to total privacy about your baby."

"Your baby." The two most beautiful words in the world. The thought of her own baby obliterated everything else Dr. Russo said.

"Secrecy, in fact," he explained. "On the other hand, there's no agency, no social workers. Are you interested?"

"Interested?" Frannie's laughter had pealed like cathedral bells. She had devoted years of her life to the dream of a child. Yearning for her own baby pierced every activity and hour. Yes, she and Phil were interested. Who cared what the rules were?

Phil was so excited about their baby that he lost weight. He couldn't eat. They didn't watch television, didn't go out for dinner, didn't do anything except shop for the baby and get the nursery ready. They laughed and hugged and bought everything. Now that the baby was almost here, they could not believe they had never discussed adoption, which was obviously the most wonderful event on earth.

When Dr. Russo called to say that they could come to the hospital and he would bring them their new baby, Frannie didn't even remember to ask if it was a boy or a girl. Phil had to call back.

"It's a girl," said Dr. Russo. "She's beautiful, she's healthy, she's perfect."

When Frances Linnehan held her daughter for the first time in her life, her heart melted. Not then and not ever did Frannie have the sense that her little girl was adopted. Her baby was hers.

Phil said, "She looks like me."

Even Dr. Russo agreed: their daughter looked like her daddy.

Phil had held his new baby carefully against his shoulder, supporting the tiny head with his hand. "She's perfect," he announced. "You're perfect, aren't you? Are you Daddy's girl?" he cooed.

Dr. Russo seemed as excited and proud as Phil and Frannie. He was not thrilled that Frannie's sister, Kitty, had come along. "I told you the rules," he said sharply. "This adoption is not to be advertised."

Ridiculous. A baby was a celebration. What was Frannie supposed to do, anyway? Fake a pregnancy? Lie to her own mother? Tell pretend stories about childbirth?

Her sister distracted the doctor. "I'm in the same situation," Kitty had confided. "We've been trying for a decade to have a baby. But—oh, well. Instead, Matt and I will be the world's best aunt and uncle," she said bravely, and then burst into tears and had to hand baby Claire back, because it hurt so much. She was not going to have a baby of her own.

Again Dr. Russo reminded them not to tell people. But surely he didn't mean friends. Frannie told all her friends. One of them listened in astonishment. "You didn't even meet with social workers? There wasn't a home study? They didn't run a background check on you?"

"It was a private adoption," explained Frannie. "Everything's different."

The friend was doubtful. "I never heard of a doctor just walking out of the hospital with the baby and handing it over."

Frannie was sick with fear. Was there something illegal about this?

And then it was time to go before the judge, and the adoption was finalized, and they had a birth certificate with Claire's and their names on it, and all was well. Or was it? In her heart, Frannie Linnehan had always known that there was something radically wrong with the way this adoption had been handled.

Now, in the car, speeding home, desperate to be with her daughter, Frannie's every nightmare seemed almost to collide with the windshield; she kept having the sense that she was crashing into them, kept needlessly braking, kept bursting into tears.

When at last Frannie made it to the house and staggered inside, Claire was not there. She didn't answer her cell phone. Phil didn't answer his, either.

Claire had mentioned a project with Wanda and Annabel. Frannie opened the school directory, a page on the Board of Education site requiring a password, and did a search. There were no students in the entire town named Wanda or Annabel.

Frannie was astonished. Claire had lied! It was so unlike her! And the morning after she'd skipped the sleepover. And this video she had made, without bothering to tell her own mother and father!

Frannie had a thought so awful she could not speak it; she could only feel it.

This video had gone out into the world. The whole world. To all people, places and ages. The birth mother—that meaningless figure in history who nevertheless had given Frannie and Phil their darling girl—might have seen the video. Had she found Claire?

* * *

The more she thought about it, the more upset Kitty Vianello was. Missy had been wired. Chattering teeth. Cold lips. Eyes open so wide it must have hurt. Could Missy be on something? At those PTA guest lectures, some speaker would always claim, "Any child can get into drugs; nobody is exempt."

Of course every parent would think, Except mine; my kid is exempt.

Kitty called her daughter's cell phone.

Missy did not answer. But trains were noisy. Possibly she didn't hear the ring, or more likely, she had set her phone to vibrate so the ring didn't bother other passengers, and in all the laughter and silliness of kids on a trip, she wasn't paying attention.

Kitty left a routine message. "Call me, honey."

Missy was just excited, she told herself. But who got that

excited over a class trip? And although Missy did love the city, she was not a big museum person. She wasn't even an occasional museum person.

Suddenly even the trip was suspect. Since when were kids allowed to tag along on other classes' school trips? Didn't they still need permission slips and insurance forms and fees paid in advance?

The phone rang in her hand. It was her sister. "I'm glad you called, Frannie," said Kitty. "I'm worried about Missy."

"You saw that," Frannie yelled, "and you didn't let me know?"

"Saw what?"

There was a pause. Her sister said, "Go to YouTube."

"But first—"

"This is first, Kitty," said her sister. "This is first, second and third."

Kitty hurried to her computer, followed Frannie's instructions and played the video. She almost fainted. "Matt! Come here! It's an emergency."

Matt trotted into her office. She pushed him into her chair. He watched the video twice.

"Matt, there's no escape now," said Kitty. "Videos have a shelf life of forever. Who might see this? What will they do?"

Her husband tried to be comforting. "I don't think anybody can 'do' anything. Not to us, not to the girls. I wish the girls hadn't taken that approach. But I think Missy's accomplished what she wanted to. We have to put the truth on the table."

"We don't know the truth!" cried Kitty. "We never have!"

Because sixteen years ago, Kitty Vianello had also gotten a

phone call from Dr. Russo. "What's wrong?" she had cried, clinging to the phone. Why would her sister's doctor call? Had something happened to Frannie? To the baby?

"Nothing is wrong," Dr. Russo said. "I was impressed by your family. I rarely handle private adoptions, but incredibly I have another one, and you meet the mother's criteria. This baby had a low birth weight. She's in Newborn Intensive Care and might not live. Right now she's not thriving. If you and your husband have the courage and want to adopt her even with the risk that she might not make it, you can visit her now in NICU. Perhaps the presence of her mommy and daddy will help. Do you want to try?"

In an instant, Kitty and Matt had grabbed their car keys. Matt drove as if they had already met their daughter, already held her, had been worrying about her for weeks. They ran up to NICU. It seemed to them that they actually recognized her, this shockingly small infant under her heat lamp.

The staff called the baby Little Miss. Kitty and Matt shortened it to Missy.

For long nights and dark days they held their tiny baby in her tiny knit cap, maneuvering around the tubes that nourished her. Their love for Missy almost crushed them. From the first, Kitty was her mother; Matt was her father. All they wanted was to bring Missy safely home.

There was some kind of birth date confusion—the electronic file gave one date and the paper file in Dr. Russo's handwriting gave a different one. Matt and Kitty cared only about the little flickering life in their hands.

One grim night they called their minister because the hospital staff thought Missy would not make it, and the minister baptized her at two in the morning. Working backward from the nickname, they had named her Melissa.

One day Dr. Russo led them into the family conference room at the hospital, never a good place to be. Kitty and Matt did not know why the obstetrician would deliver the bad news, instead of the neonatologist. They held hands. They listened fearfully.

"The birth mother has a condition for adoption," said Dr. Russo.

There's a birth mother? thought Kitty. She had actually forgotten that Missy was not hers.

"Anything," said Matt. "We'll agree to anything."

"She does not want the adoption known. It is crucial that this baby never trace its origins."

There had been no time to tell friends and acquaintances anyway, because Matt and Kitty were practically living at the hospital. As for relatives, they simply phoned everybody and extracted promises of secrecy. Matt's mother was the only relative to argue. "Don't be silly," she said. "Of course I'm telling every person I know that I'm a new grandma."

"Right," said Matt. "But don't tell them your new grandbaby is adopted."

On the beautiful day when Missy was strong enough to go home, Dr. Russo had gone out to the car with Kitty and Matt, just as he'd done with Frannie and Phil.

"And the adoption papers?" asked Matt. His mind was on

the car seat, in which his tiny daughter had way too much room and needed the padding of rolled bath towels. He was desperate to get home. NICU had saved his baby girl, but he wanted miles between his baby and that hospital.

"It always takes a while," said Dr. Russo.

* * *

Babies require space.

The Linnehans had needed a bigger house for Claire and ended up in New York State. The Vianellos had also moved. Both families were now among strangers who would never know that the baby next door had been adopted.

But relatives did know.

An uncle found it disturbing that the same doctor had given the same instructions to two couples: keep the adoption secret. "What'd he do—steal the kids?"

An aunt found it comforting. "Dr. Russo is probably trusted in scary, sad situations. Probably has a reputation for helping unwed mothers."

In time, Claire's adoption was finalized. Missy's was not. But the Vianellos had bigger things to worry about. Their fragile baby was back in the hospital twice in the first year of her life.

Matt called Dr. Russo to ask how the adoption was going. Dr. Russo didn't return his calls. Kitty left messages. No response. Matt went to the man's office, and Dr. Russo said he was working with the birth mother. Not to worry. Everything would work out.

"What do you mean, working with her?" Matt had said, almost fainting for the first time in his adult life.

"She's a little skittish. But she'll sign."

Matt and Kitty were terrified. What was there to be skittish about? What if she wanted her daughter back? Legally, Matt and Kitty Vianello had no claim on their baby.

Time flew. Missy began to crawl and then walk. She was the most wonderful toddler in the world. They could not take their eyes off her.

They forgot about the birth mother, because Missy was so completely their own. In the local paper they read a notice that children entering public school had to produce their birth certificate. Matt called Dr. Russo's office. Dr. Russo had retired to Florida. The office refused to supply a phone number. It was the work of a minute to find it online.

"I'm no longer sure," said Dr. Russo, "that the birth mother will go through the necessary motions to sever parental rights."

"She has to!" shouted Matt. "Missy is our daughter! What's going on? What does the woman need? We can pay her. We'll do anything."

"I promised the birth mother I would never discuss her situation."

"Then don't discuss it! Make her sign! We have to have a legal adoption!" Matt remembered the misgivings of his uncle. "You didn't do anything illegal, did you? Missy isn't stolen, is she?"

"There is nothing illegal," said Dr. Russo. "There is just something sad. Let it go, Mr. Vianello."

"How can we let it go? We have to have a birth certificate! We have to finalize the adoption."

Dr. Russo explained that a hospital issued a certificate of live birth, which would be superseded by a different birth certificate when the child was adopted. He would forward a copy of the original certificate so that they'd have some kind of paperwork.

Matt and Kitty argued about what to do after they had the original certificate.

"It will give the birth mother's name," said Kitty. "We'll find her and get her to a lawyer and get the papers done."

Matt refused. "What if she sees Missy and wants her back? Who wouldn't want Missy back?"

The original papers never arrived. The next time Matt Vianello telephoned Dr. Russo, his widow explained that he had suffered a fatal heart attack during a tennis game.

Their only route to a legal adoption was dead and gone.

Matt refused to hire a lawyer. One toe into the mud of this situation and the birth mother might rear her ugly head and grab Missy for herself.

Matt and Kitty Vianello's daughter had no official identity. It was a sinkhole in their lives.

* * *

Missy's father could not seem to get out of the swivel chair in front of the computer. He kept staring at the video, replaying this intensely shocking thing his daughter had done.

His daughter's entry into high school had increased the paperwork difficulty. The lack of social security number was insuperable. PSATs and driver's license tests alone would bring a halt to their pretenses. Matt had already had two unpleasant discussions with a school vice principal and it was only October. He and Kitty did not even claim Missy as a dependent on their income tax forms because they had no social security number for her. He had been trying to think up new lies, such as pretending that fire had burned their documents. Ridiculous. If the originals were lost, you'd just order copies.

He had known the truth would surface one day soon.

Today, thought Matt Vianello, watching the video again. It'll surface today.

"Frannie is scared silly," said his wife. "She can't reach Phil. He's at some construction site, probably can't hear his cell phone ring, what with power tools screaming. Turns out Claire lied about where she would be today." Kitty's voice was shaking. "Frannie thinks the birth mother found both girls."

"The video doesn't say what hospital or state or year or day those identical twins were born," argued Matt Vianello. "How could some woman see the video and say, 'There they are! My daughters! Let's do lunch!' "

"Oh, Matt," said his wife, "the poor woman has probably wondered and yearned and wept for her babies all these years. I've always believed that the poor thing regretted so much that she signed one baby away, she couldn't bring herself to sign the other one away. She sees Missy's video, and let's say our girls look a lot like her, and she guesses, and she calls."

Matt wanted to cite all the obstacles between seeing a video and phoning this house. But were there obstacles? Everything the birth mother needed she could find online, with the clues on that video.

In a high, shuddery voice, his wife said, "The girls are perfect. So their mother has to be a good person too."

He stared at her. *She* was the mother. He pulled his wife into his lap. She wept against him. "I'm trying not to be scared," she said. "Of course they want to meet her. And I'm sure she's nice."

Anybody could claim to be a birth mother, thought Matt Vianello. Some stalker out there could easily convince two girls with romantic ideas about a hidden past to meet him somewhere.

He decided not to share this thought with his wife.

Frannie called again. She'd checked with neighbors, on the chance that Claire had just gone next door. The neighbor had seen Claire take a taxi. The Linnehans lived in a town where a taxi was a rarity. "If Missy took a train, then Claire took it too," said Frannie. "If there's no art trip, then maybe there's a birth mother trip."

"You're closer to the city than we are," Matt told her. "Kitty and I are getting in the car right now. We'll come to you. Keep trying to reach Phil. The minute the girls call, we'll go get them." He and Kitty got in their SUV. They loved it for camping and hauling and general comfort. It wasn't a comfort now.

"My theory," said Kitty, who had a new theory each year, "is that the birth mother had twins. Twin number one was born in good health. The mom signed off within hours of birth, and Phil and Frannie took their Claire home. But the second twin was desperately ill and whisked to NICU. Nobody bothered with adoption papers because nobody expected the second baby to survive. Then, when it looked as if Missy might pull through after all, Dr. Russo phoned us."

Matt tried not to be a race car driver. What would be the point? There wasn't even a point in driving to his sister-in-law's. The girls would call their parents when they were good and ready, and that was that. But the adults had gotten into this nightmare together, and maybe together they could get out.

"The poor mother was just a kid herself and couldn't face those layers of attack a second time," his wife continued. "All those counselors, social workers, nurses, doctors. She begged Dr. Russo to keep everything a secret so her own parents would never find out. Maybe she drove far from home to give birth, somehow escaping notice, and by the time Missy was adoptable, the poor teen mother was back home and she had no choice but to ward off official attention."

Matt was skeptical. Had this very young mother owned her own car so she could drive all that way? Been able to spend months away from home without questions as she grew visibly pregnant? Been able to bill her parents for doctors and hospital without their noticing what the bills were for? "If Dr. Russo really wanted to separate identical twins," said Matt, "he would not have chosen adult sisters as the mothers."

"But Dr. Russo couldn't have known that Missy and Claire were identical. The weight and health difference was too great. The girls didn't look alike at birth. Even we didn't notice until elementary school."

That was true. And outsiders, who could have offered opinions, did not usually see the girls together, since Missy and Claire weren't in the same school system, church, Scout group or marching band. The only comments had come from strangers in stores. Easy to dismiss. Only the scrapbook had been hard to dismiss.

Matt suddenly pitied Dr. Russo, who had obeyed that unknown mother—separating her twins and keeping her secrets, perhaps even designing paperwork saying that the little twin had a later birthday than the bigger one, so that no one would guess the babies were related. And then at the last moment, when the first adoptive parents had backed out, Dr. Russo had gone for the gold, choosing as the tiny twin's parents the sister and brother-in-law of the woman who had adopted the stronger baby. It was a lot to shoulder: remaking a family, misrepresenting birth dates, hoping that two little girls would still have each other.

Matt's eyes stung. "The girls will be fine," he told his wife. "We made some poor decisions because we were afraid. But nobody can take away a child of sixteen. We have nothing to be afraid of now." In fact, he was more scared than she was. That video could have opened up a chasm and the girls could be falling in.

* * *

STILL SATURDAY MORNING
Long Island

NED CANDLER FELT as if he were diving into water whose depth he did not know. Water reminded him of black swans. *Three* black swans. Who could have guessed?

"Vivi," he said, trying to keep his composure, "you are not adopted. You are our daughter. I'm your father. Allegra is your mother."

"Ned, don't! Don't talk about it!" said his wife.

"Allegra, we have to tell her."

"No!" she insisted. "You're adopted, Genevieve!"

"Mother, cut it out!" shouted their daughter. "You and Dad can't have separate versions of who I am. Stop behaving like crazy people. It's *my* life, not yours."

"You're wrong, Vivi. Your life will be just the same," said Allegra. "It's my life that will change. I didn't mean it to happen. I was young. It seemed all right at the time. I didn't know it would haunt me."

Allegra walked into the kitchen. She opened a drawer and took out a knife. It was a small, very sharp knife for peeling.

Allegra gripped it in her right hand and extended her left wrist.

CHAPTER

SATURDAY MORNING
On the train

MISSY HAD CROSSED from Connecticut into New York, and at this point, her parents could neither find her nor stop her. She decided to listen to her mother's latest message. At last, it seemed that they had seen the video. They were hurt, sorry, furious and worried. Where was she? What was she doing? Was Claire with her? And then, in a tiny voice, as if adding a postscript that hardly mattered, her mother said, "Yes. You were adopted, Missy. But it never felt that way. Call me back, sweetheart. Call me now. I need to hear your voice."

Even though Missy had been sure that she was an adopted twin, and planned her television scene, and drawn her cousin in, and gladly forced this into the open—still, the bottom fell out of her heart. *I'm not their daughter.*

The train sped on, lurching and rattling and clacking. Missy tried to find joy in the fact of Genevieve, but what was the joyful part? We didn't have the lives we were born to have, thought Missy. We three babies should have stayed together. Who parceled us out to different families?

Our real mother.

If Missy had been driving a car, she would have turned around, fleeing to the safety and comfort of the parents who had always wanted her and who wanted her now. But a train can only go in one direction at a time. Missy was headed toward a collision with the truth.

When her phone rang again, it was Aunt Frannie. Missy didn't answer that either, but she did listen to the message. There was no trace of cheerleader in Aunt Frannie's voice. She was furious. Yes, Missy was adopted! she shouted. Yes, Claire was adopted! So what? Why weren't the girls answering their phones? How dare they worry their parents like this? Yes, their parents should have discussed this long ago, but that did not mean the girls could behave like children and run away and hide. Supposedly Claire was with classmates named Wanda and Annabel, but there didn't seem to be any girls named Wanda or Annabel in Claire's high school. Missy was to call back immediately and the entire family must get together.

For better or for worse, thought Missy, I'm getting together with a different family. For better or for worse was a wedding-vow phrase. But this felt more like a divorce.

The train stopped. More passengers got on. Missy didn't think she'd seen anybody get off. They were all one hundred percent going to Grand Central.

Her cell phone wouldn't quit. Now she was receiving a text. But it was from Genevieve! Missy read greedily. Parent trouble. Taking later train. Will send arrival time ASAP.

I won't cry, she said to herself. I won't break down. We've waited sixteen years. We can wait another hour.

But a tear spattered her phone when she texted back, I'll wait at Grand Central.

Claire slid into the seat next to her, shivering, panting and identical. The girls melted against each other and held hands, fingers crushing matching fingers. The comfort of her cousin was total.

Because she isn't my cousin, thought Missy. She's my identical twin. I'm her. She's me. And because she knows it now. We both know it. "How did you get to this station?"

"My taxi driver raced the train."

"I'm so jealous. I've never raced a train."

"Listen to these phone messages," said her twin, dismissing trains.

"Same as mine," said Missy, after a minute. "Do we let them suffer?"

"Starving people in war-torn countries suffer," said Claire. "Our parents are just facing the consequences of their own choices for a few hours."

How bracing to hear Claire's resentment. Immediately Missy's own resentment passed. "Genevieve is going to be late," she said.

"Good. I need time to prepare."

Missy felt that "preparing" to meet your identical triplet was hopeless. "Who are Wanda and Annabel?"

"They aren't anybody. We were going to use a fake name for Rick's interview and those came to mind, but you forgot, so I used them again. Wanda and Annabel may be at the library right now, producing an excellent paper."

The train stopped at 125th Street.

"If we were going to a Yankees game, we'd get off here," Claire pointed out.

They loved Yankees games. The stadium was awesome, the hot dogs were perfect, winning was fabulous, losing wasn't the end of the world, and through it all, you got baseball.

"This will be a home run," said Missy.

"I'm not so sure," said her identical twin. "Even the best players strike out."

* * *

When her mother removed a knife from a drawer, Genevieve vaguely assumed that toast interested her more than adoption.

Of course, she's not my mother, thought Genevieve. Maybe she's haunted by the fact that she didn't have her own child. She has me instead.

Allegra brought the knife down. Not on bread. On flesh.

Admitting that Genevieve was adopted was so awful that Allegra Candler would rather be dead? Genevieve felt as if *she* had been stabbed.

Ned Candler leaped across the room, grabbed his wife's wrists, knocked the knife to the floor, then pulled her into the living room and down onto the sofa. They stared into each other's eyes. It was more dramatic than the usual, but essentially it was still the usual. Allegra and Ned were a unit, while Genevieve stood there watching.

Ned held up the threatened wrist and examined it.

No blood. Either Dad had been quick enough or Mom had not really wanted to hurt herself.

One thing was clear. A career in emergency response was not in Genevieve's future. She hadn't even recognized an emergency, let alone responded.

Allegra wept in Ned's arms. She looked oddly like Claire in the video at the moment she was wrenched by the shock of Missy's claim.

Genevieve turned away from the parents she had failed. Even now, they're fine without me, she thought. I feel like a dead soccer ball. Not even worth kicking.

She had rarely felt as removed from parental love. They were hugging each other. Why weren't they hugging *her*?

I'll look at Missy and Claire again, she decided. When I see the video, I'll remember that at least *one* person wants my company. Which reminded her that Claire didn't.

Genevieve brought up the video.

"Vivi, don't!" cried Allegra.

"These are my sisters. I won't turn them off. They're not going away. Tell me who our parents are."

"Vivi, think of me!"

"No. This is my life, not yours. My drama, not yours. Tell me who my parents are. Tell me who my sisters are."

Ned handed his wife a small square box of tissues. Allegra bought tissue boxes with care, because color and design had to be perfect and so often tissue boxes were tacky. "You won't understand," her mother wept.

"I'm sure you're right," said Genevieve. "Tell me anyway."

Ned and Allegra exchanged one more look.

Genevieve lost the last shred of energy she possessed. She fell into a chair—across from her parents, of course, not next to them; nobody had patted the cushions to invite her to sit on the sofa—and texted Missy. Nightmare. Parents saw video and fell apart. I can't come.

Her own message frightened her. She was shutting the door on the sister who was rushing to meet her. But Genevieve could not summon the will to send a correction. My parents don't love me, she thought. Next to that, what matters? Her body seemed to break down, as if she were a chemistry experiment, separating into her original raw materials.

"Vivi," said her father sternly, "texting in the middle of a conversation is rude under any circumstance. But *now*? What message matters now?"

"A message explaining who I am would be a good message now."

Allegra looked away. Staring at her manicure, she whispered, "It's like that mother. Oh, it was years ago. I've never forgotten her. I still weep for her. She drove to work one hot summer day and forgot that she was the one taking the baby to day care. She forgot the baby altogether, and left it strapped in its car seat in the back of her car. At the end of the day, when she finished work, she walked through the parking lot and unlocked her car, and there was her baby, cooked to death."

* * *

SATURDAY MORNING
Connecticut

PHIL VIANELLO WAS framing an addition to an already large house. The addition would have an amazing view. Phil didn't care about the view. When you have been out of work, work is what's beautiful. Although his cell phone was attached to his belt, he paid no attention when it rang.

Around noon, he began to think of lunch, and assumed that Tommy was walking over to discuss lunch breaks. But Tommy said, "Frannie called. Some kind of emergency."

A car accident? Claire was hurt? Frannie was hurt? Phil grabbed his phone. "Nobody's hurt," said his wife. "But we can't find Claire or Missy and they're not answering their cell phones."

Phil had envisioned paraplegics and long-term comas. When his wife babbled about some school video, he was annoyed. "So what?"

"We don't know where the girls are," said his wife.

"Claire's the most careful girl on the planet. Spontaneous is not her middle name. She isn't doing anything reckless. Anyway, she's sixteen. She gets to decide what she does on a Saturday."

"Phil! The girls figured out that they're adopted."

"And didn't I say from the first we should have been telling Claire the truth? You went along with your sister, because Missy's adoption is a mess, and you two decided to hide the facts. I'm sorry we weren't the ones to tell them. But I'm at work, Frannie."

"Phil! They know they're identical twins!"

"That's a crock. You base that on badly focused photographs taken years ago. I've never once looked at my niece and thought she was my daughter. And Claire is older than Missy. We *know* she's older! We were there!"

"Phil!" his wife yelled.

He was sick of her shouting his name. Who else did she think was on the phone? "Frannie, I have to get back to work."

"Phil, what if they're out there looking for their birth mother?"

"What if they are?" he demanded. "It's a natural interest."

"Phil! Are you listening?" shouted Frannie.

"I'm listening," he said grimly.

"We think the birth mother saw the school video and put two and two together and called the girls."

Women, he thought. Leaping from point A to point Z without a single fact. "What are you basing that on?"

"Not much," admitted his wife. "Phil, please come home."

"I'm. At. Work."

"Okay, just look at the video on your cell phone. Please. Then call me."

Phil had large hands and thick fingers. He had difficulty with the tiny buttons of a cell phone. He used the eraser tip of a pencil he carried in his shirt pocket.

There was his niece, Little Miss Perky, beaming at the camera as usual. Then his daughter, looking frightened and unsure. The girls turned toward each other. Even in miniature, he saw it: identical profiles and hair, identical shoulder width and the same deeply set eyes, identical earlobe shape and chins. *Identical twins.*

But emotionally, the girls were no match. Missy was all excitement. Claire was all shock.

Me too, baby, thought her father.

Claire had been his child from the first thrilling moment he'd held her in his huge hands—realizing that he, Phil Linnehan, was responsible for her life, her home, her safety and her future. He had smelled her sweet baby scent and a moment later the stench of her soiled diaper, and he had laughed, and kissed her tiny cheek, and never again did he consider that she was actually somebody else's baby. Because she wasn't.

On the video, Claire wept.

My fault, thought her father. I should have overruled Frannie and Kitty and Matt. I should have told Claire about the adoption myself. Long ago.

But long ago, he had more or less forgotten. It passed through his mind occasionally, but without meaning. Claire was his daughter. Period.

The video ended.

He phoned his daughter. She didn't answer. He had the sense of something evil crawling up out of the vast galaxy that was the Internet, something evil watching that little video of Missy's and setting its hooks. He looked dizzily around the construction site. Work had just moved to second place. "Tommy," he said thickly. "I have to get home."

* * *

The train entered darkness. They were now under New York City, and would stay underground for miles, and would still be underground when they reached Forty-second Street. Missy pressed her face to the window to stare into the dark creepiness of tunnel and track. Claire did not like thinking about the underbelly of the city. Were they about to face the underbelly of their own existence on earth?

The train slowed, crawling into the terminal. Passengers lined up in the aisle to get off quickly. Claire did not move.

"We're here," said Missy, jabbing her. "Hurry up! Get going!"

"There's no rush. Genevieve texted that she'd be late."

But Missy needed to collide with their past and embrace their sister, and she needed to do it now. She stepped over Claire and butted into line. Claire could not catch up because hundreds of passengers were getting off their train and a second train across the platform, tossing newspapers, trash and recyclables into immense containers without missing a beat. Some of them were probably dealing with dread diseases and horrid divorces and difficult jobs. All Claire had to face was another person who wanted to be loved.

This did not increase her enthusiasm. She almost hated Missy for rushing on and not looking back. She followed Missy up an escalator. Now the famous high ceiling soared above Claire, azure blue with stars of gold. It always reminded Claire of a cathedral. It was, in a way: a sacred seat of New York. Balconies and stairs and banks of escalators wrapped the great space. Ticket windows and track entrances faced each other across the crowded floor. In the center was the charming circular information booth, like a gazebo in a marble park. On top was the clock, marking the meeting place of choice for visitors to New York and their hosts.

Missy was already across the floor and taking up a search position.

Be late, Genevieve, thought Claire. Be really late. Or never. Never would be good.

* * *

Missy checked her watch. One minute had passed. Now what? Stand around and read train schedules? Why had Genevieve let mere parents get in the way of meeting her missing identical triplet? They could pick up parent pieces later. Right now they had to do sister pieces.

She listened to yet more messages from her mother and father. "They don't know about Genevieve," she said to Claire. "I think they're still holding back, though."

Claire busied herself examining the ceiling.

The girls had dressed similarly. In stressful situations, they both chose to fade. Their clothing did not match, but presented the same idea. What would Genevieve wear? Would this complete stranger also lean toward beige and layers and ironed creases in pants?

Missy's phone buzzed. Another text from Genevieve. Perhaps Genevieve had caught her train after all! Maybe she was on her way over from Penn Station! Maybe she'd be here in a minute!

Missy held the tiny screen so Claire could read with her.

Nightmare. Parents saw video and fell apart. I can't come.

* * *

Claire had gotten up her courage, caught the train, arrived in New York, and Genevieve was not coming? She scanned the crowds anyway, as if Genevieve were crouching out there, biding her time. Maybe Genevieve, like Claire, was hiding from the truth. Or maybe Genevieve was indeed a fake, and couldn't face what she had started.

Missy stamped her foot. "Genevieve *has* to come! So what if her parents are upset? Everybody's parents are upset. Who cares? Nobody cares! Parents are beside the point! The point is, we are sisters. Triplets. Identical. We have to meet! We have to meet *now*."

Claire waited for Missy to run out of steam, but she didn't. "Fine!" snapped Missy, as if the world were arguing with her. "If Genevieve can't come here, we're going there."

"What are you talking about?"

"I made plans. I'm keeping them." Missy spun around and strode away.

Claire had to run to keep up. Missy was moving so fast that Claire knew her only by her black puff of hair. High over the wide hall into which Missy hurtled were carved letters that read SHUTTLE. Claire threaded desperately through the crowds. "What are you doing?" she demanded.

"I have to see Genevieve. Just the way I have to see you, Claire. If I don't see you every week, I feel as if I'm peeling off. Friday night was torture. Right now, I'm skinless. There's no person left to me. Only meat."

Well, that was the most sickening analogy Claire had ever heard. But at least Claire was needed. And to the exact same degree, apparently, Genevieve was needed. Of course it's the exact same degree, thought Claire. Because the three of us are exactly the same.

Missy bought a subway pass at the ticket machine, swiped it through a turnstile and handed the pass back to Claire so she could swipe. Missy didn't wait. She galloped down the stairs to the brightly lit shuttle station.

I could catch a return train, thought Claire. Bail out and go home.

Missy had reached the bottom of the stairs and was hurrying toward a mostly full car. Its doors were still open, but the conductor was looking out his window, assessing departure time. In moments the doors would close. The train would leave.

Claire was as unable to detach from Missy as if they were still sharing a womb. She swiped through the stile and took the stairs two at a time, raced past subway musicians and bounded into the last car as the door was closing. The shuttle jerked out of the station and gathered speed. When they reached Times Square, Missy found the southbound #1 line, and they went one stop to Thirty-fourth Street and got off.

Claire found New York only mildly interesting, except for when she found it overwhelming. There was always too much to think about in New York. But Missy adored the city and loved navigating through the crowds. She led the way down long underground corridors lined by every fast food in world cuisine. The mixture of smells Claire normally found enticing made her gag. In no time, they were in the station for the Long Island Railroad, and Missy was buying tickets from a wall machine, and ten minutes later they were headed out of New York.

The train window was dirty and scratched. Outside, rain fell in patches. There were stops. People got on and off. Claire felt as thick and misty as the weather. The speed at which Missy and the trains were changing her life reduced Claire to a puddle.

"Next stop is ours," said Missy. Missy was trembling, but Claire did not think it was fear. Claire didn't know. This time Claire did not share the feeling. "I didn't bring the map," said Missy, eyes glued to the window, "but I memorized it. Fourteen Bayberry Lane is kind of near the train station. We'll walk if there's no taxi."

"Missy, the parents flipped out at the mere thought of us. Is this wise? I mean, should we ask first?"

"Of course we're not going to ask. They'd flip out even more or else say no. Who cares about them, Clairedy? Genevieve wants to see us or she wouldn't have started this. And I have to see her. I am ninety-nine point nine percent sure Genevieve is our identical sister, but I'm not one hundred percent sure. I have to know one hundred percent. The minute I see her, I will know."

Claire had always accepted the family belief that Missy was the little one, the lightweight. But in fact, for years now, Missy had been the leader and Claire the follower. And back in the TV studio, Claire had been certain that Missy was older. What about Genevieve? What order were the girls in? Was Claire the baby of the family?

What family?

I don't want to know, thought Claire.

Next to her, Missy expanded with joy while Claire shrank with horror, in some ghastly identical twin equation.

* * *

SATURDAY MORNING
Long Island

GENEVIEVE CIRCLED HER chair and stood behind it, gripping the upholstery with both hands. The vision of an infant absent-mindedly left by its own mother to bake to death made her ill. "You didn't do that to me," she said to Allegra, unable to say "Mom." "I didn't cook in a backseat. Neither did Missy or Claire. We're all three alive."

"I did do it," cried her mother.

Suddenly her father was glaring at his wife. "Allegra, don't dramatize!"

Since normally Ned thrived on Allegra's drama, his wife was

hurt and amazed that he wasn't keeping up his supporting role. He turned his back on her. "The truth is dramatic enough, Vivi."

"And what is the truth, Dad?"

He wavered. He looked at his wife.

"I thought it was all gone," Allegra moaned. "And here it is on a video! Online! People will know."

"I'd like to be one of the people who know," said Genevieve. "Was there some crime involved? What are you afraid of? It's just adoption!"

"It wasn't criminal," said her mother defensively. "People do it all the time. We both decided. Your father and I. Together."

"I don't care who's to blame. I just want to know who I am."

Allegra Candler reached for her handbag. She got out her compact and checked her face. She powdered. For Allegra, makeup was body armor. Her moment of weakness was gone. Allegra Candler was not going to tell Genevieve anything.

"Dad," said Genevieve.

"The truth is ugly," he said at last. "I apologize for it, Vivi. We never wanted children. When we found out we were going to have a baby, though, we decided it would be okay. We were the right age, our friends were having children, it didn't look that hard. And then we found out we were going to have three. We couldn't stand it. We gave two away."

Genevieve let go of the chair. She stepped back. After a moment, she stepped farther back. Then she turned to stare down the little front hall into the darkness. She could not tolerate these people in her field of vision.

The concept of being adopted had shocked her. The sight of two identical sisters had shocked her. But more shocking was the truth. She was not adopted. She had been born to this man and woman: married, successful, well-to-do, attractive suburbanites. Who had kept one child out of three. As if their daughters had been a litter of kittens.

That was shock.

Her parents were not charitable. When there was no escape, they might write a tiny check to a neighbor collecting for a cause, or put a single dollar in the church offertory plate. Last spring when Genevieve sold grapefruit to raise money for new high school band uniforms—her parents had bought her a good flute, although they almost never saw her play—Ned and Allegra were grumpy about the cost even when they got grapefruit in return.

But they had given away one thing rather easily.

No.

Two things.

Their children.

Genevieve moved all the way into the dark little hall. She stayed in the center, as if even touching the wall her parents had painted would infect her.

I can't ever meet Missy and Claire now, she thought. How could I face them? I'm the one our parents kept. They're the ones our parents—

Genevieve's heart stopped. She walked back. Her eyes were

opening wider and wider. A cold, hideous fear was filling the back of her head.

No, she thought. No, no, no, no, no. "You didn't charge a baby fee, did you? You didn't get paid, did you? You didn't get the down payment on this house by selling my sisters, did you?"

CHAPTER

LATE SATURDAY MORNING
Long Island

ALLEGRA CANDLER HATED remembering the year she'd turned thirty. The brilliant career was plain old work. Eight or nine hours a day, plus a commute, and for what? Yes, she had terrific clothes and shoes. Yes, she was slender and beautiful. But she was old! One morning she found a gray hair. She yanked it out and the next day there was another.

It was no surprise that she felt sick and listless. Her body was going downhill. Her ankles grew thick and her ivory complexion became patchy. Allegra loved a mirror. She looked at herself in full-length mirrors and wall mirrors, the mirror in her compact and the mirror that pulled out from the bathroom wall. She looked at her reflection in every store window she passed. The occupation was ruined. It was not until her zippers would not zip that she realized she was pregnant. When she thought of stretch marks, she wanted to scream. She would be disfigured, and for what? For something that cried and whined and got wet and stinky and stayed up all night and cost money.

How were she and Ned supposed to keep up their lives?

What would happen to the parties and dances and season tickets?

And what if she didn't even love this baby? Her love didn't go as far as other people's. It was finite. She loved Ned. There wasn't leftover love waiting around for some baby.

The weeks passed. Allegra couldn't bring herself to go to a doctor. She hated doctors' examinations anyway, and pregnancy meant more of them. Ned coaxed her to make a doctor's appointment and he went along.

Enough weeks had gone by that they could view this future baby on ultrasound. "We'll be able to see the sex of the baby," said the obstetrician happily.

Once Allegra knew if it was a boy or a girl, it would be real. She would have to think about its room and its clothes and its bed and its stroller. She would have to think about diapers.

"If it's a girl," Ned said, "we'll name her for my grandmother. Genevieve. My grandmother will be thrilled." (In front of the doctor, Ned did not add, "And she'll give the baby lots of money.")

Allegra didn't like the name Genevieve. But she didn't actually care what name the baby had. I should read a book about depression, she thought. I've heard of postpartum depression, which I'm sure I will have. It stands to reason that there's prepartum depression, which I definitely have.

"Wow," said the obstetrician. "Wow."

What could be "wow" about yet another baby for a guy who saw them every day? Reluctantly, Allegra looked at the blurry black-and-white image on the screen.

The doctor was ready to high-five. "Congratulations. You're going to have triplets." With his finger, he traced the babies' outlines.

It was like a horror film. Three creatures were swimming around inside her!

"Three little girls!" the doctor told them, laughing out loud, eyes fixed on the ultrasound, as if he actually loved the little swirly shapes.

"We could delete two, couldn't we?" asked Allegra. It was arithmetic: simple subtraction.

The doctor's face went blank. His shoulders lowered. "There is such a procedure." His body language was clear. The doctor thought less of her.

Ned said, "Let's think about it, Legs."

They went home. Allegra made an error. She would pay for this error all her life. That night she left a message on her boss's phone. *I have to take a sick day. I'm pregnant and feel awful.*

Her boss telephoned in the morning. "We're so excited for you! We're already planning a shower! Is it a boy or a girl?"

There was no way now to have zero babies. Allegra said, "Girl."

Allegra became more important than she had ever been in her life. She was more important in the neighborhood. People dropped by, offered help ("We'll paint the baby's room for you") and insisted on new rules ("You can't put the baby upstairs when you sleep downstairs; you'll never hear the baby cry"). She was more important at work. She was more important to Ned's grandmother. Genevieve Candler was indeed thrilled that they would name her first great-grandchild after her.

And the others, Allegra had thought. What are we supposed to name the others? I don't want the others!

"How are you feeling?" people asked. "Has the baby started kicking yet?"

There isn't a baby, Allegra would think. There's a stream of them. A series.

She couldn't drag herself to the doctor's. Every decision, whether to have a baby or to have breakfast, was beyond her. She got nausea from pregnancy and nausea from imagining her future.

Her colleagues gave her a baby shower. Allegra forced herself to coo and clap over teensy eensy garments. She did not use the terrifying words "triplet" or "multiples."

There would be a huge awkward stroller with three babies sticking out in a row. When the babies were old enough to walk, she'd have to put them in harnesses like sled dogs. Mealtimes would be assembly lines of whiny children and boring food. She and Ned did not prepare meals. They ate out. Children were worthless in restaurants. They never liked the food and wanted to leave before it had been served anyway.

Allegra could not imagine the expense. The diapers alone would beggar them.

The decision came about one evening when Ned admitted he didn't want three babies either. He loved golf and parties and sailing. He wanted expensive things, like antique cars and great watches. Now he'd have to invest every cent in babies, who would be around for eighteen years plus college.

"We have to keep one," said Ned, "because everybody knows we're having a baby. But let's give the others up. Unmarried mothers do it all the time. We happen to be married, but what difference does that make? A woman has the right to choose. Let's choose to be a mother once."

"That's brilliant," said Allegra. "Jillions of people are desperate for kids. And who has better genes than we do?"

Allegra began her leave of absence early so nobody would see her become size-triple huge. She didn't want anybody to know that two out of three babies were being given away. If only she had ended the pregnancy the instant she suspected! Any of her friends would have gone with her and been supportive. The same friends, however, would be appalled that Allegra was getting rid of her babies *after* they were born.

Ned and Allegra lived on Long Island, where Ned had grown up. To carry out the plan, Allegra announced that *her* baby must be born in Connecticut, where she had grown up. They rented a tiny furnished apartment, where Allegra lived like a swollen plant, waiting for the births that nobody would witness. Nobody would know she was coming home with one third of the set. Ned commuted between both places and they were on their cell phones all the time, missing each other. Back then, a cell phone was the size of a brick, and hardly anybody else had one.

Together, they went to the doctor in Connecticut whom

Allegra had seen from her teens until her marriage. Yes, Dr. Russo had said. I know couples eager to adopt.

Pick the best families, Allegra told him. I want the best for them.

Dr. Russo stared at her. She knew what he was thinking: the best would be their biological parents.

She and Ned held hands. So they were unpopular with Dr. Russo. Who cared about him? They'd be *very* popular with the adopting parents. Ned and Allegra would go back to Long Island and never see Dr. Russo again, and he could never talk about them or about their decision because of privacy laws.

"The first baby," said Allegra, "will be ours. The others go to whatever mothers you choose. I don't want a trail back to us. I want total privacy. Privacy is my right. I don't want social workers and people who interfere."

"Do you want to know anything about the family? Do you want an open adoption, where you continue to visit your babies?"

"No."

"Do you want the girls adopted as twins?"

"Separately," Ned said. "Twins might want to know their background more. Twins would have twice the questions. Twins might find us. We don't want a paper trail or an electronic trail. We take one baby, we're out of there and you find places for the others."

Then came childbirth. Pain and fear, which doctors were supposed to prevent, were intense. The first one out was beautiful, which surprised Allegra until she remembered that she and Ned were beautiful. It was small and screaming. The staff wrapped it in a white blanket edged in pink and blue stripes. A tiny white hat with a tiny pink and blue pom-pom covered its little head.

The second one was impossibly small. It looked more like a fat red spider than a future human. Allegra would have thrown up if she hadn't been so busy delivering the third baby, which took its time coming. Allegra never looked at it. She fell asleep. By the time she woke up, Ned had handled the situation.

Twenty-four hours later, she and Ned left the hospital with the first one.

Dr. Russo had lined up parents. Baby Three was healthy, and its parents took it immediately. Allegra and Ned lived through the interviews and the paperwork and the signing off. Baby Two, however, was very sick. Its adopting parents didn't want it after all, because their sole criterion was a healthy baby.

Back on Long Island, Baby Genevieve was not a good sleeper and not a good eater. There was nothing she didn't cry about—grating sobs that pierced the night and lasted throughout the day. There were parades of visitors. Ned's grandmother and his brother Alan and his sister Dorothy and their spouses of the moment came. Everybody oohed and aahed. Nobody said, "Oh, by the way, did you happen to have a litter? Was there a runt? Who took them?"

Allegra let everybody hold baby Genevieve as long as they wanted. She begged Ned's grandmother to pay for a nanny, but

Grandmother Candler just laughed and said the best way for Allegra to become an experienced mother was to do the mothering herself.

Dr. Russo telephoned from Connecticut. Would Allegra and Ned care to visit the sick baby in Intensive Care?

Dealing with baby Genevieve was as intensive as Allegra could stand. No, she would not care to visit an even more intensively demanding baby. She wanted to go back to work.

People in their set did not use day care; they shelled out for a nanny, which was expensive. Allegra and Ned would have to sell one of their cars, stop going to restaurants and wear last year's fashions.

Again they approached Ned's grandmother. "Nonsense," said the older Genevieve. "Like everybody else, you'll juggle career and baby. You'll sacrifice joyfully to do what's best for your little girl."

Every now and then Dr. Russo called. Baby Two had survived after all and had been given to a different set of adoptive parents. In spite of all the paperwork and painful invasive interviews even when Allegra had specified that she didn't want to do any of that, it seemed that Allegra and Ned had not surrendered their parental rights to baby number two. It turned out they had to do it for *each* child. Dr. Russo wanted Allegra and Ned to come to Connecticut. "You promised to handle it," Allegra snapped.

"And I have, Allegra. But you have to meet the social workers, there has to be a court judgment, it has to be legal."

"I won't be judged!"

"It isn't like that. They won't judge you. But a judge has to be involved."

Allegra stopped answering his calls.

To their surprise, little Genevieve grew on them. The difficult infant became a beautiful toddler, laughing and eager and quick to learn. They began calling her Vivi, which suited her—she was full of life. It was fun to have a little girl who was good at things, and it was especially fun to shop for her clothes. Vivi was a whirlwind, racing through each day. Thankfully the nanny dealt with her Monday through Friday, and would often stay for the weekend.

When she entered school, Vivi loved it. She loved study. She loved new fields of study. "Oh! Spelling!" little Vivi said excitedly in second grade. "Oh! History!" she cried in third. "Oh! Geology!" she exclaimed in fourth, wanting to be driven to view cliffs and rock formations along the Hudson River.

Allegra signed Vivi up for flute lessons, because the flute was silvery and delicate and made pretty sounds, but the band director begged Vivi to play trombone, because he didn't have any trombones, so Vivi played both and for years carried the awkward trombone around and practiced at annoying times. She became a fine swimmer, which wasn't fun, because you couldn't tell who was who at swim meets and the humidity at pools ruined Allegra's hair.

Vivi loved knowledge. By tenth grade, she was in High School Bowl instead of something with bragging rights like tennis. She visited her annoying great-grandmother constantly, and when the old girl ended up in a nursing home, Vivi trotted by after school, willingly spending time with other wizened old women as well. When her great-grandmother's house was sold, Vivi kept the contents of her library, and was always reading books by dusty old authors that GeeGee had loved three-quarters of a century earlier.

Allegra often had the disorienting thought that *she* was the one with the adopted child.

It was about this time that the children she had not kept began to grow in Allegra's mind, like weeds in a garden. When Allegra glanced at Vivi, she would see shadows of the others. Those others were growing up somewhere. They had personalities of some kind. They played a sport and were good in some subjects and not others. They were fun or grumpy, interesting or annoying. They were people.

People Allegra did not want in her life.

Now they had popped up on a YouTube video like spam. And Vivi had found out. Allegra had never wanted anybody to find out.

How creepy that the multiples had been identical. You would not have guessed at their birth. Well, not that Allegra had looked at the third one. But that second one, the shriveled red one. It was difficult to fathom that the Claire or the Missy in this video had been that shriveled red one.

What a relief when Ned grabbed the knife from her hands. Allegra hated the thought of being hurt, let alone hurting herself. Telling the truth would also hurt. What would Vivi swallow? I rehearse presentations for work, she thought, staring at her implacable daughter. Why didn't I rehearse for this?

"I was selfish, Vivi," she confessed. "I was worried about my career. I knew that parents who yearned for a child would be better at it than I would be. And you were just right for us. You were so smart and fun and easy and pretty. I loved fixing your hair and buying you dresses and watching you learn."

Allegra could not tell what her daughter was thinking. Probably she was better off not knowing.

"How did you come to that decision?" asked Genevieve.

Easily, thought Allegra. But even she knew not to say it out loud.

Discarded identical triplets would be a scandal. Boyd sent his video links to everybody he knew, so thanks to Boyd, Allegra's life was ruined. She imagined taking early retirement. Moving to the Carolinas. There was a lot of golf there. Allegra and Ned loved golf. She'd never have to see what other people thought of her. She could just enjoy herself. This house was worth a bunch, even though it was tiny, because it was in a terrific neighborhood. Somebody would bulldoze it and build a mansion in its place.

Allegra fantasized about a house with a golf course view and a better climate.

* * *

Ned's heart sank when his daughter's eyes fixed on him next. He said nervously, "We hadn't planned on children, Vivi. We were spoiled brats. But when we got pregnant, we knew we could rise to the occasion. And your great-grandmother was thrilled when we named you for her. You just know her as an old lady with a walker, getting meals on a tray, but seventeen years ago, Vivi, she was a corker." Ned began a funny story about the older Genevieve.

"Save it," said Genevieve. "Go back to the day my sisters and I were born."

Make it sound fun, Ned told himself. "I remember when they brought you to me," he said fondly. Ned had not been in the delivery room. The whole thing made him ill. He waited in the family room on a vinyl couch. "You were so pretty, Vivi. Your dark eyes were open and you were squalling. You were swaddled in a soft tiny blanket and wearing a sweet tiny cap. We saved the cap."

He remembered the rush of emotion when he held his daughter for the first time. He knew that if he held the other two, he would feel the same rush. If Allegra wants them after all, he decided, I'm okay with it. But Allegra never mentioned the other two, so he didn't either.

"And the decision?" asked his daughter. "To discard your other daughters?"

"We didn't discard them. We gave them to adoptive parents. Our family physician, whom we knew and trusted, found excellent families." He wanted his daughter to love him. He certainly loved her. Okay, he wasn't home much. Plenty of parents weren't home that much. It had nothing to do with love. "Every day, every month, you were more delightful, Vivi. You taught us how wonderful it is to be a parent."

It wouldn't end here. Vivi would demand more knowledge. She was a file folder for facts. But Dr. Russo was deceased. Nobody knew about all his phone calls over the years. Nobody knew about his ceaseless demand that Ned and Allegra return to Connecticut to surrender parental rights to the last baby or else bring her home.

Ned had made an error in judgment back then. He had said to his wife, "Vivi's an unbelievable amount of work and noise, but I'm kind of crazy about her. If I see the other baby . . . I don't know if I can surrender it after all."

So Allegra had never agreed to a trip to Connecticut, because she knew Ned would cave.

Ned glanced back at the computer. His brother Alan was on Boyd's e-mail list. Alan was probably staring at this video right now. He was probably laughing. Phoning their sister Dorothy. They couldn't forward the video to the older Genevieve, because their grandmother did not use a computer, but they would make sure the old lady saw it.

"What did you mean by haunted?" asked Vivi, facing Allegra.

Ned hoped Allegra wouldn't cry again, because Vivi would not feel sorry for her.

"I didn't hold them, you know," said Allegra. "I didn't want to bond. I think any parent who gives up a child is haunted. Hoping it's okay."

Ned did not think Vivi would fall for this. A woman who hoped her children were okay would not have grabbed a knife from the drawer and pretended to end it all.

He thought of Boyd's e-mail. Boyd sent his stupid attachments to everybody. Neighbors would know. Golf partners. Tennis partners. Cruise companions.

His boss.

* * *

The secret that makes them exchange Dark Looks, thought Genevieve, is that they are *not* haunted by Missy and Claire. Even now, they're not referring to Missy and Claire as their daughters. Even now, they're saying "it," not "she."

She looked hard at her father. "So Mom didn't hold the other babies. Did you?"

He shook his head.

Genevieve was trembling. Her father was a bystander in his entire world. He didn't even really work at his own corporation—he did a task on the edge of it. He had been a bystander at the birth of his own three children; he had not held two out of three. "I don't see how you could have separated identical triplets, let alone given two away."

"You weren't identical when you were born," said her mother peevishly. "You were totally different when you were born. The second baby was in trouble and I believed it was my fault for thinking bad thoughts. I kept my eyes closed and let professionals help her. Besides, the obstetrician kept placing demands, and it hurt, I don't care what anybody says, it hurts, and then came the third one, and I was too exhausted to think about the others. Maybe I had too much anesthesia or something. I didn't want to get involved."

Emma had said that Genevieve had the least involved parents in New York State.

Nobody could have guessed *how* uninvolved. "In what way was your second daughter in trouble?" she asked.

Allegra flinched at the term "daughter." "Low birth weight. They put it in intensive care."

It, thought Genevieve. "How often did you visit your sick baby?"

Silence.

The pain Genevieve felt was like appendicitis. But you could cure appendicitis; you could operate and cut the appendix out.

One summer, a family vacationing down by the beach had given a cat to their children. The children loved this cat, and the litter of kittens it soon produced. When school started, the family drove away, leaving the cat and her kittens to fend for themselves. Ned and Allegra had abandoned their daughters as easily as those summer vacationers had abandoned their pets. On the other hand, Genevieve had found homes for the kitties and the doctor had found homes for the babies. When Genevieve had spoken to Missy on the phone, her new sister sounded fine. Missy wasn't haunted by the life she'd ended up with.

Oh, Missy, thought Genevieve sadly. You're in New York City right now. You're there and I'm not. I'm hearing this awful story instead.

Why hadn't Missy texted back? Was she mad at Genevieve for canceling? How was Genevieve going to make things right? How could she ever meet Claire now? She would have to tell these girls the truth, an ugly slimy thing they would not want any more than she did. "How much did the adopting parents pay you?" asked Genevieve. She was tired. She imagined that as the rain cleared, her father would golf after all and her mother would head for the mall.

"We don't know a single thing about the parents," said Ned firmly, "and nobody paid us a dollar."

"You don't know a thing about the parents? You didn't ask? You didn't set parameters or have somebody check on them and visit them?"

"They were private adoptions arranged by the doctor. The parents probably wanted the adoption secret as much as we did. We dealt with authorities on one of them but the other one's paperwork came later, and your mother and I were back at work, and we kept postpoing it."

Genevieve didn't like the sound of that. "But you got to it," she said.

"Well, not really."

"One adoption isn't complete?" Genevieve was aghast.

"It is from our point of view," said her mother.

"But those poor parents are in some horrible nonadoption limbo?"

"Oh, I'm sure over the years it just cancels out or something," said Allegra. "I don't want to deal with it. I don't want to deal with any of it. I can't believe it's come back to haunt me. How could that girl do that? What will people think? What will they say?"

"Let's worry about what Missy and Claire are going to say," snapped Genevieve.

"Vivi, you haven't been in touch with them, have you?"

"Of course I have."

"How could you!"

"They are my identical triplet sisters," said Genevieve, in case Allegra had missed the point. "You didn't let me have them. You didn't let me know. You made me grow up amputated!"

"Don't be silly. You never dreamed you had sisters."

There would have been enough space for three in her poet's attic. They would have had bunk beds and the closets would have been severely crowded and the drawers overflowing and the girls would have argued over the tiny bathroom and who got to choose the radio station—but they would have been sisters. Sharing thoughts and hopes and clothes and laughter.

"How do you plan to face Missy and Claire?" Genevieve asked. "Should we ask both families for dinner?"

"I'm not going to face them!" cried her mother. "They're out of my life. I don't want them back."

The doorbell rang.

Allegra cringed. "It's beginning, Ned. All the attention I don't want. Somebody saw the video and they've come for details, they've come to gawk. Ned, what are we going to say?"

Her parents moved closer to each other. They were afraid. Not of her, the daughter they had raised. Not even of the daughters they had not raised. They were afraid of the censure of the world.

The doorbell rang again.

"We're not home," suggested Ned.

Genevieve stepped into the little hall to look through the narrow glass panel beside the front door.

Someone had hung a mirror over the glass. How strange. She would have to take the mirror down in order to see out. What was the mirror even hanging on?

The expression on Genevieve's reflected face changed to a wide grin. Except she was not smiling. Genevieve touched her face, checking for a smile. In the mirror, no fingers moved.

She was not looking at her reflection. She was looking at her sister.

CHAPTER

NOON ON SATURDAY
Long Island

MISSY AND CLAIRE got off the train in a beautiful town where green lawns shimmered with the jewels of fallen autumn leaves. It struck Claire that the identical triplets had grown up in almost identical settings.

Missy marched forward. Claire could step out of the way of some out-of-control vehicle, but she could not get out of the way of her out-of-control cousin. She felt like a puppy on a leash: leave this station, cross this road, follow this sidewalk. She had only puppy thoughts and puppy knowledge. She was aware of sun and scent, traffic and trees.

Her cousin planned to walk up to a house whose address she had found online, knock on the front door and say to total strangers, "Hi. Do we look familiar? Do we look like your little girl Genevieve? Can we come in? Can I have a glass of water?"

She's not my cousin, Claire reminded herself. That's my sister walking two paces ahead of me.

Claire would have liked a year or two to think about this. But no, they were bolting into the foreign territory of an identical triplet.

Missy came to a halt. She pointed across the street at an adorable little dollhouse. Much smaller than other homes on the street, its shade came from other people's trees. The number 14 was visible on the red door with its white steps. There were two cars in the gravel driveway. They were home, these people who had adopted the girl who might be Claire's sister. "Stop, Missy," begged Claire. "Stop right here. This isn't the way to do it. We can't fool around with other people's lives. Let's go home."

They'd catch a train going the other way. Trains were wonderful. They ran all the time. They always had room. When there were no seats, you could stand.

"It isn't other people's lives," said Missy. "It's our lives." She crossed the street.

Claire backed up against a white picket fence with sweet-smelling flowers on delicate vines. She wrapped her fingers around a post and watched. She could not knock on that door.

Missy glanced back, puzzled and disappointed. Claire felt a literal tug, as if Missy really and truly were yanking her chain.

* * *

Missy's right foot landed on the bottom step of the tiny charming porch. Guessing who she was had been fun. Knowing might be a disaster. Missy swallowed.

So Genevieve's parents had collapsed when they saw the video. Whatever. I'll just walk around the parents. I'll comfort the mother and father and tell them they don't matter. My sister matters.

Missy took the second step. And then the third and final step. The little porch was so small she filled it, and it filled her. She felt Claire catch her breath at the same moment with the same fears, and then Missy Vianello pressed the Candlers' doorbell.

* * *

On the opposite side of the street, Claire's fingertip seemed to feel the pressure required to ring the bell. It was like a passing bell dividing class time in high school, but this bell would divide their cousin lives from their sister lives.

Let her not be our sister. Let none of this be true.

The front door opened.

There stood a girl who really and truly was exactly the same as Missy and Claire.

Missy and the girl touched. Their hands explored, testing hair and cheek and shoulder. It was like watching a zoo exhibit.

Claire felt like chopping off her hair, gaining twenty pounds, wearing thick glasses and smearing on orange lipstick—anything not to be the clone of a total stranger.

Missy and the girl began to hug. It was tentative. They were only half touching.

"Missy?" said the girl nervously.

"Genevieve?" said Missy, as if there could be a *fourth* girl inside, somebody named Estelle or Zoe.

Claire began to sob.

* * *

The girls were touching for the first time since before birth. Missy had known that she would know the moment they touched, and she had been right. Waves of knowledge passed through her. She and her new sister were laughing and crying, smiling and trembling. Then Genevieve saw who stood across the street. "Claire?" she whispered. "Missy, that's Claire!"

"That's Claire," agreed Missy.

Genevieve's touch turned to a grip. "I have to meet her. We have to be together. Hurry!" Pulling Missy with her, Genevieve took the three porch steps in a bound. They hurtled over the tiny front yard and across the quiet street.

Claire, be okay with this, prayed Missy. This is who we are.

* * *

Genevieve stopped at the sidewalk to give Claire a few feet of grace. To let Claire decide. She felt relatively sure that Ned and Allegra would not follow. She was not ready to bring parents into the mix, especially not these parents. And they were afraid of publicity, so a public street might frighten them into staying indoors.

Claire's stare was so intense it felt like laser surgery.

Genevieve held out her hands.

After an eternity, or a minute, Claire edged closer. She was quivering. The hand that touched Genevieve's cheek was cold. "Oh, Missy, you were right," whispered Claire. "You said we

242

would know the minute we touched. And I do know. Genevieve, I'm sorry. I was scared. I'm still scared. I sort of don't want it."

You really aren't going to want what it turned out to be, thought Genevieve. "It's okay," she said. "We're together now." Genevieve had a sister to the left and a sister to the right. She could have stood here for hours, gazing at each sister in turn.

Missy put her arm around Genevieve. Carefully, slowly, Genevieve put her arm around Claire. A smile began to form on Claire's face—the face that was also Genevieve's face. All three of the girls' mouths lifted in the same smile. Claire shifted, tugging at Genevieve until they were no longer a row. They were a circle.

Missy whispered, "I did a terrible thing, forcing Claire into going public when she didn't even know yet. I've been cruel to our families. But oh, Genevieve! We have *you*!"

We were all three scared this morning, thought Genevieve. All three trying to look bland and tailored and able to shrug. She said, "I don't really ever dress like this."

"Me either," said Claire. "I like lemon and turquoise and hot pink."

"Oh, yes!" said Genevieve. "And lime. Anything green."

"Why did we wear beige?" said Missy.

"To fade," said Claire. "I didn't want anybody to see. But it's pretty cool, isn't it?"

It was beyond cool. It was amazing that identical triplets could exist at all, never mind that she, Genevieve, was one of them. She couldn't laugh and she couldn't cry; she was stuck somewhere in trembling joy, feasting her eyes on her sisters.

Claire said nervously, "Your parents are standing in your doorway, Genevieve. They're staring at us."

Genevieve remembered reality. She had her back to a woman who had wanted to knife herself because Missy and Claire existed. "There's a little park down the block," said Genevieve. "We'll walk down there. They won't follow us."

"Shouldn't we say hello?" asked Missy.

"Not now." Genevieve set a fast pace. Their steps matched, as if they had had dancing class together and run up to bed together and learned songs together all these years.

They were one lawn away from Genevieve's house. Two lawns, then three.

Missy looked over her shoulder. "This feels rude."

Genevieve did not look over her shoulder. And then hedges and shrubs and branches bending low hid the man and the woman in the door of the little white house with the sweet little porch.

Missy said, "Genevieve, I'm desperate to know. Who are our parents? Did you find out? Do you know anything?"

It was the worst possible topic. Genevieve wanted it to come later. But it was the big question, and Missy and Claire needed the answer. They walked the whole block before Genevieve found the courage to tell them.

She said to her new sisters, "Be brave. That man and that woman standing in the doorway of my house? They are not *my* mother and father. They are *our* mother and father."

Claire could not make sense of this. How could Genevieve's parents be all their parents? The middle of her back still felt the pressure of those parents' eyes. From the back, she thought, they probably can't tell which of us is which. In fact, from the *front*, they probably can't tell.

The sidewalk went up a slight hill, passed several houses and headed down again, curving around.

The middle of her back relaxed. The eyes of the people in the doorway could not pierce the dirt of the hill. "Genevieve, don't talk about them," said Claire. "Talk about you." I'm not walking past that house again, she thought. I'll circle the whole town to reach the railroad station if I have to.

The park was a corner garden, with a little fountain and a small statue, some grass and a tall tree. It had one bench, wet from the rain. Genevieve swooshed her hand down the slats, removing most of the water, and mopped up the rest with her jacket. Not great for the jacket, but now they could sit.

Genevieve took the middle. Claire sat on her left while Missy sat on her right. Missy opened her cell phone, stretched her arm out in front of her and caught the three of them on its camera. They stared at the proof of their identical identities.

Claire thought, Only other people will know what identical triplets look like. I'll see the three of us just in pictures. That's why I never believed that Missy and I could be identical—I can't see us both at one time, except in mirrors. Now I have a new sister who is a mirror.

"We could have lived together," said Genevieve. "We could have been sisters all this time."

"It's not too late," said Missy. "We're not dead or anything."

They were laughing now, and it was the same melody, the same harmony, on the same pitch.

"I can't sit in a row like this," said Claire. "I can't see." She turned sideways, tucked her feet up on the bench and hugged her knees, giving herself a fine view of Genevieve. A split second later Missy did the same. We even sit alike? thought Claire.

"What did you mean about having to be brave?" Missy asked Genevieve.

"It's a bad story."

"How bad?" asked Claire. "Maybe I don't want to know."

"I want to know everything," said Missy.

"I'll make it quick," said Genevieve. Her mouth trembled. She put her hand up to steady the lips and chin that would have to deliver the news.

Claire took Genevieve's hand. I wonder if our fingerprints match, she thought.

Genevieve held tight and began to talk. The story of Allegra and Ned was not believable, so it didn't change Claire's life. It was just stuff, as if Genevieve were reading from a Weird News column. Claire had been thinking only of the birth mother. When she thought of adoption, she assumed the biological father was offstage somewhere; that he didn't know, didn't care, wasn't home, went to sea. But this birth father—*her* birth father—was down the block, standing still. Neither parent had been a sad, frightened teenager or a desperate, drug-using loser.

They had just been busy.

Again Claire felt brainless. What did that even mean—how could you be too busy to bring your own daughters home from the hospital?

"But they just stood there," protested Missy. "In the doorway. Claire and I were created by a man and a woman who didn't even cross the street for us?"

Genevieve nodded.

"They didn't run over to meet their other two babies? They aren't thrilled to find out that we're fine? That we turned out well? *That we came?*"

"I think they were hoping nobody would ever know," said Genevieve. "They were hoping it was a flub, like a bad golf score, and it wouldn't matter."

"It?" repeated Missy. "Having triplets is an 'it'?"

"I'm quoting."

Claire watched Genevieve's hair puff as the sun came out and the humidity changed and realized that she was watching her own hair, as it were. She and her sisters were breathing at the same tempo. Their foreheads wrinkled at the same time and their hands made the same gestures. Claire let herself merge with Genevieve, in just the way she had previously feared. It was a good fit.

Genevieve told them about Jimmy Fleming and Ray Feingold and the library where she'd watched Rick's video. She explained that Claire was legally adopted and Missy was not. "I guess we'll never really know why they didn't handle your adoption legally, Missy, but maybe even they felt shame. Even they couldn't face what they were doing and pretended it would go away."

It, thought Claire. Meaning us.

"Do you want to meet them?" asked Genevieve.

"Do you *want* us to meet them, Genevieve?" asked Missy. "Because I do want to, but only if it's okay with you."

"Not me," said Claire. "I have parents. In fact, I have parents who are worried." Claire picked up her cell and speed dialed. Her mother answered on the first ring. Frannie Linnehan's voice was not just loud. It was lunatic.

"Where are you?" shrieked Claire's mother. "Are you all right? How could you vanish at a time like this? I know it's mostly our fault, but you shouldn't just vanish! You should answer your phone! I am so mad at you, Claire!" Frannie Linnehan's voice seemed to cross state lines. Missy and Genevieve didn't have to lean close to hear.

"Hi, Mom," said Claire happily. It was fine to be yelled at. The people in the doorway down the street hadn't cared enough to keep Claire, never mind worry about her.

"Clairedy, that video!" Her mother's voice cracked. "I can't stand it when you cry on the video. It makes me cry. I'm crying now. Claire, where are you? I need you. Come home. We'll come get you. We're all getting in the car right now. We just need you to tell us where to drive. Is Missy with you? Tell me she's with you."

"Don't worry, Mom," said Claire. "I am so totally coming home. Things developed fast, and actually Missy and I took the train to New York and another train out to Long Island. When I explain, I want you and Daddy to remember that you are my mother and father. You were my mother and father from the minute you got me, you'll always be my mother and father, and no other person counts."

"Oh, my God. You've met your birth mother!" screamed Frannie Linnehan.

"No, Mom. I never want to meet her. I'm not going to meet her. But I have met somebody. You know that Missy and I are not just twins, but identical twins, right?"

"We didn't know, Clairedy. We didn't guess for years. You were both in elementary school before we started to grasp the situation. Even then, we were guessing. The doctor who arranged the adoptions never told us much. I don't see how you could have any facts either."

"We didn't need facts. People forwarded the video. A boy who saw it thought he had met one of us. He made sure that the video was seen by the girl he had met. But that girl wasn't me and she wasn't Missy. There weren't two of us up for adoption, Mom. There were three of us. Identical *triplets*. Our identical sister saw the video. She saw herself. She knew instantly, even though she hadn't known before. She got in touch. We couldn't wait to meet her. Actually, Missy couldn't wait and I dragged myself after her. We're with her right now. Our third sister."

Their faces were so close over the tiny phone that the hot tears inching down Genevieve's face slid onto Claire's cheek.

Frannie Linnehan screamed. "A third sister! What's her name? Let me talk to her! I have to meet her! I have to hug her! I have to know her! What could be more wonderful than another girl like you, Clairedy! Is she there? Will she talk to me? This is so fabulous! This is almost as exciting as when we got you at the hospital! Another daughter! What's her name? You have a decent cell phone! Is she there? Film her! Let me see her! Let me see all three of you! But first let me talk to Missy," she said sternly.

"She can hear you, Mom."

"Missy, your parents are mental! They are right here with me, of course, we are having a family conference. In fact, we are piling into the car to set out for Long Island, but you call them this instant, do you hear?"

✳ ✳ ✳

Genevieve tried to imagine parents who had family conferences. Who were thrilled to hear about her. Who shrieked joyfully, "Another daughter!"

Missy obeyed and called her parents that instant. Her mother was furious. Genevieve listened while the mother yelled, "I shouldn't yell! Your father and I should have talked to you long ago. Still and all, Melissa Vianello! That video was horrible. Vanishing today was horrible. Not telling us what you were doing was horrible. Not being able to reach you was horrible!"

Genevieve sopped up her tears with the hem of her long

flowing shirt. What would it be like to live with parents who were so emotional? So . . . so parental?

"I wanted it in the open, Mom," said Missy. "I wanted to stop guessing. I wanted to know."

"Then you should have asked!"

Missy's father took over. His voice was deep and raspy. Genevieve pictured somebody big and broad. "Missy, we couldn't tell you that you were adopted. First of all, in our hearts, you weren't. You were ours. It's impossible to describe how fierce the desire is to have babies. Your arms ache, your house is empty, your future is dull. You want your own kid. And when Dr. Russo said you were ours, they let us go to Newborn Intensive Care long before you were ready to come home and you *were* ours. Every minute, every crisis, every IV. But mainly, we couldn't tell you because the birth mother never surrendered her parental rights. She never tried to get you back, but she never signed anything either. You're ours, honey, but not in the eyes of the law. It's scary, we've always been scared. Sixteen years we've been scared."

My parents did that to them, thought Genevieve. All to avoid a few hours of social workers and judges glaring at them. I don't think anybody would have glared. It was just in a day's work. And maybe the authorities would have been relieved that baby Missy was getting a better mother than the one she'd been born to.

Oh, Mom! thought Genevieve.

Pain sliced her like surgery without anesthesia. She had never been first on her parents' list. Everything—cars, watches, travel, fashion, eating out—came ahead of Genevieve. She suddenly, desperately wanted to be with her great-grandmother. Nobody but GeeGee could comfort her now. GeeGee would not be surprised by this story. She had no use for her grandson Ned and less use for the woman he had married.

And then Genevieve knew something else: her great-grandmother was staying alive for her. Staying active, staying alert. Staying. Because little Genevieve needed all the love she could get.

"Don't be scared, Dad," said Missy. "I don't feel adopted either. I'm yours. I'll be home tonight. I don't want any other home. But I do want Genevieve." She whispered to Genevieve, "I'm definitely going to meet your parents. I have to give your mother—I mean, my mother—a piece of my mind. Imagine scaring my parents like that!"

Genevieve had never given her parents a piece of her mind. How docile I've been, she thought. I always try to appease them.

Missy's mother took back the phone. The yelling was over. The fear was gone. The voice of Kitty Vianello was filled with excitement. "Will Genevieve talk to me?"

Missy transferred her cell phone to Genevieve's hand. Genevieve felt as if she were not familiar with this technology. I'll be on the phone with the mother of my sister, she thought crazily. For a moment she couldn't breathe. Then she said softly, "Hello, Mrs. Vianello. This is Genevieve Candler."

"Genevieve! Oh, Genevieve! That's the prettiest name in the world! Oh! I can see you! Claire forwarded a picture of the three of you! You're in the middle, thank God I can tell. Am I telling just from clothing? Because I know what Missy and Claire own? I don't think so. I think I actually know. Genevieve, I'm having a heart attack from joy. Are you all right? We're already on I-95, heading south. Are your parents okay? Should I talk to them?"

"My parents are okay," said Genevieve, and it might be true. They would be planning how to contain this, how to spin it. They would come up with a way to protect themselves. They might even enjoy exposure, if they could not prevent it. They might relish being on some shiny talk show with some shiny host.

No, thought Genevieve. That is a deal breaker. We are not letting the media own us. I will set my parents straight on that.

"How far out on Long Island are you?" asked Missy's mother. "Which bridge do we take?"

Genevieve was appalled at the thought of six parents crossing paths. "Maybe Missy and Claire can still take the train home," she said. "Maybe we can all meet some other time. Right now I'm just enjoying your voice. You sound happy."

"I'm delirious, Genevieve. Two were perfect, but *three*! It's incredible! I love you already. I have to meet you and hug you. Genevieve, have you met your birth parents?"

"Yes," said Genevieve. "I've met my birth parents."

* * *

"My turn," said Claire's father. "Clairedy, I've been at work all morning. I haven't even seen the famous video yet."

"It's okay," Claire assured him. "You can skip it."

"Good, because I'm totally blown away by this cell phone picture of the three of you." Phil Linnehan raised his voice. "Hey, Genevieve!" he bellowed. "Hi! Welcome! I guess I'm your dad, too. Well—not exactly. Do we know who the dad is? Are we doing dads yet? What stage are we at? *Triplets*. Wow. My heart is flopping around."

The phone calls ended. The girls were left trembling in the aftershock of this family earthquake. There were a million things to talk about. Claire let Missy and Genevieve do the talking. Already the two of them seemed closer to each other than to her.

How did real triplets behave? Did two have more power and more fun than the third? Did they rotate last position? Did everybody get a chance to be first? Or did they stay equal thirds, like a geometry problem?

I don't want a problem with Genevieve and Missy, thought Claire. I want it to be perfect.

It seemed impossible to Claire that the supposed parents had not come to find their three daughters. What could Ned and Allegra Candler be talking about in their sweet little white house? She cut them a little slack. After all, she hadn't been brave enough to cross the street.

"Let's go meet your parents, Genevieve," said Missy. "It's time."

Even now, even here, Claire had forgotten how closely her thoughts tracked with Missy's.

Genevieve looked dubious. "They're not going to be like your mothers and fathers. They're not going to dance and sing for joy. But they're civilized. They'll be courteous."

"Did they ever hold us?" asked Missy suddenly.

Genevieve withdrew. In some palpable way, she became a stranger. Genevieve had been places where Claire had never been and Claire did not envy her. "No," said Genevieve finally. "They never held you."

"Ugh," said Claire. "I don't want any part of them." The whole story—those awful people—their awful decisions—well, maybe not *that* awful; after all, they didn't have to have the babies. They could have gotten rid of them early on, and then Claire wouldn't even exist—she had to give them credit for that—but not so much credit that she wanted to be part of this.

"You are part of them," Genevieve pointed out.

"Technically. Biologically. Nothing else. If you're going to meet them, Missy, I'll wait at the train station." She pointed to the intersection. "I get there by walking the rest of the way up this street, right? And cutting to the left about three blocks? And that will be the main street? And the station is there?"

Genevieve was frantic. "I can't take just *one* of you to meet my parents. And it's too soon to split up. We aren't really sisters yet. We've hardly started."

Claire looked at her watch. "Actually, we've been talking for ages." All that time, she thought, that man and that woman have been hunkered down inside their house. Or maybe not. The rain has stopped. Maybe they went out. Errands to do. Could there be an errand more important than meeting your daughters?

Genevieve's control was breaking. "Now that I've found you, I don't want to be apart."

Genevieve has to go home to those people, thought Claire. She lives with them. They really *are* her parents. Am I going to abandon her to that? Is it abandonment if it's your own parents?

My own parents, she corrected herself, and wanted to run.

Missy put her hands on Claire's shoulders. "I'll do what you want, Clairedy. I'll leave with you if that's what you have to do. But if we don't meet these people, they'll haunt us."

Genevieve flinched, jerking her hand up as if she'd just gotten a splinter.

If Missy and I leave together, thought Claire, then Genevieve is the leftover one. The one without a companion. Missy and I become twins, while she's just an extra. "Don't move," she ordered Missy and Genevieve. "Just let me solidify."

They didn't laugh. They knew what she was feeling. They knew the time it would take. They knew.

"Okay," said Claire. "We're triplets. But you two go first. You do the talking. I don't want to touch them or anything."

* * *

Ned had fixed coffee. Allegra was not drinking it. She couldn't pace, sit or think.

"They even look like black swans," said Ned, watching the video for the hundredth time.

Allegra stared blankly at the screen.

256

"The *Journal* article. I showed it to you. It's still on the counter." He read it out loud again, but Allegra didn't listen this time either. How had those girls gotten here? There was no car parked. The high school where the video had been made was in Connecticut. The girls must have taken the train.

Should she and Ned go after them? Where would Vivi take those girls? Vivi's place and person of refuge was her great-grandmother. Vivi walked there all the time. Would she bring the girls to the nursing home? Or had they parked their car someplace else and Vivi was planning to go home with them?

Allegra just wanted this to end.

The front door opened.

Genevieve walked in. How beautiful she was. The black hair clouded around her, and strange soft excitement bloomed on her face. "Hello, Mother," she said. "Hello, Dad. I'd like you to meet Claire Linnehan and Missy Vianello."

And there they were.

Two more Genevieves.

One of them must be the tiny red spider who had come second. The other was the third baby, for whom Allegra had not even opened her eyes. Allegra closed her eyes now too. They'll never leave, she thought. They'll tell their parents, we'll have to meet, Genevieve will want them to visit. We'll have to get to know them.

She opened her eyes. One of the clones was smiling at her. Genevieve's smile. It was too eerie. "It's okay, Mrs. Candler," said the girl. "It really is."

The other one stayed back, looking sober, as if in judgment.

The smiling clone walked right up to Allegra, as if it wanted to be hugged, but Allegra could not reach out. "Don't be upset," said this apparition. Genevieve's voice, but not Genevieve. Allegra gave herself points for realizing which one was her own daughter.

Then she thought, They're all my own daughters.

"I have the best parents," said the girl. "I have a great life. You were so generous to do what you did." The stranger Genevieve went ahead and hugged her. Was it the Missy one or the Claire one? Who would name a child Missy? It wasn't even a name, it was just stuff. And "Claire" was as stodgy as "Genevieve." Allegra would never have named her daughter Genevieve, but Ned had thought it would clinch the inheritance. The nickname Vivi was perfect, but Genevieve herself never used it.

She glanced at her actual daughter and saw sadness etched on Vivi's face. Every person I know is going to look at me like that. They all expected more of me.

The clones moved close together. It seemed to Allegra that they might merge and turn into one girl. Maybe they were an optical illusion anyway.

*   *   *

Ned Candler had spent his life shaking hands and greeting people, being friendly and sociable and remembering names. Laughing and chatting, asking after spouses and children, being warm and likeable. He called upon all those years of experience now, but they didn't help. The sight of three Genevieves was staggering. He knew his own daughter only because she stood slightly in front of the others, holding out her hand to guide him forward.

For Vivi, he told himself. Do everything now for Vivi. "I'm your father," he began. The admission floored him. "I'm—" He couldn't think. What was he? Other than worthless? "Stunned," he finished. "I never knew."

Of course he had known. He just hadn't known that the three were identical. He walked toward them. It was too hard. He stopped at Vivi. "I'm sorry for all our mistakes, Vivi. I love you." He was amazed, even honored, that his daughter hugged him. It gave him the courage to turn to the triplet on Genevieve's left.

She didn't smile. She didn't speak. Ned put out a hand, although it was hard to know the proper etiquette for meeting one's own daughter.

She studied his hand.

He left it up in the air.

She took it, moved it fractionally upward and dropped it. Then she took her hand back, but kept it away from her body, as if it needed scrubbing.

"That was Claire," Genevieve told him. "And this is Missy."

How bizarre: his daughter's smile on some other daughter's face. Missy's cell phone rang before he could attempt to shake hands with her. Ned was not surprised that even though she was meeting her real father for the first time, the teenager's first priority was her phone. "It's my mother," said Missy, lifting the cell phone to her ear. "Hi, Mom. Well, we're kind of okay. We kind of decided to meet—I guess you'd say—Genevieve's parents. Well, that's not the actual positive truth. Actually, they're the real ones. The parents. Genevieve's mom and dad kind of thought that one kid was enough so—well—that's where you came in."

The Claire one was flapping her hands as if she'd touched a wall of spiderwebs. She backed into the little hall. She found the front door.

Ned knew he should go after her, offer comfort, but he didn't know where to start and then Missy held out her phone. "My mother wants to talk to you."

Ned was horrified.

The Claire one was out the front door and running down the steps.

Somehow he had Missy's cell phone by his ear and he was saying, "Good afternoon." Ned had seldom had a less good afternoon.

"Mr. Candler? Oh, my. What a situation we've found ourselves in. I'm thrilled and terrified. But first, let me thank you for our beautiful daughter. We love her more than life. We're so grateful. But right now, we don't want our daughters on their own. Did you know that middle-aged sisters adopted your two girls? Well, my sister and I and our husbands started driving into the city the minute we found out you're on Long Island. We're on the Long Island Expressway, but we actually haven't the faintest idea where you are. Would you please give us directions to your house?"

* * *

Genevieve ran after Claire.

Genevieve was a good athlete. In fact, it looked as if she and Claire were exactly the same level of athlete. Genevieve figured they could run forever, with Claire fifty paces ahead. "Claire!" she shouted. "It's okay. You don't have to go back in. But this isn't the way to the train station. Let me go with you. Let me be your sister."

* * *

Missy was the only triplet still with the birth parents.

It was scary being alone with two people who had treated their babies like extra kitchen appliances. She could sneak a quick look and then had to look away. Her parents were a million times better than Genevieve's. What if that doctor had not found Missy's mother and father? What if she had had to grow up here instead of with Matt and Kitty Vianello?

Missy understood the phrases of adoption now. This man Ned was a biological parent, while Missy's father was a father. This woman was a birth mother. It wasn't such a bad phrase after all. It got the job done. And then the real mother and father could go on from there.

Missy had planned to demand that these two fill out adoption papers on the spot. Now she realized it wouldn't be that easy. Besides, it mattered less. It was a legal thing, not a real thing. She was less interested in these parents than she had expected, and far more unnerved. She could see herself in the woman's features. She could see her own eyes in the father's. She prayed she had not inherited their selfishness or coldness.

She found herself backing toward the door, just as Claire had. Is it a twin thing? she wondered. I mean, a triplet thing?

She didn't want to turn her back on these two, as if they were dangerous. The danger was sixteen years ago, she thought. Now some lawyer can take it from here. "I'm glad we met," she said, although she wasn't sure if that was true. "I think the three of us will wait at the railroad station for my parents."

"Wait!" said the father. "Your parents will be here in half an hour. You don't want to sit at the railroad station all that time."

Missy was already texting her mother. "We'll be fine," she told the father. "We have plenty to talk about." She could not seem to smile at them. She waved instead, and her hand felt silly. The stare of the mother—the real, biological mother—was without welcome. Without depth.

Missy felt a bolt of fear so intense that she stumbled into the wall. She flailed around for the door handle. A nightmare sequence of being trapped, helpless in some sticky snare, filled the tiny hall. Missy tried to be rational but nothing mattered except getting out of here. She heard herself whimper. She found the knob, turned it, yanked the door open and ran.

* * *

Claire had known that when grown-up adopted children wanted to meet, birth parents often refused contact. She had not known what it would feel like to enter, without permission, the house of people who do not want you in their lives. In the eyes of that beautiful birth mother had been horror. Then the handsome birth father—younger-looking than her dad; better kept, somehow—offered his hand for her to shake. It had been a mistake to touch him. Claire had been seized by some primitive fear. Like a little girl in an ancient twisted tale, she knew that the evil woodsman would close the door behind the wandering child and imprison her.

Claire started to throw up. When she swallowed it down, the vomit seemed to enter her veins, and she felt its poison course through her body. She could taste the poison in her arms and legs and throat.

She reached the little park. It was serene and silent. She felt safe but unclean. At least she could stop running. She let Genevieve catch up. How strange to watch herself running toward herself.

All these years, she had not really seen much resemblance between herself and Missy. But between herself and Genevieve stood nothing. They were doubles. Claire flushed. "I'm sorry, Genevieve. I panicked. I know they're your mother and father. I know you love them. But I had this awful sensation that if I stayed, I'd never get home."

"Let's not cry," said Genevieve, crying. "I'm sorry about my parents. I wish they were different, but they aren't."

The girls walked on. They reached the train station. Signs said DEPARTURES and ARRIVALS. I'm both, thought Claire. I arrived at a truth I didn't want; I'm departing with a sister I do want. She put her arms around Genevieve. "Thank you for running after me. Thank you for contacting us to start with. You said it was a matter of life and birth, but now that I've met you, I think maybe the real phrase fits. This really was a matter of life and death. We absolutely had to meet. Missy knew and I didn't."

"I want to keep meeting. But my parents are who they are, Claire."

"Your parents gave me the best gift there is. I exist. And I ended up with the right parents for me. Missy has the right parents for her." Claire did not pretend that Genevieve had the right parents. She was out of courteous closing statements. She didn't want to talk. She wanted to take a shower and wash those people away.

* * *

Ned sat down. Allegra sat down. They did not touch.

"What do you call baby swans?" said Ned softly. "I forget the word. Anyway, the girls grew up without us. They're swimming fine without us. They just live on another lake."

Allegra had no idea what he was talking about. "I'm not swimming. I'm drowning."

"Drowning in what?" he asked.

She knew the answer Ned wanted: that she was drowning in

regret. That she wished they had kept the other daughters. That the final daughter had not raced out of the house as if Ned and Allegra carried a communicable disease.

But Allegra was drowning in wasted years. "We kept Vivi, Ned. But I didn't love her enough or enjoy her enough or laugh with her enough or admire her enough. Ned, those other parents are coming. She'll go with them. We'll lose her. I can tell it's going to happen. I deserve it. But I don't want to lose her!"

Ned jumped up. "Let's go after Vivi."

"How can I face those other parents?"

"Allegra, the adopting parents think you're a goddess. You gave them each a beautiful daughter. We don't have to worry about them. We have to worry about Vivi. Let's hurry."

"We have nothing to offer!"

"We can show up," he said. "We haven't done a whole lot of that."

What would she say to those parents? Because she couldn't avoid them now. They had actually driven to Long Island already! She had said way too much to Vivi and it was impossible now to rewrite history. Allegra softened the edges of the decision in her mind, structuring phrases that would make it all ordinary and acceptable.

She could pull it off with those parents. But what about Vivi? What could she say to Vivi?

Hanging by the door to the garage was a photograph, enlarged, matted and framed, of little Genevieve with her beloved great-grandmother. The inherited traits of hair, eyes and chin were obvious. Vivi smiled at it whenever she entered the garage, which never failed to annoy Allegra. The photograph was a clue. "We'll say what GeeGee always says. We'll tell Vivi she's our sweetness and light. Vivi loves that line." I haven't been paying attention to Vivi, Allegra thought. I've been going to parties. Fixing my face. Staring at my career. But Vivi is my sweetness and light.

She flushed. Was she just mentally preparing a publicity release? Working on damage control?

"Those girls and those parents will want Vivi to spend the rest of the weekend with them," said Ned. "We have to be charming, and agree to it, and wave her off, and stay cheerful. That's the kind of parent she needs."

For sixteen years, Allegra Candler had cheerfully waved good-bye and pretended this was the parent Vivi needed. "No," she said to her husband. "We have to refuse. She can't go."

"Are you crazy? What kind of strategy is that?"

"We've thrown her away, as if we gave Vivi up for adoption, too. We have to bring her home, Ned." And they'd have to talk. She knew that Vivi would prefer talking with her great-grandmother. Allegra dreaded telling old Genevieve about the decision she'd made years ago. Those terrible harsh eyes would judge her. When the older Genevieve showed her contempt, the younger Genevieve would follow suit. Allegra had to take the offensive. "We'll drive to the nursing home. We'll tell GeeGee everything. If we offer to visit GeeGee immediately, I think Vivi will stay with us instead of going with those others. At least for now."

Ned paled. "My grandmother will kill me when she finds out."

Allegra smiled at him. "She can't move fast enough." She took her husband's hand. Their only hope in this scandal was their daughter. If Vivi stood by them, they might make it.

In her car, she slid the keys into the ignition. She seriously considered driving away and starting a new life under a false name. I want to, she thought. But I can't abandon Vivi. Although I have abandoned her. Year after year.

How Allegra had resented GeeGee for taking Vivi's heart.

But I never offered my own, she thought. That's all Vivi wants. My heart. My small, ungenerous heart.

Allegra Candler prayed the first real prayer of her life. *God, open my heart.*

* * *

An immense SUV drew up at the New York–bound side of the train station. It was a big sprawling family car, the kind Genevieve's parents sneered at. Doors flew open, and mothers and fathers leaped out. Missy and Claire received enough hugs and kisses from their parents that the girls might have been kidnapped and kept prisoner in a basement for weeks.

And then Genevieve was lost in the embrace of Missy's mother. Kitty Vianello enveloped her, saying how wonderful it was, what a miracle it was, how lucky that Genevieve's friend had seen the video, how beautifully this was going to work out. How even though she was furious with Missy for the hoax, she was joyful that it had led to Genevieve.

Genevieve had never been hugged like this. GeeGee was too frail and her own mother lacked enthusiasm.

Missy's mother traded her over to Claire's. You would never have known that Kitty and Frannie were sisters. They didn't act, look or sound alike.

The dads weren't as effusive. They didn't hug as hard. They didn't know where to look—at their own daughters, who were safe and sound, or at the other daughter. Not theirs, and yet the same.

Then everybody had to take pictures. They posed like any family at any reunion. Then everybody had to laugh and hug again. Missy kept saying to her mother and father, "I'm so glad you're my parents!" which Genevieve certainly understood. She yearned to be loyal and stand up for her own parents, but there was no defense for Ned and Allegra's actions.

It's all about parents, thought Genevieve. Missy and Claire have learned a biological fact, but they'll go on with their lives, which aren't going to change. But I can't unlearn what I've found out about my parents. My situation isn't identical to theirs, even if my genes are. I don't get another set of parents.

"Can you come home with us for the rest of the weekend, Genevieve?" asked Claire's mother, clapping with excitement and dancing in place. She must be the Jazzercise one, thought Genevieve. "We'd love to have you. There's plenty of room for seven of us in the car."

"I'll phone your mother and ask," said Missy's mother. "They'll want to meet us before they let us take you away and I'm a little scared of meeting them, but of course I'm hoping to coax them to finish up the little eensy legalities we need. It won't be any trouble for them. We'll pay all the costs."

Genevieve felt as if she were standing in front of BB guns. Even though these grown-ups were throwing affection at her, it felt like steel pellets. It wounded her to see what her parents had done, to have to present excuses for them. "I think they might not be that eager to meet you. They've tried not to think about this for a long time. They won't want to think about it anymore today." Or ever, she thought. Missy and Claire will go home and talk and talk. I'll go home and nobody will say a word.

"If you want to spend the night," said Missy, "you don't even have to pack clothes." Missy's eyes were sparkling. "Everything I have will fit you perfectly."

"And be in the right colors," said Claire.

"Every Friday Claire and I have a sleepover," said Missy. "We'll have it tonight instead. I used to call them Claire-overs."

"Have you girls eaten?" said Claire's mother. "Let's stop along the way and have a great meal to go with all this great news. Genevieve, are you a hamburger person? A spaghetti person? A salad person? Burrito? Help me out here."

The adoptive parents were adopting Genevieve. She could go back and forth, part of each family. Not only could she have another set of parents, she could have two more sets.

"I want to have the first Gen-over," said Claire. "My house is closer anyway."

The one who wasn't even going to talk to me wants me to

spend the night, thought Genevieve. She wants to name the sleepover for me. A Gen-over.

It was like standing in front of a Thanksgiving buffet. All the best food, all the good china, all the gleaming silver—and you can eat all you want and come back for seconds, and dessert is yet to come. Six people, offering platters of love.

"We'll bring you home again on Sunday, of course, Genevieve," added Claire's father.

Six people beamed at her. Two of the smiles were identical to her own. Genevieve felt a despair so great she thought she might collapse. To be loved the way Missy and Claire were loved—what would that be like?

She felt the cool wind and the taste of autumn in the air. She smelled coffee from the kiosk down the platform. She felt tears burning the back of her eyes.

If I go with these people, I will shred what's left of my own family. When I come home after a weekend with my new sisters, my parents will have even thicker shells. I'll be even more in their way. They'll keep exchanging Dark Looks. We'll speak in formal tones and they'll dream of the day I leave for college.

What do I want? The affection of excited strangers? Or the love of my parents? Not that I get a whole lot of love from them. I get a roof over my head and—

Her mother's car pulled up.

Genevieve stared.

Her mother got out of the driver's seat. Her father, always the passenger, got out from the other side. They walked toward her. Her mother called, "Vivi?"

Genevieve's eyes blurred. To come here had taken courage and resolve. Ned and Allegra didn't have much of those. This was huge. They had done it for her. They were going to meet the adoptive parents and admit the past. They weren't going to hide.

A sob escaped Genevieve.

Her mother ran toward her. Genevieve could not remember when Mom had ever left Dad's side to come to her. Genevieve held out her arms. It was extraordinary to comfort the woman who had never learned to give comfort.

"Oh, Vivi, I got here in time," said her mother. "You haven't left yet."

Say it, Genevieve willed her. Say the three words. Say them out loud.

But Allegra did not.

Genevieve took the deepest breath of her life. It went from her toes to the sky. She would have to teach her parents. Could they learn? Did she have the energy? "I love you, Mom," she said quietly.

For a moment, Genevieve thought Allegra might ask for a definition. And then Allegra Candler swallowed and said, "I love you."

Her father took pictures of Genevieve and her mother. "We need pictures of everybody else, too," he said. "I just called GeeGee. We're going over there tonight. The three of us."

"You told her already?" Genevieve was aghast.

"I told her we have something to celebrate," said Ned. "I told her we'd be there shortly."

The three of them never visited GeeGee, no matter what there was to celebrate. GeeGee will think it's a college discussion, thought Genevieve. She'll expect them to ask for money. But they'll ask for understanding and forgiveness. Way harder than money.

What would the older Genevieve Candler do?

All her life GeeGee had said to her, "It's about choices, my darling girl. Every single moment is a choice. Will you be good or mediocre? Will you be kind or indifferent? Will you be generous or cold? Every choice is always yours. Never somebody else's."

"Vivi," whispered her mother, "the parents and the girls are waiting. I have to go up to them. I'm a little scared."

"It is scary. But they're nice, Mom. And my sisters? They're just like me."

Her mother struggled to smile. "They're that wonderful?"

The most uninvolved parents in New York State were trying to be involved at last? Ned and Allegra were weak. They were going to need a lot of help. Genevieve considered her choices. She could shut them out or take them in.

Genevieve led her parents forward. She locked eyes with Claire and then with Missy. We're about to find out, she thought, whether identical twin-triplet communication actually exists. Are we on the same wavelength? Will they know what I want? Will they give it to me?

I need you, she told her identical sisters. I need you to embrace my mother the way your mothers embraced me.

And then Genevieve Candler knew that she was a triplet. From Missy and Claire came tiny nods and starter smiles. We're here, they said. We're yours.

* * *

LATE SATURDAY AFTERNOON
The Cross Bronx Expressway

ON THE DRIVE back, talk was ceaseless. Everybody had opinions and stories, recriminations and questions, excuses and hopes.

"I'm so proud of how nice you were to those Candlers, girls," said Claire's mother. "Considering the ghastly version you're giving us of their lifestyle."

"It was a one-time thing," said Claire. "I don't feel any need to be around Ned and Allegra again."

Missy didn't feel any need either. But how could Ned and Allegra be avoided, if she and Claire were to have Genevieve in their lives?

"But you were so polite, Clairedy," her mother said. "Especially to the mom. I thought you liked them."

"Who could *like* them?" asked Claire. "Genevieve wanted us to be nice. So we were nice."

We're all pretending, thought Missy, that nobody here is actually related to anybody there. We're pretending that the sort-of parents of Genevieve are just walk-ons, and that we can walk away. We loved crossing that bridge and leaving Long Island behind. The water barrier is a fear barrier too.

"Genevieve needed us to forgive her parents," said Claire, "but Missy and I ended up exactly right. It's Genevieve who has to forgive. We did two thirds of it. That'll make it easier."

No, thought Missy. You and I did none of it. Genevieve still has all of it.

"What do you mean, you did two thirds of it?" asked Claire's father.

"We're triplets," said Claire breezily. "Two forgave. One's working on it."

Missy marveled. Claire had decided to give the biological parents only a minute of her time, only a shrug. Would that work? Or would Missy and Claire have a thousand nightmares where they were trapped in the little dark hall with the mother and father who wished they had never come? Would Missy and Claire, every day of their lives, shiver inside the knowledge that they were just recyclables? Soda cans put out by the curb?

It was decided to stop at a favorite restaurant because everybody was starving. The grown-ups argued about traffic and the best route to the best food.

The mystery, thought Missy, was not the existence of identical triplets. The mystery was how Genevieve had learned about love. Perhaps love was inborn, and you didn't acquire it from observing your parents. Perhaps love came along with heart and lungs; you just had it from birth.

It could take years to stumble through the moral fog that was Ned and Allegra. No matter how fast they drove, no matter how often they stopped for food, they could not drive away from those parents.

Or, thought Missy, I could do what Claire's doing, and give Ned and Allegra an hour. Claire's dismissing them, because they were our parents in the beginning, but they are not, in the end, our parents.

They reached the restaurant. They had just placed their orders when the third text of the hour arrived from Genevieve. "They're at the nursing home," Claire reported. "Genevieve sent a photograph."

Missy stared at an incredibly ancient woman, smiling cheek to cheek with their sister. Big and Little Genevieve.

"I can see us in her face," whispered Claire. "Same jaw. Same eyes."

Same love, thought Missy, and the mystery of where Genevieve learned love was solved. From the gamble of her hoax, Missy had had a splendid haul: an identical twin, an identical triplet, and the great-grandmother who had made sure that somebody loved Genevieve enough.

* * *

Claire was wondering where Genevieve wanted to go to college. I could go there too, she thought. We could be room-mates. We didn't get the first sixteen years together, but we could have four at college. We're both high school juniors. In two years, we could be sisters under the same roof.

Claire didn't feel like discussing this in front of parents. She texted Missy. What about college? Roomies—me and G?

No fair! You two would have a year without me!

I'm texting G. I want to know what colleges she's thinking of.

What do I have to do, graduate a year early?

"What are you girls doing?" asked Missy's mother.

"We're bickering by text message," said Missy. Next to her, Claire wrote to Genevieve about college. Missy considered what she wanted to say in her own message to Genevieve.

Whatever she wrote now would commit her to another trip to Long Island and another sighting of the sort-of parents. But our next visit won't be about parents, she thought. It will be about sisters. And love.

CAROLINE B. COONEY is the author of many books for young people, including *They Never Came Back; If the Witness Lied; Diamonds in the Shadow; A Friend at Midnight; Hit the Road; Code Orange; The Girl Who Invented Romance; Family Reunion; Goddess of Yesterday* (an ALA-ALSC Notable Children's Book); *The Ransom of Mercy Carter; Tune In Anytime; Burning Up; The Face on the Milk Carton* (an IRA-CBC Children's Choice Book) and its companions, *Whatever Happened to Janie?* and *The Voice on the Radio* (each of them an ALA-YALSA Best Book for Young Adults), as well as *What Janie Found; What Child Is This?* (an ALA-YALSA Best Book for Young Adults); *Driver's Ed* (an ALA-YALSA Best Book for Young Adults and a *Booklist* Editors' Choice); *Among Friends; Twenty Pageants Later;* and the Time Travel Quartet: *Both Sides of Time, Out of Time, Prisoner of Time,* and *For All Time,* which are also available as *The Time Travelers,* Volumes I and II.

Caroline B. Cooney lives in South Carolina and New York.